Blood Lines

Kit Tunstall

Ellora's Cave
Romantica Publishing

What the critics are saying...

ജ

BLOOD CHALLENGE

5 Rating "This novel in my opinion can stand alone in the series. The chemistry between Rica and Ellie nearly made ME howl at the moon. [...] The Mating Moon Ceremony was very erotic and powerfully sexy!!! [...] All in all it is a very good read and I very much recommend it, this book is very much a keeper. I can't wait for the rd installment of this series." ~ *Just Erotic Romance Reviews*

BLOOD BOND

Delicious Threesome Erotica "BLOOD BOND is book three of Tunstall's Blood Line series, but well capable of standing alone. While some benefit may be gained by knowing the characters from previous volumes, both characters and storyline are clearly explained. [...] The characterization is well-done and the storyline intriguing, as well as very sexually oriented. The highlight was, of course, the three-partner (one female, two males) relationship, portrayed carefully and yet erotically. BLOOD BOND is a great, fast read for when those threesome- story cravings get nasty, and a tempting story in what looks to be a very promising series!" ~ *SensualRomance Reviews*

An Ellora's Cave Romantica Publication

www.ellorascave.com

Blood Lines

ISBN 9781419958038

Edited by Ann Richardson.
Cover art by Syneca.

This book printed in the U.S.A. by Jasmine-Jade Enterprises, LLC.

Trade paperback Publication September 2008

BLOOD LINES

BLOOD CHALLENGE

Chapter 1

"Ms. Adare?"

At the sound of her name, Ellie turned away from the attendant stacking her luggage. She eyed the large man with black hair and green eyes before her gaze moved to his shorter companion, noting what a contrast they presented. His lithe build and tamed brown curls looked strange next to the large one's wild hair, barely contained in a short ponytail. "Doctor," she corrected.

The larger one shrugged. "*Doctor*, your visa has been revoked."

Her eyes widened. "What? On whose authority?"

"Anca Draganescu, the ruler of Corsova," the shorter one said. He seemed faintly apologetic, but his voice was just as firm as his partner's.

Ellie shook her head. "But why? I filled out the proper paperwork weeks ago."

"Yes, ma'am, but you're required to fill it out honestly."

"Sorin," the shorter one said in a low tone of voice.

Sorin continued, ignoring the warning. "If you had been honest about your reasons for visiting Corsova, you'd have been saved a long trip."

Her hands settled on her hips as she glowered at him. "A social anthropologist does their best to blend in when the opportunity is presented to them. I may have omitted part of the reason for my visit, but I've done nothing wrong." She tried pasting a coaxing smile on her heart-shaped face as she glanced at the shorter one. "Couldn't we work this out?"

His eyes widened. "You can't bribe us, Doctor."

She sighed. "Fine. I want to see your ruler. I'm certain she'll be reasonable." After all, from what Ellie had been able to determine in her initial research, their current queen was a native New Yorker. She should be able to use the career-woman approach to get her visa reinstated.

Sorin crossed his arms. "That isn't possible. Lucian." He inclined his head.

Lucian extended a folder of documents to Ellie. "You'll find a ticket for the train leaving in a few minutes, along with the documents you submitted when you applied for entrance."

Sorin walked over to the employee who had been unloading her bags. "Load these back on the train. Dr. Adare will be returning to Constanta."

"Leave them right there," Ellie snapped. "You can't do this to me. Just let me—"

Sorin turned to her, towering over her. "It would be unfortunate if we have to physically restrain you during your return to Romania."

Her eyes widened. "You can't threaten me."

"It isn't a threat," Lucian hurried to say. "It would be temporary custody, for the duration of the train ride. However, we have no wish to restrain you. If you'll join us on the train, we'll see you back to Constanta." He gave her a small smile. "There isn't any need for unpleasantness."

Ellie grasped her carryon case, resisting the urge to swing it at both men and make a run for it. That wouldn't be the best way to start her three-month stay in Corsova. No, she would have to outwit the brutes. She took a deep breath and gave them a charming smile. "Of course not. I'll be happy to return to Romania. There are interesting groups there too."

Lucian nodded. "Excellent. We'll see you back—"

She frowned. "Excuse me?"

"We've been assigned to see you returned to Constanta," Sorin said, crossing his arms. "I must insist you board the train, Dr. Adare. It will be leaving shortly."

She swallowed down her protests and walked to the stairs, conscious of them shadowing her steps. She pushed down her seething anger and tried to accept the situation. She would ditch the goons in Constanta and rent a plane. She hadn't spent two years earning her pilot's license just because it was a fun hobby, and she hadn't spent the last year studying the Corsovan language just to turn back now.

Once she returned to Corsova, she would have to keep a low profile. Studying one of the mountain groups would be ideal. She could gather her data about the modern-day culture that chose to live at an early twentieth-century level of technology, put together a paper to publish, and win the position as chair of her department at Columbia before Dr. Ludlow. Being denied legitimate entrance into Corsova was a minor inconvenience, but it wouldn't stop Ellie.

* * * * *

Ellie huddled deeper into the parka she had purchased in Constanta and squinted out the windshield of the small Cessna she had rented with her expense account from the university. She knew she would have to reimburse accounting for a three-month plane rental, but that was the least of her worries right now.

She was lost in the mountains, in the middle of a blizzard. One moment, tiny snowflakes splattered against the windshield, falling from a moderately overcast sky, with the sun still visible. The next, she was flying into wind gusts, with snow so thick she couldn't see. Even her equipment was no help. It had stopped working within minutes of crossing the Corsovan border.

"Just calm down, Ellie," she whispered to herself. She had enough gas to backtrack to Romania. She could attempt to fly in later, once the storm lifted. There wasn't any reason to panic.

With careful movements, she began turning the plane, intent on heading back the way she came. She tried to keep the plane level, but it dipped down on the left side, seconds before she heard a cracking sound that drowned out the noise of the wind and blinding snow. The plane shuddered at the impact, and it took all her strength to hold it steady.

She let out a small yelp of alarm as the Cessna nose-dived. She no longer had any idea of her altitude and feared crashing into the side of the mountain. She struggled to slow the plane's descent, but it smashed into a barrier much too soon.

The collision threw Ellie forward against the seatbelt. It snapped loose under the force of her body, and she went flying toward the instrument panel, striking her head on the hard surface. She was vaguely aware of the rocking motion of the plane tapering off as she lay against the panel, attempting to keep her eyes open.

Waves of blackness flickered behind her eyes, and her head was a throbbing mass of agony. Ellie tried to lift her arm to examine her forehead, where she could feel warm blood flowing freely, but couldn't find the strength to move.

She blinked as the darkness behind her eyes expanded, obscuring her vision. She knew slipping into unconsciousness would be signing her death warrant, and tried focusing on the pain to stay alert. It had the opposite effect, making her want to sleep to escape the anguish.

Ellie tried once more to move, and succeeded in putting her palms against the control panel and heaving herself backward into the bucket seat. She could feel the buckle of the belt digging into her back and, as her eyes closed, made a mental note to demand a refund on a portion of her deposit. She tried to fight off the darkness, but it crashed over her and swept her away.

The sound of wolves howling nearby brought Ellie back to a state of semi-consciousness. Shivers racked her body, and her head ached so badly she could barely open her eyes. She knew it was important to wake up, or she would become dinner for the wolves she heard getting closer. Her head didn't feel like cooperating, and she lost consciousness again.

It might have been minutes or hours later when she awakened again. Ellie groaned when she felt something soft against her face. She blinked open her eyes and would have screamed if she'd had the strength. A large brown wolf lay across her lap, with its muzzle pressed against her cheek.

Her eyes blurred, and she thought she saw the countenance of a young woman appear on the wolf's head as it drew away. "Remain calm. Help is on the way."

She couldn't help noticing the wolf had a thick accent, and its English wasn't perfect. Oh, yes, she was about to die or already had. Ellie closed her eyes again, surrendering to sleep. It seemed preferable to hallucinating or experiencing the agony of the wolf tearing into her.

When she next awoke, it was to the din of raised voices. She blinked open her eyes, stunned to find herself in a small room, nestled under a mound of blankets. She was warm and dry. Her head still ached, but she could manage to keep her eyes open.

She turned her head, and a groan escaped as pain flared with the motion. She saw a fireplace, complete with a roaring fire. It provided enough illumination to make out the room's contents—a small table, a dresser, and a closet with the door partially opened.

Ellie cautiously touched the wound on her forehead, finding a thick bandage covered it. Someone had found her, but the question was, who? "Hello?" She winced at the raspy quality of her voice. The angry voices didn't diminish, so she assumed they hadn't heard her. She cleared her throat and tried again. "Is someone there?"

The shouting ended abruptly, followed by two or three seconds of silence before footsteps approached the room. When the door opened, a beam of light arced into the room, catching Ellie in the face. She winced and shielded her eyes. She waited for the person to speak, but they stood in the doorway silently.

The light backlit their frame, which she believed was a man's. Surely, few women got that tall and broad. The long hair she saw flowing down his shoulder might have caused her to doubt her original conclusion, except it didn't seem feminine. The ebony shade gleamed in the light, but it didn't have that fussed-over quality of most women's hair.

Although he hadn't moved forward or spoken, a chill of fright darted up Ellie's spine. There was a menacing air about the man, and she found herself recoiling into the soft mattress of the single bed.

She couldn't find her tongue to break the quiet. Ellie resisted the urge to fling back the covers and run screaming from the room, simply to break the eerie silence. Her heart raced as he continued to stand there, not moving except to cross his arms over his chest.

She didn't know how much longer the silence would have lasted if someone hadn't pushed open the door and walked past the man. As she got closer, Ellie recognized her as the woman from her hallucination. She must have been the one to find her. Ellie didn't know why her mind had added the touch about the wolf. Who could fathom what images an injured brain might producc?

"How are you feeling?" Her English was as stiff and accented as it had been before. "Miss?"

Unexpected tears welled in her eyes as the woman reached out to stroke her arm. She looked down and realized she was wearing her own pink flannel gown. She was touched that they had gone to the trouble of retrieving her luggage when they rescued her. "O-okay," she finally said.

The woman touched her bandaged forehead. "Nasty." She clicked her tongue. "You were asleep for a long time."

"How long?"

"Two days."

The hairs on Ellie's neck prickled, and she knew the man had stepped into the room even before she turned her head and saw him walking toward her. She tried to smile, but her lips were as numb as the rest of her when fear seized her. She held her breath.

"You're better now." He nodded. "You can leave." His pronunciation was better than the woman's, but his accent was just as thick, with the trace of a growl.

Ellie gasped at the same time as the other woman, although she suspected for different reasons. Hers sprang from the surprise of discovering how attractive he was when he stepped into the light. His well-formed features gave him more than a hint of masculine beauty. He could be a statue, carved in stone, but it would have been the perfect marble favored by the Greeks. His high forehead denoted intelligence, and his sharp cheekbones highlighted his round, dark-blue eyes.

His scowling eyes, she realized. A frown drew his thin lips downward. She didn't doubt he was annoyed, but she didn't know why. She watched his muscles bulge as he shifted position, and she knew he could hurt her easily. However, the image that flashed through her mind was one of pleasure, rather than pain. She blinked it away, attributing the brief thought of having him cradle her against his chest to the aftereffects of the concussion she must have sustained.

"Rica," the woman said, and her tone held a note of reproof. "The miss is not yet well enough—"

"Davinia." He glowered at her before his gaze turned back to Ellie. "You'll understand we don't like outsiders."

She nodded.

"My people chose to rescue you," his tone left no doubt his choice would have been different, "but now you are well enough to leave, yes?"

She shrugged, and pain fanned down her spine. "I don't know where I am."

"Necheau," Davinia said. "High in the Bulgain Mountains." She glanced at Rica, and her eyes held a mixture of anger and fear. "Rica knows you can't leave, miss."

Her eyes widened. "What?"

"The pass."

Ellie frowned. Was that supposed to answer her question? "Huh?"

"We are snowed in until the spring thaw."

Rica growled, and the menacing sound echoed through the small room. "You will fly back the way you came."

Ellie shook her head, immediately regretting doing so as pain flashed through it. "I can't. The plane crashed. I don't know the extent of the damage, but I doubt it'll fly anytime soon."

"No, it won't," said Davinia. "It is a miracle you survived, miss. You can't fly that contraption."

"I don't care if you walk out. You will leave tomorrow morning."

She shuddered at the conviction in his harsh tone. Ellie inclined her chin a notch and tried to paste on a charming smile. "Please, sir, let me stay until I recover." *That'll only take three months. It will be a long recovery.*

She bit back a delighted giggle. Who would have guessed a plane crash could be serendipitous? She had the perfect excuse to stay and observe these people, at least for a few days. If she could ingratiate herself with this man, who seemed to be their leader, she might even be able to stay the full three months. Three months would be a cinch compared to the two years she lived with a small tribe in Africa, or eleven months in the rain forests of Brazil with another tribe.

His scowl deepened. He glared at Ellie, and then Davinia, before turning on his heel and striding from the room. He slammed the door, and the sound reverberated through her aching head.

"Ignore Rica's temper, miss," Davinia said in a whisper, after shooting a glance at the closed door. "He is too used to getting his way, with everyone kowtowing to him. He is sometimes like a little boy." She let out a little giggle before clapping her hands over her mouth. She looked alarmed by her revelation.

"Who is he?"

"He is the Alpha." She hesitated, before adding, "He leads us."

"Thank you for saving me, and for sticking up for me." Ellie smiled at the brunette when she sat beside her on the bed. "It couldn't have been easy to contradict your leader."

Davinia shrugged. "It is the way of women, to watch out for each other." A sad expression flitted across her face. "Of my people, anyway. The Pack is different about such things."

Ellie's eyes widened. "'The Pack'?"

She busied herself straightening the quilt, seeming to be avoiding Ellie's eyes deliberately. "The villagers call themselves this." She stood up quickly. "I should let you sleep, miss."

"I'm not really tired," Ellie said, as a yawn tried to free itself from her. "Well, maybe a little."

She nodded and turned to the door. "Sleep well."

"Oh, Davinia?"

"Yes, miss?"

"Call me Ellie." She didn't try to keep in the yawn. "Thanks."

"Of course." With a small curtsey, the woman left the room, closing the door behind her with a soft click.

Ellie smiled at her thoughtfulness. If the others in the Pack were as welcoming as Davinia, she wouldn't have any trouble integrating into their culture and getting a firsthand point-of-view for her study. Her smile faded as she realized how difficult it would be to get them to warm up to her if the others were like their leader. Surely, no one else in Necheau was that cold or unyielding.

Or that attractive, a sly voice whispered in the back of her mind as she slipped into sleep once more.

Chapter 2

When Ellie next awoke, the headache had gone. She stretched in the small bed and pushed back the covers, shivering at the chill in the air. She eyed the primitive log room with interest. Instead of electricity, oil lanterns stood on the table and above the mantle of the fireplace. No fire burned now. Ellie padded to the closed drapes, wincing at the coolness in the wood floor against her bare feet. She pulled them open and cried out with shock, stepping backward.

Four children had their faces pressed against her window. When they saw her, they too fell back into the snow. Three scattered in various directions, but the smallest stayed. She couldn't have been more than four. She cautiously approached the window, sniffing like a dog. A smile blossomed on her face, and she waved before darting off to catch up with her comrades.

Ellie grinned as she watched the little one run away. Her eyes were still on the window when she heard the door open. She turned and smiled at Davinia as the other woman entered with a pail of water, soap, and a towel. "Good morning." She ventured a guess of the time based on the sunshine streaming through the window.

"Good morning, Ellie." Davinia set down the pail. When she did so, her dress pulled taut over her stomach, revealing she was far into a pregnancy. "Did you sleep well?"

Ellie nodded. She walked over to join the woman, glancing down at her stomach. "When is your baby due?"

"Three weeks." A fleeting glimpse of sadness darted through her eyes.

Ellie frowned. "What's wrong?"

Davinia shrugged. "Nothing. I'm excited, but worried. I had hoped my aunt would be beside me during the delivery, but she died last year."

It was instinctive to reach out and pat the girl's hand. Ellie guessed Davinia was a few years her junior, but it wasn't a mothering instinct that had her reaching out for the girl. She just seemed so lonely and lost. "I'm sorry. What about your mother?"

"She died when I was very young. I was a late baby." Davinia seemed to make a determined effort to push away her sadness. "Viggo has given me permission to name our daughter after my aunt."

Ellie's interest piqued. "Who's Viggo?"

"My husband. Rica's brother. He's the beta."

She nodded, wondering why this group had fashioned their culture after a wolf pack. It wasn't unheard of to still find primitive groups, but it was rare to find one in the middle of Eastern Europe, when the surrounding countries thrived on progress, technology, and science. "Is it normal for the men to choose the names of children?"

Davinia frowned. "Not so much, but I'm not a recognized citizen of the Pack. I can't stand in during the Naming Ceremony, so Viggo will be alone. He's agreed to the name I picked for her." She rubbed her stomach, seemingly in an unconscious movement.

Ellie led her to the bed, getting her to sit before sitting beside her. "What does it mean, that you aren't recognized?"

"I'm not one of them. I don't have any rights. I'm not even a real person to most of them." She lowered her voice after glancing around the room, as though looking for someone who might be listening in. "They are clannish, these people. Not at all open to outsiders. If I didn't love Viggo so much, I wouldn't be able to tolerate life here."

"Where are you from?" What she wouldn't give for the recorder in her bag. Ellie would settle for a piece of paper and a pen, but didn't want to alarm Davinia and risk missing this information.

"I lived nearest to Bulgainia. I grew up at Castle Draganescu." A melancholy smile flashed across her face before disappearing. "I wouldn't have met Viggo if I hadn't gotten a little lost in the forest and ventured farther than I planned on a nightly hunt—" She suddenly broke off, and her eyes widened. "I have chores to do. You should bathe. You'll find your cases in the closet. I didn't dare unpack until Rica approves your stay." She got up quickly and made for the door.

"Davinia, wait."

The girl paused at opening the door, but didn't turn around. "Yes, Ellie?"

"When will you have time to talk more? Your people fascinate me."

Davinia turned around. "They aren't my people." She shook her head. "I suppose I would have time to talk tonight, if you're still here."

Ellie frowned. "Why wouldn't I be?"

"A meeting's been called. Several members of the Pack are demanding you leave. Rica will hear the arguments and decide tonight."

"He can't send me away. I have nowhere to go."

Davinia bobbed her head, but she didn't reply to that. "I have to go."

"Davinia, how do I go to the meeting?"

The girl quickly shook her head. "Oh, you mustn't. It's closed to all except adult members of the Pack. I won't be going either."

Ellie felt a twinge of fear, realizing the only person who seemed to be on her side wouldn't be allowed to speak in her favor. Despite her plan to blend into the fringes of the Pack, she knew she would have to go to the meeting and make herself heard. She bit her lip, considering her options. She didn't want to get Davinia in trouble, but the girl was her only option. "I need to go to the meeting. Will you help me?"

Davinia hesitated. She seemed to be debating her options. Finally, she nodded slowly. "I'll come for you after sunset."

"Thank you, Davinia."

"You might not thank me when you see the Pack. They won't be shy about their desire to get rid of you."

Ellie firmed her shoulders. "I'll be fine."

Davinia made a non-committal sound and left the room. The silence pressed on Ellie after her departure, leaving her with only her thoughts. And what heavy thoughts they were. It looked as if this group would be the most challenging one of her career. She could handle it. She knew how important it was to finish this study so she could get tenure and the chair of her department. She wouldn't let a little thing like the group's close-mindedness drive her away. Besides, she didn't have anywhere to go until the snow thawed.

* * * * *

Ellie awaited Davinia's arrival in a state of nervous excitement. She jumped when the door opened, although she had expected Davinia more than an hour ago. The sun had been down two hours now. She got to her feet and shrugged on the parka hanging from a hook when she saw the other woman wearing a floor-length fur wrap. "Where are we going?" she asked, following Davinia from the room.

"The meeting spot. It's a bit of a walk."

As they left the room where Ellie had spent her time, she looked around. The room was part of a larger cabin, designed in the same rustic manner, and built from logs. It was reminiscent of pictures from frontier days in the west. "Does everyone live like this?"

Davinia led her to the wide front door, pausing to look back. "Like what?"

"In cabins," Ellie eyed the profusion of dimly lit lanterns scattered throughout the room, "without electricity?"

"Necheau isn't equipped to have electricity. Some families don't even have running water, but Viggo and I do. He installed it when I agreed to marry him." A small shudder racked her frame. "I can adapt to the lack of electricity, but I'm not running to the lake for a bath every day."

They stepped outside, and Ellie immediately hunched into her coat. She huddled behind Davinia's taller frame, using her as a buffer against the fierce wind blowing through the night. Fat flakes accompanied the wind, slapping her in the face as they landed. She slogged through the foot of snow on the walkway, eyeing the drifts on each side of the walk. They rose to her waist. "Where's the meeting spot?" She hoped it wasn't far, because her designer leather boots were no match for the piled snow.

"About half a mile." Davinia moved lightly through the snow, seeming not to have any trouble navigating.

Ellie plodded along. It wasn't long before the snow penetrated her boots and pants. Soon, the damp feeling turned to an icy sensation. Breath smoked from her in plumes, and she was about to call a halt to the endeavor when Davinia stopped walking. She paused at her side and glanced down, seeing nothing. "Is this it?"

"Down the hill and around the corner." Davinia bit her lip. "Wait here. I need to make sure everyone's…" She trailed off and rushed down the hill without so much as a cloud of snow following in her wake. How did she move so fleetly with her heavily pregnant frame?

Ellie began to jog in place and blow on her hands, hoping to bring warmth back to her extremities. She was half-convinced the blood had frozen in her veins. She thought longingly of the Árvore tribe, living in the sweltering jungle. What she wouldn't give for the high temperatures and even higher humidity she had hated during her eleven-month stay in Brazil. It was paradise compared to Necheau.

She had progressed to heavy foot stomping by the time Davinia returned. She stopped in mid-stomp with a sheepish grin. "I can't feel my toes."

Davinia smiled, but didn't respond to her comment. "You can go down. I'll show you the way. You must be quiet. Don't make your presence known. I beg you. The others would be upset, and Viggo would take the brunt of my shame for disobeying."

She made a non-committal sound and picked her way down the steep incline carefully, staying two steps behind Davinia and a little off to her side, in case she fell. Ellie didn't want to hit the woman and knock her down the hill.

They followed the slippery slope to the bottom, where the land evened out. She followed Davinia a few more steps before pausing when the other woman held up her hand. She pointed to a large tree, and Ellie ducked behind it. Davinia did the same with another tree beside it, and they leaned out cautiously to watch the meeting being held in a clearing. A bonfire provided illumination, and those in attendance crowded around it. Some sat on logs, and others stood up.

Ellie's eyes widened as she saw those assembled. Men comprised the majority of the gathering. Hairy, bare-chested men, whose chests gleamed in the firelight. Her gaze unerringly picked out Rica among the group, and her pussy clenched when she saw the sheen of sweat glowing on his impressive frame. She followed the line of black fur down his stomach, to where it disappeared inside the waistband of his snug jeans. She leaned out farther, struggling to get a better view.

As soon as she realized what she was doing, Ellie darted behind the tree again, feeling a flush heat her cheeks. She couldn't believe she was lusting after that man, when it was obvious he hated her. Not her, specifically, she suspected. Rica seemed to be the type to hate anyone who wasn't like him.

She forced herself to focus on the meeting.

"She can't stay. She isn't one of us," said a burly man with greasy hair. He shook his fist as he spoke.

"What choice is there?" another man replied. He was slim, but with muscles that rippled as he paced across the clearing. He was handsome, with an even tone that conveyed calm.

"You and that wife of yours should have left her out there. That's a solution," yet another man shouted.

"Take her back," said a huge woman sitting on a log. She was also shirtless, and her large breasts jiggled when she got to her feet. Graying-brown hair cascaded down her front to hide her sagging breasts, but they continued to bounce as she raised her voice. "Leave her there. It's not our responsibility if she doesn't find her way out of the mountains."

"You would leave her to die?" Rica spoke without a trace of emotion in his tone.

"Surely you don't want her to stay, Alpha?" There was a note of deference in the woman's tone, but she didn't back down. "She isn't one of us." She turned her glare to the younger, calmer man. "We've had enough outsiders brought into the Pack lately."

"You dare speak about my wife?"

Ellie's eyes widened further at the man's display of temper. She had pegged him as a peacekeeper, until that moment. She turned her head to look at Davinia, finding the other woman huddled against the tree, with her head down. It must be Viggo down there, speaking up for his wife.

"The subject of Viggo's wife has been settled." A hint of anger laced Rica's voice. "The issue up for discussion is what to do about the outsider." He took a few steps forward, taking time to meet the eyes of each member assembled. "I'll allow a vote on the matter, but the decision rests with me."

The greasy-haired man shook his head. "But—"

Rica turned to him, snarling. "Do you challenge me, Istal?"

The other man sank to his knees in the snow, bowing his head. "No, Alpha."

Rica nodded with satisfaction. "Voice your opinion. Yea, she stays. Nay, she goes."

Ellie held her breath, awaiting their reaction. Her heart sank at the overwhelming majority of nays that rang out from the clearing below. She looked at Davinia, and her frightened expression didn't improve Ellie's confidence.

Once the voices died down, Viggo stepped forward. "The decision is yours, Rica, but know I won't support cold-blooded murder. If you decide to leave that woman in the mountains, you aren't the leader I thought you were."

Ellie couldn't hold back a gasp as Rica leaped at his brother, landing gracefully before him. She heard Davinia cry out when Rica grasped Viggo by the throat and lifted him to his toes. She saw her friend start to rush forward and hurried to intercept her, holding her around her thick waist. "Remember what you told me. Viggo would be in trouble if they see us."

Davinia's lips trembled. "He won't hurt him. Rica wouldn't hurt his brother, his Beta...would he?"

Ellie shrugged, having no answer. They ducked behind the tree together, holding hands, as they watched the scene unfold.

"Are you challenging me, brother?" Rica's soft purr barely carried to them, but his anger seemed to resonate around the clearing and up the hill. "Do you question my ability to lead?"

"Not if you make the right decision," Viggo said with a gasp.

"I see." Rica thrust him away, causing Viggo to land on the ground. "You'll support me if I make the decisions you want." He turned his back on his brother. "The woman stays."

Ellie expected a flurry of protests, so the eerie quiet surprised her. She looked at Davinia. "Why aren't they arguing?"

"They wouldn't defy the Alpha. Only someone planning to challenge him would."

"Will Viggo challenge Rica?"

Davinia shook her head. "He's allowed more leeway, because he's Beta...I think. I've only been to one meeting."

"What happened?"

Davinia looked away from the meeting. "I was summoned to hear the decision of the Pack about whether I could join or not. They had already decided when they sent for me. I thought Viggo had convinced the Pack to allow me to marry him and live here, but now I suspect Rica was the one who made the final decision." She blinked, but a tear still streamed down her cheek. "That would explain their attitudes toward me."

Ellie patted her shoulder, but her attention returned to the group when Rica began speaking again.

"We don't want her here. None will deny that, but we can't force her into the mountains. We aren't savages, despite what some think. She has my protection until the thaw. Do any challenge this decision?"

Once again, silence greeted his statement, although there seemed to be a wave of anger flowing from the group. Ellie jumped when Davinia pulled on her sleeve. She turned her head. "Yeah?"

"It's time to leave. Your fate has been decided, and the rest of the meeting isn't our business."

Ellie nodded and turned to follow Davinia. She looked back briefly, and her heart stuttered as her gaze locked with Rica's. She tried to convince herself he couldn't see her from so far away, and sheltered by the tree, but she wasn't sure about that as she hurried after the other woman. She shivered, wondering what the penalty was for eavesdropping on one of their meetings. Would he change his mind about allowing her to stay?

* * * * *

That must have been the end of the meeting, because Davinia and Ellie had barely returned to the cabin and settled by the fire when Viggo entered. He had put on a shirt and coverings, and his expression didn't betray anything.

Davinia got to her feet, rushing to remove Viggo's fur cloak. "Ellie, this is my husband, Viggo. Viggo, this is Ellie."

He nodded to Ellie. "She can stay."

Davinia nodded her head, but gasped when he lifted her hand and held it to his cheek.

"Your hand is cold as ice. Have you been walking, Davinia?" The question was light, but his tone carried a hint of suspicion.

She shrugged. "I showed Ellie a bit of the village. She's feeling better today."

"Hmm." He eyed them both, and his lips compressed. Finally, his gaze settled on Ellie. "He wants to see you."

She didn't have to ask whom he meant. "When?"

"Right now. Since Davinia gave you a tour, I'm sure you won't have any trouble finding his home."

"Oh, we didn't get that far, Viggo," Davinia said in a rush. "I'll show her."

"No. You've been out too much already. It's not good for the baby." He gestured to Ellie. "I'll show you. Come along."

She got to her feet reluctantly, increasingly convinced Rica had seen her at the meeting. She suspected he had told Viggo, judging by the other man's behavior. She didn't argue with him as she slipped her feet into the damp boots and shrugged on the thick parka.

She walked behind him silently. They turned the opposite direction from where Davinia had led her, and Ellie eyed everything. The village was roughly a square, with a clearing in the middle that held only a well and water pump. Small and medium-sized cabins took up three sides of the main square, but three buildings dominated the last side of the square. A church held center position, with a huge wooden cross affixed to its roof. The buildings on each side were smaller, but not as small as the other cabins.

"What are those?" she asked.

"The general store and post office, but there's no mail this time of year." He pointed to the building on the other side of the church. "That's the school and library."

She didn't ask any other questions as they walked to the end of the square. His succinct answers hadn't invited more probing. They stopped in front of a medium-sized cabin. Viggo pointed to the gate. "He's expecting you."

She swallowed, resisting the urge to plead with Viggo to accompany her. She didn't feel comforted by his presence in any sense except she didn't want to face Rica alone. Ellie squared her shoulders. "Thanks for showing me the way."

"You can find your way back?"

"If I'm still alive," she offered with a hesitant grin.

"Yes," Viggo agreed, deadpan, and turned to walk back to his home.

She watched him go, delaying the inevitable moment of confrontation. Finally, she couldn't put it off any longer and walked to the fence, opening the wooden gate. She walked up the wooden walkway and stepped onto the porch. His house was charming in a quaint way. The sort of place her parents might rent if they ever lowered themselves to take a roughing-it vacation.

She eyed the intricate wood moldings around the door and traced a finger down the ornate design of the wood. She was about to reach for the knocker—the head of a wolf, with a ring in its mouth—when the door opened. She took a step back, bracing herself, wondering what he would do to her.

Chapter 3

He hadn't put his shirt on. That was the first thing she noticed. The second was his hard expression. He stared at her without speaking. Ellie took a deep breath and tried to smile. "Viggo said you wanted to see me."

He nodded, taking a step back to allow her to walk inside. "Come in."

She swallowed and forced her feet forward, brushing past Rica's impressive frame as she entered the dim living room. Lanterns provided a surprising amount of cozy light. She walked into the main room and looked back at him, waiting while he closed the door and walked over to her.

He moved silently, with inherent grace. Rica stopped a couple of feet from her. He didn't sit on the overstuffed sofa, and he didn't offer her a seat. He crossed his arms. His gaze swept over her. "What is that ridiculous stuff on your face?"

That wasn't the question she had expected. Ellie unconsciously pushed back strands of short blonde hair to reveal the complete tattoo on her cheek. It was an intricate design of blue lines. Each line was of varying lengths, and all met in the center of the design. The lines represented the lifespans of the chiefs of the Árvore tribe, while the dot in the center of the tattoo stood for the heart of the people.

"It's a symbol of the Árvore tribe of South America. I stayed with them for a while." She touched the silver spike in her left brow, above large gray eyes. "A product of misspent youth." She extended her left forearm. "This is a marker of the different groups of people I've lived with through the years."

"Why have you lived with these people?"

Her mind raced for an answer. She couldn't reveal she had written books about a few little-known tribes. Ellie thought Rica wouldn't have any trouble grasping what her profession was, or what her purpose was in coming to Corsova, if he knew that. "I took an extended vacation for a time. I felt like staying with the groups and learning from them. It was a growing experience."

"What were you on vacation from?" Again, his gaze swept over her. "You don't strike me as the hardworking, useful type."

Her eyes narrowed at the insult, but she couldn't retort and maintain the façade she had adopted. She shrugged and tried to project a simpering smile. "Oh, whatever strikes my fancy. Mother and Daddy don't care if I hold a real job. They know I'm gaining life experience."

He snorted, leaving no doubt of his opinion about that. "Well, don't expect to gain life experience with us. I'm permitting you to stay until the spring thaw, but you aren't a guest. You'll help Davinia with whatever chores she has. You'll also be available to the other women, if they ask for help." He shook his head. "That's doubtful."

"Thank you. I appreciate your hospitality. You're too kind." She couldn't hold back a trace of sarcasm.

His eyes narrowed. "It wasn't kindness that motivated me. I don't relish leaving you to die in the mountains, and there's nothing else to do with you. Just stay out of everyone's way."

She frowned. "Like poor Davinia? She's been married to your brother for how long? A year? Two? More? And she's still not treated like one of you."

"It's not your business." His arm snaked out, and he grasped her wrist. "Speaking of other things that aren't your business, you weren't invited to the Pack's meeting. Davinia's a biddable girl, so I know where to place the blame for that. You keep to yourself while you're here."

Anger sizzled through her, and she batted her lashes up at him. "Why, Rica, I planned to become best friends with your wife. Maybe I'll corrupt her as I've so obviously corrupted Davinia."

To her surprise, he didn't look angry. Instead, he seemed grimly amused. "I have no mate, woman, and if I did, she would be more than a match for you. I know your kind."

"Really? Because it seems to me, you don't know much about anything, except this little village and its way of life. Yes, you're a…small man." Her eyes widened at the rejoinder. What was she doing? It was her job to blend in with these people, to gain their confidence, so she could get an insider's perspective on their lives. Alienating the leader wouldn't help her accomplish that goal. She opened her mouth to apologize, but a gasp escaped her instead, as he jerked her into his arms.

"I know a great deal about many things." He pressed his face closer to hers. "Probably more than you do," he said with a growl.

She couldn't help noticing how close his mouth was to hers. Her lips felt dry, and she moistened them with her tongue. Her gaze didn't stray from his. Ellie meant to apologize, but couldn't find the words. She couldn't seem to gather her wits. Her thoughts were a confusing whirl, centering around one thing: How would it feel to have his lips on hers?

He began to sniff her, but still didn't touch. Ellie held her breath, wondering about his actions. *I wonder if I smell good to him?* The thought was disorienting, but not so much as the one that followed. *He smells good to me, with his sharp, woodsy scent. He's so male.* She cleared her throat. "Rica, I'm sorry—"

He cut off her apology with his lips, molding them to hers with firm pressure. His arms engulfed her, pulling her against the hardness of his body, the firmness of his cock. Ellie realized Rica most certainly wasn't a small man as his hard cock swelled against the confines of his jeans.

She wrapped her arms around him, pressing her palms against the smooth skin of his back. She ran her hands down his back, pausing to trace the line of his spine to the waistband of his jeans. He deepened the kiss. When his tongue invaded her mouth, she opened under its assault. Her fingernails dug into his back, and her nipples beaded.

She groaned when her pussy spasmed. How long had it been since she had a man? Nine months. Nine long months. Her body craved Rica's touch, even as her mind tried to caution her against the attraction. She couldn't become involved with a subject. It might skew the results of her study completely.

Still, she couldn't make herself break free from his arms. In fact, she snuggled closer, thrusting her hips so that her denim-covered pussy brushed against his thigh. She made a wordless sound of need, straining against him.

He pushed her away suddenly, and with so much force, she stumbled into the couch. Ellie's eyes widened, and she pressed a hand to her chest, as if trying to hold in her racing heart. She looked at him uncertainly, wondering why he had broken the kiss so abruptly. She held out her other hand. "Rica?"

He stepped back to avoid her touch. "Get out. Stay out of my way while you're here."

She frowned. "Did I..." Ellie trailed off, realizing she was about to ask if she had done something wrong. She should be thanking him for ending things before they got out of hand. She should definitely apologize for her snide remark, accept his kiss as a deserved response, and leave as an adult. She shouldn't be contemplating throwing herself into his arms and begging for his possession.

That thought brought a return of sanity, and she squared her shoulders. "I'm sorry for my thoughtless remarks. I don't feel quite like myself tonight. It must be from the concussion." Or the amazing kiss. She blocked that thought. "Regardless of your reasons, thank you for allowing me to stay. I'll do my best to stay out of your way."

He nodded, but didn't speak. Ellie steadied herself and hurried to the door, not looking back until she turned the knob. She glanced at Rica, unable to resist noticing the way the light shimmered on his skin, or the loneliness of his pose. She swallowed down an unexpected lump of moisture and hurried out into the night, intending to honor her promise to avoid him. She had to, if she hoped to complete her study.

* * * * *

"Was he cruel?" Davinia asked as she helped Ellie make the beds the following morning. They hadn't had a chance to speak last night, because Davinia and Viggo were in bed by the time she returned. Ellie had stayed up half the night, tossing and turning in the small bed, wishing Rica had taken care of the ache he had created between her thighs.

She tucked in the corner of the sheet, shaking her head. "No, not really. He told me to keep to myself and not expect a free ride."

Davinia nodded. "The women here have so much work. It's just silly they won't put in electricity."

"Why is that?" Ellie tried to sound casual as she kept her attention on smoothing the sheet.

"The Pack doesn't like to rely on anyone for anything. That applies even to utility service. The rest of Corsova put in electricity in the '50s, but Rica's grandfather refused to allow it in Necheau." Davinia stood up straight, rubbing her lower back.

Ellie saw her grimace as she stood up to retrieve the quilt. "Are you all right?"

Davinia shrugged. "I suppose they are the typical pains of pregnancy."

"Maybe you should see the doctor." She unfolded the quilt across the bed as she spoke.

Davinia grasped the other side. "We have no doctor. Belia, that horrid woman who spoke out against Rica last night, is the midwife, but she won't see me."

Ellie paused in the action of tucking in the quilt. "What? Why not?"

"I'm not one of the Pack."

She was concerned for her new friend. "Have you seen a doctor at all?"

Davinia shook her head. "It's not our way. I would know if there's a problem."

"Hmm." She wondered how many live births the women of Corsova had each year. "Is it the same with the people in the village where you lived before?"

"It's the same with all our people." Davinia laughed lightly. "Bulgainia isn't a village. It's the capitol of Corsova, and quite modern. I used to go shopping with my aunt. I could buy clothes right out of the store, rather than make them myself." She looked sad. "That was before I married Viggo."

"Are you happy?" Perhaps it was an impertinent question, but Ellie sensed her friend wasn't.

Davinia sat on the bed. She was careful not to meet Ellie's eyes. A sigh escaped her. "I love him, and I'm thrilled about the baby, but I wish things were different. If he weren't the Beta of the Pack, we could have lived at the castle or in Bulgainia."

Ellie sat on the other side of the bed, trying to commit to memory everything Davinia said. Part of her wished she didn't have to be so analytical. She wanted to listen just for the sake of listening, not to learn something she might be able to use in her study. It was the same situation each time she integrated into a culture. Her conscience always warred with her academic side.

"Viggo wouldn't have been happy there. I know that."

Ellie touched her hand, moved by the pain in her voice. She ignored the twinge of her conscience that told her it was wrong to gain Davinia's trust. "Would your people treat him as an outsider?"

"No, not at all. Everywhere else, our two groups have become almost a hybrid. It's only here that the Pack—" She broke off, wiping her eyes. "Never mind. It's not that interesting. They're a close-minded group of people, and nothing will change them. I have Viggo, and soon Ylenia." She patted her stomach before standing up. "There's washing to do, if you don't mind helping me?"

"Of course not." Ellie followed her from the bedroom, wishing circumstances were different. When Davinia found out her purpose for being here, she would assume Ellie had used her for information. The other woman would never believe she had liked her, or that it was difficult to do her job and be her friend. She probably wouldn't believe Ellie didn't have any close friends and hadn't since she graduated from college. They were transient, and the budding friendships always ended when her true purposes were revealed.

* * * * *

Later that afternoon, Ellie ventured outside. They had completed the chores, and Davinia was napping. Her friend hadn't said anything about staying inside, and she had deliberately avoided asking. She knew what she would hear if she mentioned she planned to explore the village. Davinia would try to discourage her.

At least her friend wouldn't get in trouble for her walk, since she was asleep and couldn't have stopped her. Ellie strolled along the square, mostly cleared of snow, admiring the homes along the way. Although they were all the same basic design, each had unique touches to set it apart. Almost every door was a carved masterpiece, and she wondered who had done them. It might have been each owner of the houses, but the doors looked as if the same artist did them.

As she neared the well in the center of the square, she saw an old woman shuffling toward it, carrying a bucket. Swollen joints betrayed her arthritis, as did her slow pace, and the way her back curved, as if weighted by years of burdens.

Ellie hurried forward to the old woman, reaching her at the same time she reached the water pump. "Ma'am, may I help you?"

The woman turned her face in Ellie's direction. Myriad wrinkles mapped her face, telling the story of her age in vivid detail. Her hair was whiter than the snow on the ground. Her nose twitched. "Who's that? I don't see too well these days."

"My name's Ellie. My plane crashed in the mountains."

The woman nodded. "Ah, so you're the one." She didn't sound unkind. "The outsider. I heard about you this morning from Lia."

"Who's Lia?" She took the bucket from the woman when she didn't reject her offer. Ellie put her weight into the pump, finally getting it to go after two or three tries. She maintained a steady pumping rhythm as water poured into the bucket.

"A silly young thing. She's convinced Rica will challenge for her at the next Mating Moon, now that she's of age."

"Oh." Her heart lurched at the thought of Rica taking a mate. She forced a smile, even though the woman probably couldn't see it. "Would you like me to carry this back to your home, ma'am?"

"Please." She grasped her cane and began to shuffle back to her residence. "Call me Golatia."

Ellie grasped the bucket, straining to hold it steady. She followed Golatia, glad for the older woman's slow pace so she wouldn't spill the water. "Have you lived here all your life?"

"Of course. Where else would I live?"

She smiled at the answer. "I don't know. Maybe Bulgainia. Davinia said it's a beautiful little city."

"Bah, cities stink." The woman drew in a deep breath, twitching her nose. "Smell the mountain air."

She breathed in obligingly. "I smell pine from the trees."

Golatia shook her head. "It's a pity you can't smell it all. Bless you for your limitations, young one."

Ellie didn't know how to respond to that, so she remained silent.

The old woman stopped in front of a small house. It was closest to the well. "Rica gave me this home when my strength faded." Golatia growled low in her throat. "There were those like Belia, who said cast me out. It was the old way." She snorted. "Sometimes, the old way is not the best way, you understand?"

Ellie nodded before remembering her sight problem. "Yes, ma'am." She was surprised when the woman took her free hand and squeezed it.

"You ignore what they say when the time comes. Be strong and have faith in your man."

She frowned. "I'm sorry. I don't understand."

Golatia's laugh was a honest-to-goodness cackle. "You will, young one. Now, give me that bucket, and make sure you come visit me soon. Bring Viggo's wife. The poor dear doesn't need to be sitting at home by herself all the time."

"I could carry the water in for you, ma'am."

"Golatia," she corrected. "Ma'am makes me feel every one of my ninety years." She took the bucket, holding it with surprising strength. "Never you mind. I'm strong enough for the bucket yet. Don't forget to come see me."

"I won't." Ellie couldn't resist grasping the woman's hand and squeezing it in the same way Golatia had squeezed hers. It didn't matter if the woman was strange and possibly a little off. She had shown Ellie the first kindness from anyone other than Davinia since her arrival. "Good day." She watched until the woman made her way inside before turning away. Pleasant warmth flowed through her, and she felt optimistic about winning over the Pack for the first time since the meeting. Maybe they weren't all bad.

* * * * *

It took some convincing, but she managed to persuade Davinia to accompany her for tea at Golatia's house two days later. Ellie had spent most of her time stuck in the cabin, and she was bored stiff. It wasn't polite to simply invite themselves over, but the woman's invitation had been open-ended. Something about the other woman suggested she too was lonely, and Ellie didn't think she would mind the imposition.

"I don't know," Davinia said for the tenth time, as they approached Golatia's small cabin. "I don't even know this woman. I think it's best if we keep to ourselves."

"Davinia, you'll never fit in with these people if you hide in your house." She threaded her arm through her friend's and walked forward, bringing her along. "She's a nice old woman, and she specifically told me to bring you along."

"Okay." She gave a heavy sigh, but her steps didn't falter as they walked onto the porch.

Ellie knocked loudly, figuring Golatia's hearing was probably bad too. It was a long time before the door opened.

"Sorry, dears. I knew you were coming, but it still takes me a time to rattle my old bones from the kitchen to the door." Golatia stepped back to give them room to enter.

Ellie wondered if she had heard right. "You were expecting us?" Had the woman been preparing for their visit every day, only to be disappointed?

"Yes, Ellie. I knew you'd finally convince Davinia she was welcome." Golatia grasped Davinia's hands. "You're welcome anytime, child. Come sit, and I'll bring in the tea."

"Let me," Ellie said quickly.

Golatia nodded, allowing Davinia to assist her to a rocking chair.

Ellie walked into the kitchen through the living room. The floor plan of the cabin didn't provide a break between rooms, other than doorways. There was no door barring the kitchen from the living room.

She saw a tray on the counter, and her eyes widened when she counted three cups and saucers, and six biscuits. Golatia really had prepared for their arrival. She shivered, remembering the other woman's strange words about having faith in her man. Ellie had seen some extraordinary things in the last few years, and she couldn't discount the idea that Golatia had the gift of Sight.

She lifted the tray and carried it into the living room, setting it on a large coffee table made from a slab of trunk from an ancient tree. Whoever made it had sanded the wood and added gloss, but allowed its natural imperfections to shine through. An uncountable amount of rings swirled around it, making it impossible to guess the age of the tree the table had come from. "This is beautiful."

"Oh, yes." Golatia leaned forward to touch the smooth wood. "Rica made that when he was just a cub, learning at his father's side."

Ellie poured the tea, smiling at the affectionate term for Rica as a child. "He has a gift."

Golatia nodded. "Of course, so does Davinia's man. Their father taught them everything about the art of wood. Their family's been intimate with the ways of wood since before I can remember."

Ellie passed them both a cup before taking one and leaning back into the chair she had chosen. "Did Rica make your door?"

"Yes, he made Mrs. Cosminstan's door. Either he or Viggo make all the doors. They sell them too," Davinia said. "The others in the Pack gather the wood and prepare it for use from its raw state. Some farm for our needs and sell the remainder, but the main economy is supported by Rica and Viggo."

Ellie should have been making neat mental notes, but all she could think of was Rica's skilled hands shaping wood into art. It wasn't long before the wood in her mental image melted into flesh—her flesh. She closed her eyes and took a deep breath, struggling to compose herself.

"I have something for you, Davinia." Golatia pointed to a chest in the corner. "Go and fetch that for her, would you, Ellie? It's not good for her to be lifting in her condition."

Ellie got to her feet and retrieved the small trunk. It was ornate in its design, with Golatia's name carved into the chest. "This is gorgeous. Did Rica make it?"

Golatia laughed. "No, 'twas his grandfather's brother, back when he planned to court me. Unfortunately, Ivan lost the challenge for me. I mated with Yuri, who died the next winter, before I ever conceived. By then, Ivan had moved in with his brother Victor and his wife." Sadness flashed across her face, but then she shrugged, and the emotion disappeared. "It's all in the past, while your little one is the future."

Davinia eyed the chest. "Should I open it, Mrs. Cosminstan?"

"Golatia, and yes, open it, child. Everything inside is for you."

She opened the chest, and a gasp sprang from her. Davinia lifted a tiny baby outfit, crotched from the finest yarn. "Oh, it's beautiful."

"Mind, they might have yellowed a bit with age. I haven't pulled them out in years." Golatia winked. "There never was a young woman I wanted to have them until now. If they've aged, you can bleach them easily enough, but you'd best get it done quickly."

Davinia lifted her head from examining the other garments. "Thank you, Mrs.—Golatia. I've yet to finish any of the clothes I started for Ylenia. My fingers aren't nimble with sewing, and the order I placed from Bulgainia didn't arrive before the snow blocked the pass."

Ellie had fastened on Golatia's words about bleaching the clothes quickly. She opened her mouth to ask about it when the old woman turned to look at her. There was a hint of worry in her expression, and she pursed her lips after shooting a glance at Davinia.

Ellie got the hint and held her tongue as Davinia talked about the baby. Before she knew it, more than an hour had passed.

"Oh, we must get back, Ellie. Viggo will be home soon." Davinia was slow on her feet when she got up and walked to Golatia. She pressed a kiss to her cheek and whispered something that sounded like, "Thank you."

Ellie followed suit, waiting until Davinia had returned to the trunk and gathered up the stack of baby clothes before kneeling beside Golatia's rocker. "You know things, don't you?"

"Yes." She grinned, displaying her remaining teeth and a large amount of pink gums. "I know many things, and some I can tell. Some I can't, and some I just plain won't."

"Is her baby coming soon?" She was careful to keep her voice to a whisper.

A troubled expression crossed the old woman's face. "Very soon, and she'll need you, Ellie." She lifted Ellie's hand and squeezed it. "You think you know why you're here, but that isn't the only reason. No, indeed. There are many reasons for why things happen." She released her hand. "Now, off with you both. I need a nap. I'm not as young as I used to be." The words must have amused Golatia, because she cackled. "Come see me again soon, the both of you."

She lowered her voice to a whisper, shooting a meaningful glance at Ellie. "Bring the little one."

Ellie stood up, deciding not to pressure the other woman for answers. She had plainly said she wouldn't reveal everything she knew. Golatia was old, but she was too sharp to trick into answering what she didn't want to answer, and too close-mouthed to reveal more than she wanted to. It was with a strange feeling of dissociation that she followed Davinia from the cabin, grasping an armful of baby clothes.

* * * * *

Ellie found herself unable to sleep. She tried finding a comfortable spot, but eventually gave up. She decided to make notes in her journal to pass some time until she felt sleepy. She slid from the bed and padded across the cold wooden floor to the closet, where she had hidden her journal.

As she passed the window, she looked out. She froze when she saw Rica standing outside in the square. The way the moon backlit his frame gave him a melancholy air. She had the compulsion to join him. Although she tried to stop herself, she couldn't seem to rein in the impulse. She slipped her feet into the boots and left the room quietly. She decided the parka would cover enough of the pink flannel gown to still be modest.

She paused at the front door to grab her coat and slid her arms into it as she left the cabin. Her feet crunched through the snow, which rose to the level of her boots or higher in places. She shivered in the bitter cold and knew she should turn back, but couldn't get her feet to obey her.

By the time she reached Rica, he had turned in her direction. His expression was neutral as he watched her walk toward him. It was below freezing, but he wore nothing except a flannel shirt and jeans.

When she was beside him, Ellie had no idea what to say. Why had she come out here to join him? It had been an illusion, his loneliness. Yet, she couldn't just turn around and walk away without saying anything. "Couldn't sleep?"

He grunted.

She took that for a yes. "Me neither. I'm worried about Davinia."

That sparked a glimmer of interest. "Why?"

"Golatia said she's going to have her baby soon."

The change in his expression was startling. It went from inscrutable to gentle. "You've met Golatia?"

She nodded. "She's very kind, isn't she?"

"Yes. She helped raise Viggo and I after our mother died." Rica sighed. "She's good with children."

"Do you have any?" What made her blurt out that question? She already knew he didn't have a wife. It seemed unlikely he was divorced, living in this environment.

He shook his head. "I haven't mated yet."

"Oh. Why not?"

He lifted a brow. "You're inquisitive."

She gave him a coaxing smile. "Don't tell me you're the stereotypical stubborn male who never answers questions or reveals anything about himself."

He hesitated a moment before answering. "I haven't felt the compulsion to join with a woman." His voice had dropped an octave, and his eyes seemed to focus on her breasts, revealed by the unzipped parka.

She licked her lips, sensing a change in atmosphere. "I see. Does that mean you're…inexperienced?"

He laughed. "It means I haven't found a woman who touched my heart. There have been a few who touched my cock, of course."

She was startled at the bluntness of his speech. A blush crept up her neck, and she cleared her throat. "Uh, what are you waiting for? How will you know when she has touched your heart?"

His sigh was long and drawn out. "When I was younger and asked about such things, Golatia told me I would just know." His expression bordered on brooding. "She didn't tell me what to do when I knew the feelings couldn't be right."

"Hmm." A wind gust blew under her nightgown, bringing a rush of cold air that washed over her panties. It did nothing to soothe the heated flesh inside the material. She couldn't recall the last time she had felt such an intense and instant attraction to a man. She ached for him to reach for her, but knew she couldn't let him. If she had understood him, he couldn't allow himself to reach for her either. It was frustrating to know he shared the attraction, but was equally helpless to act on it. "I should go in."

"Why did you come out here?"

She shrugged. "It's silly."

"Tell me."

She licked her lips, which had chafed in the cold air. "You seemed lonely. I..." She shrugged again and turned away from him. Logic compelled her to run back to Davinia's and put as much distance as possible between herself and this temptation. Yet, she made no move to pull away when his hands cupped her upper arms, and he pulled her back against his chest.

"I am lonely in many ways, Ellie. I want to find my mate, the one woman meant only for me." Her head spun as Rica's head lowered, bringing his mouth to her ear. "I ache for her," he said in a rough whisper. One of his hands moved to cup her breast, through the opening in her parka. The soft flannel was an unbearable abrasion against the sensitive peak when he thumbed her nipple.

She closed her eyes and relaxed against Rica. When he thrust his cock against her lower back, a moan escaped her. She felt his cock spasm, and her pussy convulsed with sympathy. She wanted to turn in his arms and feel his lips on hers again. Not in punishment or anger this time, but with perfect passion. The crotch of her panties dampened when he squeezed her nipple between his thumb and forefinger.

His mouth moved down her throat, leaving breathy kisses in its wake. She moaned again when he nipped the bend where her neck met her shoulder. "Rica."

He lifted his head, and his hand moved from her breast. He continued to hold her for a long moment, and then his hands fell away. "You should go inside."

She turned to look at him, with confusion in her eyes. "Rica—"

His eyes were sad, and his fingers were gentle when they pressed lightly against her lips. "This wouldn't work. I have responsibilities to the Pack. Certain things are expected of me. I can't do this."

She found herself nodding. Inside, she was numb, although a tear splashed down her cheek. It felt like goodbye when she turned away from him and hurried back to Viggo and Davinia's. It was ridiculous to feel actual physical pain at the separation. He meant nothing to her. They had shared a brief moment of loneliness, and nothing else. She tried to believe that, but her heart still ached when she entered the cabin and closed the door behind her.

Chapter 4

Two mornings later, Viggo shook her awake in the early hours. Ellie rolled over and stared up at him, blinking. He said something, but her fuzzy brain didn't recognize the words. "Huh?"

"The baby's coming. Davinia wants you."

So soon. Had Golatia known? Of course she had, Ellie decided, as she slid from the bed. She wasn't aware of the way the neckline of her flannel gown gaped open until she saw Viggo avert his eyes. A blush warmed her cheeks, but she put aside her embarrassment and slid on a robe with brisk movements. "I'm ready."

She spoke confidently, but her stomach was a mass of nerves as she followed Viggo from the small guest room to the main bedroom. How could she really be ready? What did Davinia want from her? She prayed it was only the comfort of a female companion, because she didn't have any experience delivering babies. She only knew what she had observed during Árvore births, silently watching the midwives and mothers perform the miracles, while she took notes.

The room was icy, and Ellie huddled in her robe, shivering. She realized why it was so cold when she saw Davinia. Her face was bright red, and her hair hung in damp strands. Pants issued from her, interspaced with low moans. Her eyes darted around the room, and she appeared on the edge of panic.

Ellie acted instinctively, going to the bed and grasping her friend's hand. "How are you holding up?"

"Fine." She sounded anything but fine though. She shot a fearful look at Viggo, and then brought her gaze back to Ellie's.

"Just fine." She seemed to be communicating that she wanted Viggo to leave.

Ellie frowned as the thought blossomed in her mind as clearly as if Davinia had spoken aloud. She cleared her throat and looked at Viggo. "Could you bring some hot water and fresh towels? Also, a blanket for the baby."

Viggo nodded and hurried from the room at a running pace. As soon as he was gone, Davinia's grip on her hand increased tenfold. She tried to keep her tone soothing. "How soon do you think it will be, Davinia?"

"I don't know. I've been having pains since yesterday."

Ellie's eyes widened. "Why didn't you say something?"

She shifted. "I hoped they would stop. I can't do this, Ellie. I'm not ready."

She pushed the hair off her face. "I don't think you have a choice. You can't reschedule, you know."

Davinia shook her head. "I don't want to do this. I don't know how."

She didn't like the note of hysteria creeping into the other woman's voice. "Shh, it's okay. We'll send Viggo to fetch the midwife. She'll come for the Beta." Wouldn't she?

"No, she won't. You'll see. I'm going to die, and no one in this goddamned place will care." The anger in her tone faded as another contraction hit. Davinia bent forward, grasping her stomach, and grunted.

"You aren't going to die." She stroked Davinia's hand, racking her brain for something to say. "Try to breathe." Ellie recited something she had heard on TV programs a hundred times. "Small pants, okay? Follow your instincts. You know what to do." But she didn't have a clue. Her stomach churned with nausea as she acknowledged she had at least an inkling of what to expect, but no experience. Although she had watched a few births, with the mothers' permission, that didn't make her qualified to deliver a baby.

Viggo returned in record time, bearing a bucket of hot water, an armful of towels, and a comforter large enough to wrap the baby at least a dozen times, when she arrived. As soon as he dropped the items on the bed, he was at Davinia's side. "How is it? Is she coming?"

"Soon."

Davinia's equanimity shocked Ellie, in contrast to her behavior of a few minutes ago. She stepped forward, touching Viggo's shoulder to get his attention. She didn't miss the way he stiffened, and she hurriedly dropped her hand. "Will you fetch the midwife, Viggo? It's about time for her."

Viggo frowned. "I don't want to leave Davinia."

"Go on. It won't take long at all. You'll be back in plenty of time." Ellie tried to sound positive, and she was pleased when he nodded. Viggo paused to drop a lingering kiss on his wife's mouth before hurrying from the bedroom. They heard the front door close less than a minute later.

"I hope he took a coat," Davinia said amid pants.

Before Ellie could respond, another contraction came, following the last by little more than a minute. She watched the hands on the clock tick off the minutes, as Davinia's labor intensified. By the time fifteen minutes had passed, she knew her friend couldn't wait any longer for the midwife. She swallowed her nervousness, knowing she had no choice. "I'll be right back."

She gave Davinia a calm smile as she went into the bathroom and washed her hands after removing the robe. She left it draped over the door and returned to Davinia. She tried to keep her tone steady. "I think we're going to have to do this by ourselves, Davinia." When she saw the panic in Davinia's eyes, she rushed to say, "I've seen it done. That is, I've watched a few deliveries. I'm no expert, but we'll manage."

"No." Davinia shook her head, even as she bent forward under the force of a contraction.

"Yes." She spoke firmly, not allowing a hint of her fear to show. "Your body knows what to do. All I have to do is catch."

Davinia eyed her uncertainly, but the next contraction seemed to convince her she had no choice. Ellie gave her a reassuring smile, while secretly wondering how they would manage. She prayed Viggo and the midwife would return soon as she knelt before Davinia and hoped all she really had to do was catch Ylenia when she entered the world.

Time had passed, but she didn't know how much. It felt like an eternity, but also an instant. "I think this is it. I can see her head. Push, Davinia." She was too busy to look at the clock, but she wasn't too distracted to wonder what had happened to Viggo. It seemed obvious Belia wasn't coming, so where could he be?

"I want to wait for Viggo."

"You can't. She isn't going to wait that long." Even as she said the words, she saw Davinia straining to push. It seemed to happen in a rush. Seconds later, the baby was in her hands. She was slippery and screaming. Tears of reaction gathered at the back of Ellie's eyes as she examined the infant. She didn't know if she was small for her age, but Ylenia appeared perfect in every way, except for a profusion of dark hair all over her body.

"She's gorgeous, Davinia. Let me finish here, and then you can have her." She dipped a towel into the cooled water and washed the baby as thoroughly as she could. Ellie bypassed the comforter and wrapped her in another towel before handing the impatient baby to her equally impatient mother.

She smiled as Davinia immediately unwrapped the towel and counted her fingers and toes. "She's beautiful." Davinia's voice broke, and she began sobbing. "Look at all that fur."

Ellie frowned at the odd words, but her attention turned when the door slammed against the wall. Viggo strode in, looking ready to murder. "What's wrong? What have you done to my wife?"

Ellie's eyes widened. "Nothing."

"I'm all right," Davinia managed to say amid sobs. "She's just so beautiful."

Viggo froze for a minute. His gaze dropped to Ylenia, and he rushed forward, pushing Ellie aside in his eagerness.

She didn't mind. She smiled as she backed away, right into a solid body. She tilted her head and saw Rica. She immediately dropped her chin and tried to step away, but froze when his hands settled on her shoulders. She bowed her head, wondering if he would berate her for assisting Davinia.

"It's over?" Viggo couldn't seem to absorb it, even as he lifted the baby from the towel and held her against his shoulder. She howled with outrage as the snow from his clothes seeped into her skin. He jerked and shoved her back to Davinia, looking on the verge of panic.

"You did this?" Rica's voice was meant for her ears only.

She didn't detect any anger in his tone, so she mustered her courage and turned to face him. She nodded.

He nodded in return. "We owe you our thanks."

She resisted the urge to downplay her involvement. She didn't want gratitude, but she didn't want it to become a big deal either. "She saved my life." The explanation was succinct, but should suffice. She cleared her throat. "The midwife should probably examine Ylenia and Davinia though. I don't know anything about…after." She swayed as her head grew light.

His arms were there instantly, bracing her. She looked up at him with blurred eyes. "Who am I kidding? I didn't know anything about before or during either. I've seen a few babies born, but I could have killed her." A wave of nausea rolled up her throat, and she heaved. Fortunately, there wasn't anything in her stomach to bring up.

A wave of weakness followed the incident, and she didn't protest as Rica lifted her into his arms. She didn't do anything except snuggle closer, reveling in his strength, as her own faded.

Viggo and Davinia didn't pay any attention as Rica carried her from their room and down the hallway. Ellie tried to gather her wits, but all she could think about was the damage she could have done to Davinia or Ylenia. She didn't realize her fears had poured from her in a babble of words until Rica spoke.

"You were brave enough to try. She needed you, and you were there."

She nodded, trying to stop shaking as Rica kicked open the door to her room and carried her to the bed. She looked up at him uncertainly as he lowered her to the mattress. Her eyes widened when he followed, stretching out beside her. She wanted to ask what he was doing, but she didn't care. She didn't want him to leave. Tentatively, she curled closer, wondering at her own show of vulnerability, but unable to rein it in.

He didn't protest when she laid her head on his shoulder. She marshaled her thoughts, returning the subject to Davinia. "Where is Belia? She has to examine them."

"She will." He spoke grimly. "She refused to come, because Davinia is not one of the Pack."

She stiffened. "That's nonsense. She's married to your brother." She frowned. "I'm not surprised though. It's no wonder they don't accept her, since you don't even acknowledge her existence. I haven't even seen you speak to Davinia in the days I've been here. I guess it takes an *outsider* to notice." She expected an angry response and realized she wanted one. In her overwrought state, she was spoiling to rid herself of excess energy.

"You're right." His mild tone surprised her. "The others have followed my lead. I never meant to deliberately ignore her, but I have had difficulty getting past what she is. I allowed her to stay because my brother told me he would leave the Pack to be with her if I didn't." He hesitated. "Perhaps I have allowed my resentment to cloud my judgment. I promise you this will not go on any longer. She and the cub could have died." His voice lowered to a growl. "Belia will come. I assure you."

She nodded her satisfaction, and her cheek brushed against the cold flannel of his shirt. A yawn surprised her. How could she even think of sleeping after everything that had happened? Another yawn followed, forcing her to recognize her exhaustion. The adrenaline rush had faded, and she could barely keep her eyes open. "Make sure she isn't alone with Davinia. Your sister-in-law has tender feelings, and the woman might hurt her."

He sounded amused. "Have you appointed yourself her caretaker, Ellie?"

"Someone had to," she said in a whisper as her eyes closed. She thought she felt Rica's lips brush against her mouth, but it might have been part of a dream that followed her immediately into sleep.

Rica looked up as the opened door swung open all the way a few minutes later. He saw Viggo framed in the doorway, but made no effort to disengage his hold on Ellie. She had curled against him so trustingly, and she smelled so good, that it was difficult to imagine parting from her. His cock had reminded him how long it had been since he had taken a woman, and it took all his determination to keep from waking her up, rousing her into a frenzy, and burying his cock inside her pussy.

He forced away the thoughts as Viggo took a step into the room. Rica bit back a sigh as he rearranged Ellie and stood up. He took time to get an extra blanket from the chest at the foot of the bed to cover her, not wanting to risk waking her by lifting her off the covers and putting her under them. When he was satisfied she would be warm enough, he turned to his brother, glad the tail of his checked shirt covered his hard cock. "How are your wife and the cub?"

"They seem well, but I don't know. Belia will have to examine them."

"You should have come for me before going to her." Rica's eyes narrowed. "She wouldn't have refused me."

"I would have, if I had been thinking." Viggo ran a hand through his dark hair, further tousling it. "All I could think of was alleviating Davinia's pain." He snarled. "Damn that woman for her insolence. I've a mind to teach her a lesson about the old ways." His pitch increased. "She dared quote to me about tradition of the Pack. Said it wasn't our way to help outsiders. My wife is not an outsider!"

Ellie twitched in her sleep and made a soft sound. "Lower your voice." Rica frowned. "She's exhausted." He gestured to his brother, indicating they should leave the room. "Go be with your wife. I'll bring Belia."

Viggo paused in the hallway, staring at Ellie before Rica closed the door. "She did a great thing for Davinia and Ylenia. I owe her."

"No, we owe her. Davinia is my kin too. The obligation belongs to us all."

"Have you figured out how you'll repay her then?"

Rica nodded once. "I have."

Viggo frowned, looking at him. "How, brother?"

"I'm making her a member of the Pack."

Viggo's eyes widened. It was clear he knew there was only one way to make her a member. A chuckle escaped him. "Somehow, I don't think she'll appreciate your show of gratitude."

Rica shrugged. He didn't care if she was happy about the change in circumstances. She would adjust.

Chapter 5

It was early afternoon before Ellie awoke, feeling refreshed. She bounded from the bed with a surge of energy. How chipper she felt surprised her, after the harrowing ordeal of last night. She hurried to wash and dress so she could check on the baby and new mother.

A few minutes later, she found them in the bedroom. There was no sign of Viggo, but Golatia sat in a rocker brought in from the living room. She held Ylenia and crooned softly to her in a cracked voice. Davinia watched from the bed, looking tired but serene. She smiled when she saw Ellie standing in the doorway. Tears leaked down her cheeks as she held out her hands. "Come join us. See the baby this morning."

Ellie crossed the room and took her hands, squeezing. They didn't need to exchange words. A sodden ball lodged in her throat. She cleared it away with a cough before turning to the old woman and baby. She sat on the edge of the bed and leaned forward. Golatia pushed aside the blanket to reveal Ylenia.

She gasped. "She lost all the hair." Could it be the same baby? This one was as fresh and hair-free as any baby in a commercial. It was a marked contrast to last night.

Golatia smiled. "Most of our babies are born covered in fur. It falls out within a day or two, not to reappear until the first moon of puberty."

Ellie arched a brow at the strange information. Before she could probe for more details, Golatia passed the baby to her. Her arms seemed to know exactly how to curve around the small, wriggling body, and she put her nose against Ylenia's head, breathing in her baby scent. The tug of maternal longing surprised her. She had always thought she didn't want children, but this baby made her think differently.

"Davinia has painted a heroic picture of you," Golatia said, leaning forward to pat her on the leg.

Ellie blushed. "I didn't do much more than catch her." She nodded to the baby.

"Of course you did. I couldn't have done it without you." Davinia lowered her gaze. "Viggo and I would like you to be Ylenia's godmother."

She blinked, searching for a delicate response. "I'm flattered, but I can't, Davinia. When the snow melts, I'll be gone." She twisted slightly to reach for her friend's hand. "I'm touched that you would trust me with this honor though."

Davinia hesitated, seeming as though she wanted to say something. Ellie didn't miss Golatia's subtle headshake, and she frowned.

"Very well. We want Ylenia to share your name. Is Ellie your full name?"

The gesture overwhelmed her. It was difficult to force her mouth to work. "It's Eleanor." She blinked back tears, struggling to remember when she had felt so welcomed by someone.

She had spent the last few years living on the fringes of foreign cultures, always integrating herself, but never quite blending in. No one had ever opened to her the way Davinia had. None of her friends in college, and not even her mother or father. Again, she questioned her motives and had to bite back the urge to confess her reasons for coming to Corsova.

* * * * *

Golatia stayed until after dinner. Viggo didn't join them, but Ellie didn't have a chance to ask about his whereabouts. She assumed their customs were different from those of Western men. He was probably back to work, knowing Davinia and the baby were fine.

When Golatia managed to tear herself away from the baby and decided it was time to return home, Ellie volunteered to walk her. She kept a supporting arm curved around the woman's shoulders as they stepped onto the walkway. She noticed more snow had fallen and huddled in her parka. "I wish there were streetlights," she said when they left the path and stepped into the square.

"Don't worry. My feet know the way. The old dogs will sniff out the path, come snow or hail."

Ellie laughed.

"I shouldn't have stayed so long though. I promised Rica I'd be home well before dark when he brought me to Davinia's this morning." She sighed.

"Are you on curfew?" The idea outraged her.

"No. I just couldn't tear myself away from the cub. I always wanted one, but Yuri, my useless mate, died before he put one in my belly. Did I tell you that?"

She patted Golatia's shoulders. "I think you mentioned it."

"It wasn't to be, but Rica's grandmother didn't mind the help with her cubs. I think she knew how much I loved Ivan, but she didn't mind that either. She was a good friend to me. About the only one I ever had in the Pack. She never treated me as a burden, being a young widow who couldn't hunt." Tears sparkled on Golatia's cheeks, freezing instantly in the bitter wind. "It was a sad day for this bunch when we lost Bianca. She was a good woman."

"She sounds special." Ellie was confused and wanted to ask about Ivan. She had thought he was Rica's uncle, not grandfather. Hadn't Golatia said he moved in with his brother and Victor's mate? She decided not to ask for clarification, thinking the older woman had gotten confused during one of the tellings. Or perhaps Ellie was the one who had become confused. Instead, she returned her attention to Golatia as she spoke again.

"Oh, she certainly was. Her children became much like my own. When Rica's mother died having Viggo, Peter asked for my help, and I stepped in, even though I was old by then. It didn't take much more energy to help raise those two than it did to raise Ivan and Victor's."

Now she was really confused. Ellie shook her head. "I don't understand. I thought you helped Bianca and Victor with their children. Did Ivan marry someone else?"

Golatia paused in mid-step. She cleared her throat, sounding uneasy. "I forgot you aren't one of us, Ellie. My mind tends to wander these days, finding its way back muddled sometimes."

Ellie gave her a smile, but didn't reply. What could she say to that, besides some useless platitude?

"Ivan took Bianca as his mate."

"Had Victor died?"

Golatia resumed her slow gait. "No. The Pack's way of isolating themselves has led to less growth among our people. Fewer babies are born, and there are fewer possibilities for mates. Why, Lia is the fourth cousin of Rica, and everyone assumed she would be his mate, until…" She trailed off, shaking her head. "For some reason, we have more boys than girls born, which makes it even harder to find a mate. Sometimes, brothers or friends share the same wife."

"Fraternal polyandry," Ellie said under her breath.

"What?"

"It's called fraternal polyandry…rather, it is among brothers sharing a wife. I suppose it would just be polyandry when it involves friends." She bit her lip as a disconcerting thought occurred to her. "Will Rica and Davinia mate someday?"

"No. There can be no question about the paternity of the Alpha's first son, since the first son is the successor, unless another male in the Pack challenges during the Succession Ceremony. The next Beta is usually the previous Alpha's second son, but he doesn't have to be his biological offspring. He only has to be claimed by the Alpha. Bianca and Victor already had Peter when Ivan joined with her, so it caused no conflict about inheritance rights." Golatia's tone lowered. "You do not like the idea of sharing him, do you?"

She averted her eyes, although she knew the other woman couldn't see her expression in the dark. She strove for a distant tone. "I don't know what you mean, Golatia. It looks like we're near your home."

The older woman cackled. "If you are looking for him, there's a meeting tonight. You know the spot."

"Is there anything you don't know?" she asked, with mingled exasperation and amusement.

"Oh, this and that, dear." Golatia stopped at her gate, pausing to hug her. "Thank you for the escort home." She turned and shuffled up the walk.

Ellie stopped by the gate, making sure Golatia made it inside. Her feet itched to run to the meeting, but her head was trying to caution her against it. She didn't want to incur Rica's anger again, after their hesitant truce. She tried telling herself it was none of her business.

Golatia got to the porch and turned around. Her voice carried through the blowing wind. "They're discussing you and Davinia at this meeting."

Ellie struggled to sound disinterested. "Really? I'm sure Rica will settle whatever problem there is."

The older woman cackled. "It's already settled, Ellie. Call on me when you need a Guardian." She pushed open her front door and stepped inside with surprising speed, not allowing Ellie time to question the strange statement.

She turned and trudged across the square, telling herself she wasn't going to spy on the meeting. She was still telling herself that as she passed Viggo and Davinia's, making her way by memory to the clearing where the Pack met.

* * * * *

She took up position behind the tree she had used before, peering out with careful movements, determined not to attract Rica's attention again. She looked down into the clearing, seeing a larger turnout even than at the last meeting. There were children present this time. It looked like they had packed more than two hundred people into the clearing. Was that everyone except Davinia, Golatia, and herself?

There was an audible grumble of dissent sweeping the crowd. Whatever they were protesting, Rica didn't seem to care. He stood resolutely in the center of the clearing, backlit by the roaring fire. Naked from the waist up, his skin shone with the sheen of perspiration, but he seemed unaffected by the heat. Viggo stood nearby, and he was shirtless and sweating. He looked nervous.

"Don't grumble like old women. If you have a challenge, speak it now."

The man that she thought was named Istal rose to his feet. "I challenge what you say. The Beta's wife isn't one of us. I won't treat her like Pack when she's a vampire. You know how they are. Can't trust them not to bleed you out while you sleep."

"My wife would never steal blood, and certainly not from the likes of you." Viggo surged forward, until he was inches from the other man. "She prefers clean skin."

Before Ellie had time to attempt a logical explanation for the information gleaned from their exchange, Istal growled and leaped forward. One moment, he was an overweight man with a hairy chest and dirty hair. The next, in mid-air, he became a large wolf with greasy fur, snapping at Viggo.

Reflexively, she rubbed her eyes, blinking several times. She wished she wore contacts. That might provide a reason for the hallucination.

Viggo jumped out of the way, not losing a second before transforming. His pants and shoes fell from his changed form as he leapt at Istal. They met in mid-leap and crashed to the ground, with Viggo on top. Their bone-chilling growls carried through the clearing.

Ellie expected one of them to kill the other at any second. Her heart raced with fear, although she couldn't precisely identify the origin. Fear of the unknown, fear of Viggo being injured, and even fear of the Pack itself mingled together to form an overwhelming onslaught. She dropped to her knees, not even noticing the snow seeping into her jeans.

Rica pushed between the two of them, still as human as he had ever been, she noted thankfully. With what seemed like no effort, he separated them, tossing the combatants several feet away from each other. "Change back. Now." His tone was steady, but the anger in it resounded throughout the clearing and up the hill.

Viggo and Istal changed, both retrieving their clothes without looking at the other. Rica waited until they had taken up posts on opposite sides of the fire before continuing. "Marriage has joined Viggo and Davinia. She is part of our family now. You will accept her."

"I won't," Istal said. Several members nodded their agreement.

Rica whirled to face him. "Then you will challenge me for leadership of the Pack, if you defy my word."

Istal shuffled his feet, looking down. "I've no wish to usurp you, Alpha, but I can't accept that woman."

"Then leave." Rica said the pronouncement viciously. "Any who won't follow me and won't challenge me, will walk away right now."

Ellie held her breath, awaiting their reaction. To her surprise, no one made a move to leave, and no one stood up to challenge him. She slowly regained her feet, wondering at the sense of detachment she felt. On some level, she knew she was in the presence of werewolves, and that she had befriended a vampire, but she couldn't accept it. It wasn't possible.

Rica allowed the silence to grow before nodding his head. "Then you accept mates of Pack members are part of the Pack."

There wasn't a murmur of protest among the assembly, although plenty of hot glares focused on Rica. He remained impervious. "I have one last thing to tell you. Ellie Adare will join the Mating Moon Ceremony."

Her mouth dropped open, and she barely resisted screaming the questions circulating in her mind. What did that mean? What was Rica talking about? What was the Mating Moon Ceremony? And what part was she expected to play in it?

Belia getting to her feet distracted her. She switched her attention to the older woman, even as her mind tried to process all she had learned.

"You can't mean it, Alpha. She isn't one of us. It's bad enough to taint our bloodlines with a vampire, but to add a human…it's unthinkable. She doesn't know anything about us or our ways."

"She'll adapt. You would have me waste a perfectly good female when there is a shortage?" His eyes swept the group, pausing to rest on a few members of the Pack. "How many girls do we have for the Mating Moon this season? Three? The woman will infuse our bloodlines with new purity. She will give her mate cubs to continue our way of life. It would be foolish to send her away, just because she's human."

"She's not one of us!" A beautiful girl jumped to her feet. Her long hair flowed down the back of her fur robe like a waterfall of moonlight. "I won't have my Mating Moon Ceremony upstaged by a human."

Rica fixed a hard stare in her direction. "I suggest watching your tongue, Lia, unless you plan to challenge me." He said the words calmly, but the others didn't hold back their derisive laughter. Rica raised his arm, and they fell silent. "If she can best me, she can be Alpha. Do you want to try, child?"

Lia's head bowed, obscuring her features. She sounded humble when responding, but the proud line of her spine didn't soften. "I am content to lead by your side, Alpha."

Rica didn't reply. He turned his back on her and raised his voice. "The men will meet at this spot in three days to announce who they will challenge for. Next week, we claim our mates."

Ellie saw the group getting to their feet and moving up the hill. She darted away from the tree and ran through the snow as quickly as her boots would allow, desperate to outrun the Pack and her own thoughts. How did she begin to process everything she had learned in the space of a few short minutes? Everything she had believed about the natural order of the universe was wrong. She had an agile mind, but how could she hope to accept revelations of such magnitude?

* * * * *

She didn't return to Viggo and Davinia's. Instead, Ellie sought shelter in the forest, detouring away from the village. She knew she would have to return to Necheau soon, but she had to process her thoughts first.

She slowed down as she approached a fallen tree. Ellie bent down to brush off the snow before sitting. The log was cold, and snow still seeped into her jeans, but she didn't notice. She focused on taking deep breaths.

Breathing deeply, practicing a modified form of meditation, she wondered why she wasn't more frightened or disbelieving. Already, a strange calm had filled her. Was it because she hadn't truly begun to believe what she had seen, or was it because that wasn't the first time she had seen something extraordinary?

During her first few months with the tribe in Africa, she had witnessed the funeral of the leader after he was killed during a hunt. The tribe gathered at night around a fire, passing a bowl of some noxious-smelling brew among them.

Ellie had taken a cautious sip and immediately felt light-headed. She passed it on without taking her full share.

Minutes later, when the medicine woman began chanting as she danced around the fire, Ellie had watched with fascination. She attempted to make notes in her notepad, but her eyes had blurred. She had looked up just as the medicine woman transformed into a cheetah and draped herself over the leader's body. Later, she had convinced herself she had imagined things because of the dram. Surely, the woman had only slipped on a cheetah skin during the seconds she had been distracted.

Now, she wondered about that conclusion and countless other things she had dismissed over the years as illusion. She certainly couldn't blame what she had seen on a potion, and she wasn't ill. She couldn't doubt what she had witnessed, especially in relation to the culture of the Pack. No wonder they modeled their community after a wolf pack.

She jerked with surprise when she heard footsteps behind her. Ellie's thoughts scattered as she turned her head to see Rica standing behind her. She looked at him impassively, while wondering if he were a wolf too. He had to be, or he wouldn't bear the title of Alpha. Judging from the stir Rica's announcement about her inclusion in the Mating Moon Ceremony had created, werewolves wouldn't allow a human to lead them.

He kept walking, until he stood in front of her. She followed with her head, craning her neck to look up at him when he stopped moving. Ellie remained silent.

"Is it possible for you not to spy on us?" He didn't sound angry.

She shrugged. "I have a curious nature, and Golatia told me I was a topic in your gathering." She automatically slid over as Rica turned and sat beside her, not bothering to brush away the snow as he did so.

"How much did you see?"

"Most of it."

"Did you see Istal and Viggo transform?"

"Yes."

Rica looked at her with surprise. "You're taking it calmly."

Ellie gave him a small smile. "Oh, not as well as I appear. I'm shocked, to say the least."

"Do you have any questions?"

It surprised her that he was willing to be open about his culture. She felt a twinge of guilt, imagining how he would react when he discovered her profession. She tried to dismiss her contradictory feelings when she replied. "Thousands, but I can't seem to sort through them all right now."

"Hmm."

She shivered as he leaned closer, brushing his leg against hers.

"Are you cold?" He put his arm around her as he asked the question. His bare skin provided a surprising amount of warmth.

Ellie resisted the urge to curl against him. "What's the Mating Moon Ceremony?"

"What does it sound like?" His voice was a whisper against her ear as he leaned closer still, bowing his neck.

"It sounds like the women are fought over."

"That's exactly what it is."

She stiffened as he licked her ear. "What are you doing?"

"Tasting you."

"Why?" Was that breathless moan really her voice?

"Because I want to." He growled the answer in a rough tone, but it held no anger. Only passion.

She cleared her throat and tipped her head away. "Do you always get what you want?"

"Always."

She tried to blot out the rush of sensations that accompanied his hand as he trailed it up her thigh. She had to ask him about something important, if only she could remember what that was. Oh, yes, the Mating Moon. "What's the female's part in this ceremony?" Even as she asked, she knew the answer on a deeper level.

"Men will compete for you to be their mate."

She shook her head. "No. I won't do it."

Rica grasped her chin and turned her face to his. "You don't have a choice, Ellie. We've claimed you as Pack."

"So you men just decide who the women will mate with." She strove for an outraged tone, even as her heart raced in her ears. Liquid heat invaded her pussy as Rica's hand went higher, brushing against her mound.

"On the surface, but most of the women end up with the mate or mates they want."

"How?" She bit back a moan as Rica's fingers tugged at the button and zipper of her jeans. When his hand touched her bare waist above her panties, she couldn't resist a small sound of pleasure.

"There are two theories. The first is, women are naturally drawn to the strongest male. It's an evolutionary instinct, to protect themselves and their offspring." His voice lowered to a whisper as he finished.

She gasped when Rica leaned forward to brush a soft kiss against her lips, as his fingers breached the barrier of the elastic waistband on her panties. She closed her eyes, praying for strength to withstand his desire and her own. "What's the other explanation?"

He withdrew from her mouth, but she could feel his breath on her cheek when he answered. "It's more sentimental. Love gives them power to win." He sounded amused by the idea. "That idea is popular among the younger girls."

"Of course." She was proud of her level tone. "It allows them to think they aren't just property won by the strongest."

She opened her eyes and met his. Somehow, she found the strength to lean away from his tempting lips. She couldn't make herself pull his hand away from her pussy as he stroked her soft curls. "I won't participate."

"You will."

She frowned. "You have to stop this nonsense. You know I'm leaving as soon as the snow thaws."

"No, you aren't. I'm claiming you, Ellie."

Her eyes widened. "What the hell's that supposed to mean?" She would have crossed her arms if there had been sufficient space between their bodies to do so.

Rica met her eyes. He wore a resolved expression. "I'm challenging for you."

She felt a dart of fear, but not for the most obvious reason. Rather than being afraid of ending up his mate, she was terrified he would be injured. "You can't."

"I can. I'm the Alpha." Rica's lazy grin was entirely too sexual for her comfort. "Will you challenge me in order to stop me, Ellie?"

She gasped as his finger slid down her cleft, pausing to circle around her clit. She tried to draw away, but Rica's arm moved around her waist, anchoring her to him. "You can't just keep me."

He chuckled. "I can. It's our way. We're what you might consider primitive, Ellie. We eat when we're hungry, catching the prey ourselves. We're superstitious about such things as the phase of the moon and alignment of the stars." His voice lowered to a husky rasp as he lunged forward, pushing her down sideways across the log. "And we fuck when we're horny. I wanted you the minute I saw you, and you made it possible for me to keep you by helping Davinia."

She swallowed thickly as he pushed her more fully onto her back and parted her legs. His hand had dislodged from her panties, and now he used it to hold her against the log. She didn't even notice the snow under her coat and hair. "So fuck me. That doesn't mean we have to mate."

He looked surprised. "I have more in mind than a fling for the next few months. I want you by my side, Ellie. I want you to bear my young."

She shook her head, struggling to compose her thoughts as Rica settled between her legs, pressing his hard cock against her pussy through their jeans. She moaned when he thrust against her. "Are you saying you're in love with me? That's nonsense. You don't even like me."

Rica's laugh was more of a purr as he thrust against her again. "I don't dislike you. I just don't trust outsiders."

"How can you marry me if you don't trust me?"

"You aren't an outsider anymore. You're staying."

"I won't..." She trailed off as Rica's hand pushed under her coat and shirt to cup her breast through her bra. "Don't do this, Rica."

"Sorry." He sounded anything but. "I can't let you leave now."

She closed her eyes when he ground his cock against her. She was prepared for more, and her eyes snapped open when he moved away. "What are you doing? You can't stop now."

He got to his feet, grinning. "You know what to do if you want more."

She glowered as she sat up. "What?"

"Don't resist when I claim you. You and your Guardian both have to accept me. I can still force the issue by claiming you for a moon-cycle, but I don't want it to be like that." He bent down and lifted her from the log, setting her on her feet. His fingers moved quickly to zip up and button her jeans. "Come to me willingly, Ellie. It will be good between us."

"I don't doubt the sex would be incredible, but I'm not going to be your mate." The rest of her words cut off under his mouth as he branded her with a long kiss. She melted under his touch, opening her mouth to allow his tongue inside. As it thrust into her, mimicking the motion of his cock from a minute ago, she pressed herself closer. Once again, he pulled away, eliciting a muttered expletive from her.

"Come on. I'll walk you back to Viggo's." He took her hand casually to lead her out of the forest.

Ellie allowed him to pull her along, not speaking as her mind whirled with thoughts. Uppermost was his claim on her. Most disconcertingly, she couldn't seem to come up with a good reason not to accept him as her mate…at least for the next three months, until the snow thawed.

What an amazing study she could write about the existence of werewolves, from the perspective of having lived among the Pack as the Alpha's mate for three months. Dr. Ludlow wouldn't stand a chance of usurping the chair position if her study was scientifically verifiable and documented. But could she do that?

Chapter 6

After a restless night, Ellie rose early. She washed and dressed quickly, slipping from the cabin before Viggo or Davinia were even awake. The first streaks of dawn were just painting the sky as she made her way to Golatia's, knowing the old woman would have the answers she needed.

More snow had fallen during the night, and no one had cleared the path yet, so it took Ellie longer than usual to walk to Golatia's. She knocked on the door, hoping the older woman would be awake this early. A few minutes passed without anyone appearing, and she was just about to return to Davinia's when she heard the latch lift. Seconds later, Golatia opened the door, still wearing her nightdress and robe, with her white hair bound into a single long braid.

Ellie stepped back. "I'm sorry. I didn't mean to wake you. I'll come back—"

"Come in." Golatia opened the door wider. "I wasn't asleep. Merely reading. The old bones don't cooperate with a full night's rest any longer."

She stepped inside. The smell of baking bread and coffee met her, and she inhaled. When Golatia had closed the door, Ellie turned to her. "I need your help."

The older woman nodded, gesturing Ellie to follow her into the kitchen. "You want to know about the Mating Moon Ceremony."

"Yes. I want to know the implications of being challenged for."

Golatia took two mugs from the cabinet and filled them with coffee. "Have you eaten, dear?"

"No." The way her stomach churned, she wasn't sure if she could.

"Have some cinnamon bread. It will be out of the oven in a minute."

"Sure, thanks."

"Be a dear and fetch the butter from the pantry." She pointed to a little door in the wall.

Ellie walked over to the pantry and opened it. She saw shelves of jarred preserves, but no butter. "Where—"

"Lift up the trapdoor. There's a cool storage there, dug directly into the ground. It never gets very warm here in the mountains, and the groundwater keeps the spot nice and cool, even in summer. You might have to get on your knees."

Ellie knelt down, reaching for a crock of butter on a low shelf. Steps descended into the storage area, and she frowned, imagining what could happen to Golatia if she fell. She stood up and brought the container to the counter where Golatia was putting the bread, fresh from the oven. "Do you use that space often?"

"No, not these days. I stick to the top shelf, mostly." Golatia took a knife from the drawer and laid it on the counter by the butter. "Now, let's have a talk while the bread cools a bit."

"Rica told me he's challenging for me. What do I do, Golatia?"

Golatia led her to the small wooden table, where she placed their mugs of coffee and took a seat. She patted the other, waiting until Ellie sat down before speaking. "What do you want to do?"

A blush warmed Ellie's face as the erotic images that had paraded through her mind all last night and kept sleep at bay raised up to haunt her again. She couldn't tell that to this sweet old lady. It would be like confessing such a thing to her grandmother. "I can't stay, so it wouldn't be right to let him do this."

Golatia laughed. "You'd be hard pressed to stop Rica from doing anything he wanted. He wants you, Ellie."

"He said I or my Guardian could reject him." She clasped her hands around the mug, drawing warmth from the ceramic.

"You can reject him, but he can still claim you for a moon-cycle."

"He mentioned that. What does it mean?"

Golatia sipped the coffee before answering. "He takes you as his mate for one month. At the next full moon, you both appear before the Pack. You would say at that time if you will accept him. If you won't, he has to relinquish his claim on you, and another may challenge. If there are no challengers, one of those who lost the challenge for you can claim you, but that seldom happens."

"Why? Is it a virginity issue?" Ellie blushed brighter, embarrassed to discuss such a thing with an elderly woman. "Because if that's the case, I should tell you right now—"

She cackled. "No, not at all. Our kind mates for life, but we aren't averse to tumbling beforehand. Mostly, the reason girls aren't challenged for again is that they're perceived as difficult. If one man—the strongest who challenged for her, I should add—can't satisfy the girl, then who else can? You'll have the reputation of being picky."

Ellie shrugged. "That doesn't bother me. I plan to leave when the snow thaws."

"Hmm. You think you must return to your university."

Ellie jumped, slopping coffee on the table. "I…what…?"

Golatia smiled. "I know more about you than you've told everyone. I know why you think you're here, but I also know something else about you."

She swallowed, wondering if Golatia would expose her. "What's that?"

"You're a lonely soul. You aren't close to your parents, and you haven't a real friend in the world. At least, you didn't until you came here. You can dismiss it as nonsense, but I'm telling you Rica is meant to be your mate."

She flinched away from the words. Golatia's tone was matter-of-fact, without a hint of pity, but Ellie felt pitied just the same. How could this woman know that much about her? She cleared her throat. "I'm content with my life, Golatia. All I want is the position I've worked toward for the last few years. I don't need a mate to be happy."

Golatia sighed. "You're missing out if you reject him."

"You won't tell anyone, will you?"

She shook her head before getting to her feet. "I won't say a word about your reasons for being here. If you choose to reject Rica, I'll stand by you. I'll even try to fight his claim of the moon-cycle, although there's really no easy way to do so."

"Thank you."

Golatia snorted. "Don't thank me. I still say you'll be sorry if you turn your back on Rica. He would make a fine mate. He's Alpha, which makes his mate's position coveted. I'd much rather have you as his companion than that vapid Lia." She shuffled to the stove as she spoke.

A dart of jealousy tore through Ellie. "He wouldn't choose her. She's just a child."

"Hmm. Rica will have to choose someday soon. He's not getting any younger, and he needs to provide an heir." Golatia nodded her head as she cut into the bread. "If not this year, he'll certainly have to pick a mate by next year. Yes, I'd say within three Mating Moons, if you reject him."

"But won't it hurt him if he picks me? I'm an outsider. The other members of the Pack won't like me being his mate."

Golatia shrugged. "He's the Alpha. We follow him, for better or worse, unless someone stronger deposes him." She brought down two saucers and placed a large square of bread on each. "The others don't have to like your union, but they must accept it."

Somehow, that didn't reassure Ellie. She remembered the debate from last night and knew there were those in the Pack who wouldn't accept her as Rica's mate. She sighed, trying to dismiss her thoughts. She sought to tell herself it didn't matter if they liked her. She wouldn't be in Necheau long enough to stir the Pack into a frenzy, even if she didn't reject Rica.

* * * * *

Viggo was gone by the time she returned to the cabin, but Davinia was in the living room, along with Ylenia, who slept in a bassinet. As soon as she entered the room, Davinia came toward her, looking apprehensive. Ellie took off her parka, looking at the other woman questioningly. "Is something wrong?"

"No…" She trailed off into a sigh. "I don't know. I guess I want to know how you feel about me now that you know what I am."

Ellie blinked. She had completely forgotten Davinia wasn't human. Her mind had been too busy dwelling on other issues. She searched for a way to answer and saw the hurt in Davinia's eyes grow in proportion to her silence. She finally blurted out the first thing that came to her. "I thought vampires couldn't have children."

Davinia paused, looking surprised. Then she giggled. It was a high-pitched, nervous laugh. "I thought you might ask if I had stolen your blood, or if I were evil. That wasn't what I expected."

"I wasn't exactly prepared to deal with this situation." Ellie smoothed a hand through her hair and approached her friend. "It's a shock, just like learning I'm staying with a group of werewolves, but it doesn't matter." She touched Davinia's arm to reassure her. "I can tell you I have a million questions though. Do you feel like answering some?"

Davinia flashed a bright smile. "Sure."

As Ellie followed her to the couch, she tried to push back her guilt. On the surface, she was just asking questions about something she didn't understand. Only she knew she would make notations on the notepad in her room tonight, after everyone had gone to bed. She wasn't using the information for fame or wealth. Surely, the world deserved to know about the existence of these creatures. She shouldn't feel guilty for educating others. So why was she thinking "guilty"?

Chapter 7

By the night of the Mating Moon Ceremony, Ellie had decided to accept Rica as her mate if he won the challenge. She didn't doubt he would, assuming anyone else even challenged for her. She wasn't exactly popular among the Pack, as evidenced by the large purple bruise under her eye. Yesterday, Lia and three other young women cornered her by the well as she pumped water for Golatia.

Lia had spit on her. "You don't belong here."

Ellie had wiped off the spittle and attempted to handle the girls with grace. "No, I don't."

"Don't patronize me. You think you're going to be Rica's mate, don't you?" She could still hear Lia's cold laugh in her head. "The Pack won't allow it. I'm the one he's going to choose. I'm the most beautiful woman in the Pack. My mother gave her approval for me to participate a year sooner so I could get Rica."

Knowing she was a jealous child hadn't helped keep Ellie's temper in check. She had given an equally cold laugh, raked her eyes up and down the tall girl's frame, and shaken her head. "He wouldn't pick you. You're pretty, but you don't have a brain in your little head. Rica wants an equal."

Lia's response had been quick and vicious. Ellie leaned forward to look in the mirror, touching the mark the girl's fist had left on her face. She supposed she was lucky Viggo had been nearby and scattered the girls before they could do any further damage. His warning about avoiding that group hadn't been necessary. She planned to stay away from them during her time in Necheau.

There was a knock at the door, and she said, "Enter."

Davinia stepped inside, holding her parka. "Are you ready?"

Ellie felt a moment of apprehension. "Can I say no and get out of this?"

Davinia shook her head. She was careful to keep her eyes lifted upward.

Ellie tried to ignore her nudity as she crossed the room to take her coat. The only thing she wore was a scarlet band around her hips and a pair of boots. She didn't know the significance of the cloth, but she thought she knew why the girls appeared wearing only that. It gave the men a chance to see what they were fighting for.

Davinia had told her it was to evaluate her build for ease of birthing, but Ellie was cynical about that being the true reason. What man looked at an unclothed woman and sized up her hips for childbearing the first time he saw her naked?

She slid on the parka and tugged at the hem. Thankfully, the coat fell to mid-thigh, so she wouldn't have to walk stark naked through the village. Ellie didn't want to think about the moment when she had to remove the coat, in front of whomever chose to show up for the Mating Moon Ceremony. From what Golatia had told her, that was everyone in the village who could get to the meeting spot.

When they stepped out of the cabin, they blended into a large crowd moving toward the clearing. "Where are Viggo and Rica?" she whispered, leaning closer to Davinia, who had bundled Ylenia into a mound of blankets and strapped her in a sling to her front.

"Already at the clearing. Since Rica's challenging and unmated, he can't officiate the ceremony. The duty falls to Viggo."

She tugged at the hem of the parka when she noticed an older man eyeing her legs. "What about Golatia? I don't think she can walk that far."

"Rica carried her."

The opportunity for conversation lapsed as they started down the hill. Ellie focused on picking her way down the slippery slope amid the others, careful not to bump anyone. She noticed they all gave her plenty of space and tried not to let their avoidance hurt. What had she expected? They weren't happy about Rica's decision to include her in the ceremony, and they were even less thrilled that he planned to challenge for her.

Once they reached the clearing, those not participating faded into the background, forming a large, loose circle around the fire. Three young women, including Lia and one of the girls who had been part of her group, already waited on one side of the fire. A man or woman flanked each. All wore fur robes. Davinia waved her toward them.

Ellie took a deep breath and forced herself to walk in front of the larger group of men gathered on the other side of the fire. She could feel their eyes raking over her, but didn't know if any liked what they saw. She hoped not, because she didn't want Rica injured challenging for her. Far better to be humiliated by not having any others interested in her. It didn't matter to her who won anyway. She supposed being the mate to any would give her a unique perspective for her study.

That academic theory disintegrated when she stepped into line beside the last girl and looked up to meet Rica's eyes. Her stomach clenched with excitement, and she found herself anticipating the consummation ceremony. Golatia had sketched the details for her, and she knew after she accepted Rica, they would become lovers. She gave him a small smile, which he didn't return. His expression remained impassive. He seemed as blasé about his nudity as the other men did.

As if signaled, the crowd quieted as one, and Viggo stepped into the center of the circle. "It is the duty of every Pack member to take a mate. Offspring ensure the survival of our species. Choose wisely, because we mate for life." He allowed a moment to elapse before speaking again. "Those who plan to challenge have already spoken up, but it is not too late to announce your intent." He eyed the men before he gestured to the girls.

Ellie watched as they removed their robes by opening them and handing them to their Guardians. She felt a hand on her shoulder and saw Golatia standing slightly behind her. She tried to give her a shaky smile.

"Your coat and boots, Ellie."

She nodded, stepping out of the boots as her clumsy fingers fiddled with the zipper. She finally opened it and forced herself to strip off the coat in one quick movement. As soon as she handed over the covering, she became aware of how cold it was, even this close to the fire. Her nipples beaded, and gooseflesh puckered her exposed skin. She resisted the urge to hug herself, noting the proud stances of the other girls. She tried to mimic it as a few men broke from the circle and joined the already-large group.

She was vaguely aware of the eyes examining her, but was only reacting to Rica's, as they skimmed over her. He didn't betray his reaction, except for the way his cock visibly hardened. She bit back a smile, striving to keep her expression as closed as the girls standing near her.

"Who challenges for Clara?" As Viggo spoke, a girl in the middle of their line stepped forward. She was short and stocky, with a solid build. Her breasts were large, as were her hips. She wasn't beautiful, but she was striking. She used her dark hair to cover her bosom.

Ellie wondered if that was why all the girls had long hair. Did they grow it out in anticipation of this moment? She wished she hadn't favored practicality over femininity for the last few years. Her short cut wouldn't hide anything, except her ears. She didn't think there would be many eyes on her ears when it was her turn to step forward.

Immediately, four nude men surged forward, breaking away from the group of challengers. Two men similar in appearance, with brown hair and brown eyes, took another step forward. "Belo and I will challenge for her."

"The Jescu brothers have announced their challenge."

"I'll challenge." This challenger was on the short side, but with massive muscles that didn't quite look right with his slender frame. He had a challenging air about him before he even spoke up. He seemed arrogant to Ellie.

"Eugen."

Another man stepped forward. He couldn't have been much older than eighteen, with light-brown hair and dark eyes. He crossed and uncrossed his arms several times as he stuttered, "M-m-me too." His flaccid cock indicated he was either cold or nervous.

"Paul." Viggo motioned the brothers forward. "Who will begin the challenge?"

"I will," said the one who hadn't spoken before. He must be Belo. "I will challenge Paul."

Ellie couldn't help noticing Paul looked close to wetting himself as he stepped up to meet Belo. They didn't shake hands or bow to each other. Instead, they immediately began circling each other. Paul seemed close to tripping on his own feet. Each time Belo lunged at him, he flinched. He didn't seem to be an offensive fighter. Rather, he looked like he was bracing himself for attack.

When it came, he wasn't prepared. Belo leapt at him, transforming into a wolf in mid-leap. Paul put up his arms and backed away, but the wolf landed on him, snarling. Paul cried out when teeth ripped through his shoulder. He tried to transform, but apparently couldn't summon the ability in his distress. Within seconds, he was crying, "I yield."

Immediately, Belo withdrew and transformed back into his human form. He offered a hand to Paul, assisting him to his feet, and clapping him on the back. He whispered something to the younger man before walking back to his brother. Paul slunk off into the crowd.

Ellie felt reassured by the combat. She had wondered if it might be a fight to the death, but it appeared civilized. Well, as civilized as such a barbaric custom could be.

She had been wrong, she thought a few minutes later, watching as Eugen circled the unnamed brother, lying on the ground. They were both in wolf-form, which made it easier to pretend the blood flowing from the brother's wounds wasn't real. He was whimpering continuously as he struggled to gain his feet. Each time he tried to rise on his front paws, Eugen lunged forward and bit him again.

"Enough," Belo said, stepping forward. "Cedru concedes."

"Do you forfeit your challenge, Belo?" Viggo asked.

"No. I will take my brother's place."

That seemed a little unfair to Ellie, but she didn't voice her protests. She had a feeling this ritual was as old as the Pack, and they had obviously decided the best way to conduct it. She held her breath as Cedru returned to his human form with much difficulty. Two men not waiting to challenge stepped forward and carried him away from the circle.

The fight between Belo and Eugen was just as vicious, although Belo was clearly a better fighter than Cedru. In the end, he finished up pinned under Eugen's paws. He transformed to human form, saying, "I yield."

Eugen backed away and transformed to his human form. He didn't offer his hand, although Belo clearly needed some assistance to rise. Once more, men not waiting to challenge came forward and helped him to his feet. They supported him as he limped from the circle, presumably to join his brother.

"Will any other challenge for Clara?" Viggo scanned the circle and waited at least a minute. No one spoke up or stepped forward. "Eugen, claim your mate."

Clara didn't look thrilled as Eugen stalked toward her. Blood smeared his chest, but he didn't pay attention to it as he crushed her against him, branding her with a hard kiss.

Viggo approached them, subtly interceding between the couple. He faced Clara's Guardian, a middle-aged woman in a black fur robe. "Will you give this union your blessing, Guardian?"

The woman traded looks with Clara, who hesitated before nodding. "I will."

Viggo turned to Clara. "Will you accept Eugen as your mate?"

Clara bowed her head. Her blush was evident in the firelight. "Yes." The word was barely out of her mouth before Eugen pulled her back into his arms. He kissed her once more, but it was quick. His hands kneaded her breasts as he held her against him.

Ellie turned to Golatia, lowering her voice to a whisper. "What's he doing?"

"Mating with her." She clicked her tongue. "He needs to learn finesse. I suspect he is insecure about his prowess and intends to rush through the consummation."

Ellie's eyes widened. "What?" She was aware of eyes turning in her direction and lowered her voice. "What are you talking about?"

"I told you about the consummation, Ellie." Golatia was frowning.

"You didn't tell me it was in front of the entire Pack."

Golatia blinked. "I didn't? It must have slipped my mind."

Ellie shook her head. "More likely, you figured I would back out if I knew all the details."

The older woman gave her an innocent smile. "I've never doubted you would complete the ceremony."

"Hmm." She growled the sound under her breath as she turned back to watch Eugen and Clara. She felt like a pervert, watching the man stroke his new mate, but it was compelling. She couldn't seem to tear away her gaze.

As Eugen lowered Clara to the ground, her eyes caught Rica's. She could see the heat in them. He was aroused, but she didn't think it was from watching the young couple before them. No, his arousal came from picturing them in the same position, she knew, because it was the same for her. Imagining them together caused her heart to race and moisture to drench her pussy.

Clara's cry caused her gaze to drop to the couple on the ground. The girl appeared to be struggling with pain and pleasure as Eugen thrust his cock into her. She seemed to like his hands playing with her nipples, but wasn't responding to his thrusts.

"He better make that up to her later tonight, or he'll never hear the end of this," Golatia said with a low cackle.

The mating ended in a couple of minutes. Eugen stiffened and cried out, surging inside his mate. She looked relieved when he rolled away and stood up. His now-limp cock looked forlorn. Ellie almost laughed, although she didn't really find the situation funny. If anything, it was sad that Clara's first time with her mate had been short and obviously not enjoyable.

She wondered how it would be with Rica. She didn't doubt his skill, but was afraid she wouldn't be able to get past all the eyes watching to enjoy the act. Ellie half-hoped Rica would rush through the consummation and make it up to her later.

Once Eugen and Clara left the circle, Viggo called the next challengers for Lia. She stepped forward, revealing her glorious beauty, but refusing to look at any of the ten men who stepped forward to challenge for her. Instead, she kept her gaze fastened on Rica as she cupped her own breast and tweaked the nipple before stepping back to stand in front of Belia.

Most of the matches went quickly, with one fighter clearly superior. The only one to become bloody was the last match between two equally worthy combatants. They had the same build and equal strength. The only obvious difference was one had black hair and the other had blond hair.

After ten minutes of a stalemate, Viggo paused the fight. He drew the two contestants away from the group and whispered with them. Ellie saw both exchange glances, say something to Viggo again, and shake hands. Together, the three of them approached Lia.

"Lasile and Jan have formed an alliance." He stood in front of Belia. Ellie couldn't help but notice Viggo's stiff posture and the dislike he tried to keep hidden when his eyes rested briefly on Belia. "Will you give this union your blessing, Guardian?"

Belia turned her back. Viggo glowered at her before turning to Lia. "Will you accept Lasile and Jan as your mates?"

Lia tossed her hair, still refusing to meet the gaze of either man. "No. They aren't worthy of me."

Viggo nodded before turning back to the men. "Will you invoke a moon-cycle claim?"

The two men whispered together for a long moment. Finally, the blond took a step forward. "We will claim her as mate for one moon-cycle."

Lia looked outraged, and she began to screech. Belia stepped forward, adding her own opinion in loud tones. It took Viggo several seconds to restore calm. He raised his voice to a shout so everyone could hear. "You know there are only three things that will allow a girl to refuse the moon-cycle claim. Is Lia carrying another man's child?"

Lia glowered at Viggo when she shook her head.

"Has Lia made it known she intends to leave the Pack? Will she accept banishment to deny the claim?"

"No," Belia said sullenly.

Viggo nodded. "Does Lia intend to take no mate ever? Remember, if she announces that intention now, she will not be able to change her mind. She has given a vow to live chastely, and should it be broken, she will be banished."

"It's not fair," Lia said, with more than a hint of whining in her tone. "If I don't take these two, I can never have a mate. I don't want this."

"This is our way. Do you give your vow to live chastely?"

She shook her head. Her anger was obvious. "I'll accept the claim." She didn't seem happy about it.

Ellie expected the men to take her, but all they did was gather her between them. Viggo removed the sash around Lia's hips and used it to bind one hand of all three together. "The moon-cycle begins tonight. You have until the next full moon to convince this woman to accept you as her mates."

As the three walked away, Lia obviously unwilling, Ellie turned to Golatia again. "What about the consummation?"

"That will happen if she accepts them as her mate at the next full moon. The deed is required to bind the union. Much as an exchange of vows in front of a religious officiator, like a priest, in your world."

Ellie lifted a brow. "So, the sex is the marriage ceremony?" Did she really want to marry Rica, knowing she would be leaving him? It should reassure her to know the ceremony wouldn't be legally binding anywhere except Corsova, but it didn't. It still felt dishonest, even though Rica knew she planned to leave him.

Golatia nodded, but didn't speak as Viggo called forth the next girl. She didn't have as many challengers as Lia had, but the battles were more intense. When the victor finally emerged, he was battered and bloody. Tenica, the other girl who had been part of Lia's group, and her father didn't hesitate to accept Veelad. He was more skilled than Eugen, or less concerned with the audience, and her cries of pleasure echoed around the circle as he made love to her.

Ellie was surprised how it increased her own ardor, watching these two consummate their union. Once more, she met Rica's eyes, finding them locked on her, and not paying any attention to the couple. Her breasts tingled, but not because of the cold. In fact, it had gotten hot, and the sash around her waist seemed to chafe her skin. She wanted to throw it off and go to him.

She didn't even care about the others who would be watching their consummation. Right then, she wanted him any way she could have him, even if it meant in front of a gathering of two hundred. All thoughts of rejecting him had fled in the face of her desire. She ached to have Rica, even for a few months.

She would soon have her chance, because Viggo called her name.

Ellie stepped forward, conscious of the eyes examining her nude body, but only caring about Rica's, as they caressed every inch of her. She could feel her pussy warming, and electric tingles ran under her skin wherever his gaze paused.

"Who challenges for Ellie?"

She held her breath as Rica stepped forward. The crowd of men had thinned to four, and those remaining shuffled their feet. Two blended back into the larger group, but the other two stepped forward. The taller one spoke. "We challenge for the outsider."

There was a definite growl in Rica's voice. "I challenge for Ellie."

The shorter, stocky man stepped up to Rica. He inclined his head, sending long strands of dark-blond waving around his face. "I will begin the challenge."

Viggo nodded, raising his voice. "Vitoro and Tristin challenge Rica for Ellie. Vitoro will fight first."

Ellie didn't think Vitoro could beat Rica, but she wondered what would happen to his position of Alpha if someone did defeat him. Would they take over leadership of the Pack too? She bit her lip, watching the two men circle each other after they transformed.

Rica made the first attack. He made a low leap at his opponent, catching Vitoro's front paws and knocking him to the ground. The other man howled his anger, but he wasn't hurt. He was quick to regain his feet. Even as he appeared to be steadying himself, he leapt at Rica. Vitoro's teeth ripped into Rica's side, but he didn't make a sound.

He backed away and watched Vitoro with a wary stance. His attention was focused on Vitoro, who feinted forward, but didn't actually attack. Ellie's eyes remained glued to the battle, until she saw movement with her peripheral vision. She turned her head in time to see Tristin morph to wolf-form and leap. She called out a warning, and Rica's head snapped in her direction, instead of Tristin's.

He yelped when the other man landed on his back, as Vitoro darted forward to join the attack. Ellie found her feet carrying her toward the men, and she intended to throw herself into the fracas. Viggo caught her around the waist. She glared up at him. "Stop this. It isn't fair."

"It is, Ellie. It isn't an honorable way to fight, but it's accepted. If your man is strong enough, he will defeat them."

Her glare intensified. "What happens if they defeat Rica? Will they get leadership of the Pack as well?"

He nodded.

She wrenched free of his hold, but forced her feet to stay in place as Rica battled his opponents. She heard a long, low cry of pain and held her breath. Seconds later, the brownish wolf limped away, dragging his rear leg. A few steps from the ring, he collapsed and returned to his human form.

She felt a stir of hope when the match was once again fair. The hope fled when she caught sight of Rica. Blood smeared his coat, and he seemed to be moving with effort, while Vitoro's feints were still lithe and full of energy. He was faster than Rica too, darting in and out to nip at him.

Ellie clasped her hands together as Rica's muscles bunched. He crouched low to the ground, and his sides heaved. She couldn't tell if he were about to collapse or attack. As Vitoro lunged forward, Rica moved with a burst of energy.

He blocked the other man's assault, using his greater size to propel Vitoro back and pin him to the ground. His teeth clamped over Victor's throat, without penetrating the skin.

Viggo walked over to them. "Do you yield, Vitoro?"

Vitoro gave a barely perceptible nod. Rica withdrew and transformed into his man form. A cry of shock escaped Ellie when she saw the wounds marring his body. She wanted to run to him, but knew how important it was to follow the ceremony. She retraced her steps to take her post in front of Golatia, while watching him through the veil of her lashes.

He moved slowly, with a visible limp. There was blood smeared across his body, and he swiped a heavy patch from his chest without care as he stopped in front of her. The air sizzled around him, and when Ellie met his gaze, she forgot how to breathe. Primal feelings stirred in her. She had to resist the urge to throw back her head and howl at the tumescent moon. She blinked, wondering where the compulsion came from.

She stood before him, trembling under his hot gaze, not from the coldness of the snow she stood on, nor the chill wind cutting through the clearing. Ellie bowed her head, as her instincts told her to submit. When Rica briefly caressed her shoulder before dropping his hand, she shivered at the contact.

Viggo came to his brother's side, and Golatia stepped forward. "Will you give this union your blessing, Guardian?"

Golatia nodded her consent before stepping behind Ellie.

He turned his gaze on her. "Will you accept Rica as your mate?"

Now was the time to let reason reassert itself. She should give a resounding no as her answer and walk away, before the culture of the Pack absorbed her. Ellie raised her head to give her response. Rather than the strong negative reply she knew she *should* give, she whispered, "I will."

She was in his arms in the blink of an eye. Ellie looked up to meet his gaze. The heat in his blue eyes made her burn. It was so intense, she felt a trace of fear. His mouth descending on hers washed away any emotion but desire. She opened her mouth as Rica's tongue swept inside. Whether or not she had yielded, he would have branded her with his kiss. She recognized that on an instinctive level. Rather than stir her feminine ire, the notion stoked her desire.

She was vaguely aware of him moving her into the center of the circle, but tried to block out the presence of the others. It was only she and Rica, sharing this night under the moon. Gradually, her awareness of the others faded completely, as she got lost in his kisses.

His mouth traced a hot line from her lips to the column of her throat. He nuzzled at the bend of her neck, inhaling her scent. Ellie clung to him, unable to stand on shaking legs. Rica must have realized she had lost her strength, because he lifted her against him, supporting her as his nose moved lower, to nestle between her breasts. She threw back her head and buried her fingers in his hair as he inhaled her scent.

"Rica," she said with a moan when he lifted her higher and moved his mouth to take possession of her nipple. His tongue was hot and urgent as it laved the beaded peak. She wrapped her legs around his waist and pressed his head against her, urging him to take more. She closed her eyes and whimpered.

He responded to the invitation by nipping the tingling bud. The slight wrench of pain heightened her pleasure when he cupped her other breast in his hand. He rolled the nipple between his fingers, tugging in a rhythm simpatico to his suckling. Ellie arched her pussy against his stomach, aching for more. She couldn't remember ever being so turned on so quickly. All she wanted was for Rica to bury his cock inside her and claim her as his.

Her arms tightened around his neck as he lowered her to the ground. She tensed, anticipating contact with the snow. Instead, her back encountered soft fur. Someone had thoughtfully laid down a robe while she had been immersed in

Rica's touch. Her eyes snapped open with the reminder. It took a moment for those surrounding the fire to come into focus. When her eyes adjusted, she saw the Pack watching them.

What she glimpsed in those few moments surprised her. She might have expected anger from some, and there was that in Belia and Istal's eyes. She certainly would have expected to feel as though they were gaping at her, but most of the expressions bordered on solemn. They were the same expressions one might see at a wedding or funeral. The consummation was about more than sex for most of the Pack. Only a few of the young men and women showed signs of arousal.

Was she depraved for not being able to regard making love with Rica in a holy light? Her body clamored for his possession. All the eyes on her served to increase her ardor, rather than diminish it. She couldn't think about the solemnity of the ceremony with Rica's mouth feasting on her breast. Was it the same for all the brides, or was it because she was an outsider?

Rica distracted her from her thoughts when his fingers plunged inside her. Ellie winced. Her pussy was tight from having gone without a lover for several months, although she had gotten an injection on a regular basis, out of habit. She briefly wondered if the Depo-Provera shot she had taken three months ago would still guard against pregnancy, but then his thrusting finger washed away practicality.

Ellie arched her hips as Rica brought another finger inside her. He plunged both into her pussy as far as they would go, giving her a deliciously achy sensation of fulfillment. He encountered no resistance. Her body was slick and welcoming, without the residual muscle tightening. She couldn't wait any longer.

"Rica," she managed to say again, with a gasp. She wondered at her inability to speak her mind. Was it another effect of the primitive atmosphere lingering in the air? All she seemed capable of doing was grunting and moaning.

The sound of his heavy breathing swayed her thoughts. Ellie parted her thighs further, as Rica settled between them. The soft hair on his legs chafed her thighs when she wrapped her legs around him. His fingers withdrew from inside her to open her lips. She cried out with pleasure when Rica's cock surged inside her. He filled her to her limits. Still, she arched her hips, struggling to take in more of him, although she had his full length already.

His fingers moved to caress her clit as he withdrew and thrust into her again. Ellie moaned when her tight muscles loosened even further, allowing more of his cock to fill her. She tightened her thighs around him and returned his thrusts as best she could. He didn't break rhythm as he thrust in and out of her, while caressing her clit. She didn't need the extra stimulation, but she couldn't find her voice to tell him his cock driving into her was enough.

It was almost painful to have him stroking her clit while his cock plunged into her, but the line between pleasure and pain was too fine to allow her to separate the emotions. Ellie dug her nails into Rica's back as he surged inside her with a hard thrust. Her pussy spasmed around him, and his cock reciprocated. An orgasm washed through her as his fluid pumped into her. Her supersensitive clit recoiled from his stroking fingers, and he withdrew them.

She pressed closer to Rica, milking his cock for the last bit of his satisfaction. Her heart raced in her ears, and a cry burst from her. It sounded eerily like a howl, and the members standing around the circle echoed her. It was a shocking reminder of their presence, but not an intrusive one. Somehow, it felt right to lie with Rica in front of them, to not hide their passion from the Pack.

She briefly wondered why civilized marriage ceremonies didn't conclude this way, but couldn't imagine her straight-laced parents consummating their marriage in such a fashion. She didn't think any of the people she knew in her real life could give in so uninhibitedly to their desires in front of strangers. She wondered at her own ability to lose control as Rica stood up and lifted her into his arms.

She decided to save the analysis for later. Right now, she owed it to herself and all those who would read her study of the Pack someday to immerse herself in the ceremony. She snuggled against Rica, but made no move to hide her nakedness. She felt him wince and raised her head. Lines of pain grooved his face, and she wondered where he had found the stamina to mate with her when he was obviously in a lot of pain.

She tried to withdraw from his arms, to ease his pain, but his hold only tightened. Ellie ceased trying to pull away. She turned her head when she felt someone draping something over her shoulders. She smiled at Golatia as the older woman wrapped her parka around her.

"Welcome to the Pack," Golatia said with a twinkle in her eyes.

Chapter 8

Ellie didn't remember the trip back to Rica's house. Although in pain, he had carried and tucked her into his large bed. She remembered him brushing a kiss on her cheek before covering her with a warm quilt, but she didn't recall if he had come to bed then or not, since she had fallen into a deep sleep as soon as her eyes closed.

When she opened her eyes early the next morning, she turned her head and saw Rica lying beside her. His eyes were wide open and watching her. She licked dry lips, feeling shy. Her gaze darted around the room, and she heard inane chatter pour from her. "The carvings on the footboard are marvelous." She studied the intricate swirls that formed an abstract design as if the answers to life were in the wood.

His hand on her chin brought her back to face him. "Thank you."

She forced herself to look at him. She wanted to cringe with embarrassment when she remembered how they had made love with such abandon in front of the Pack. There wasn't a trace of shame in his gaze. Her eyes dipped lower, and she noticed the gash on his shoulder had healed. Her hand insisted on touching the place, finding it baby-smooth. "How is this possible?"

"I transformed after I brought you to bed. My body was on its way to healing by then, and the process sped up with turning into a wolf." Rica shrugged. "Maybe it's because when we transform, our molecules get rearranged. Our natural state reasserts itself."

"So you can heal from anything?" Why were they discussing this when he was so close, and his warm hand was trailing up her thigh under the blanket?

He shrugged again. "Almost anything, I guess. If I were seriously injured, I probably wouldn't have the strength to change until I began healing."

"Oh." Her response turned more to a moan when Rica's hand brushed against her pussy before moving onto her stomach. He pressed his palm against her skin, and the heat he transferred to her seeped directly into her womb. She shifted impatiently, earning a low chuckle.

"Last night was too fast." He said it as a statement of fact.

"It was perfect." Ellie frowned at him. Why was he torturing her by skimming her mound with his pinkie, but not touching her? "I forgot where we were."

"That's the mating frenzy." His voice lowered an octave as he slid closer, bridging the gap between them. He threw his leg over hers, immobilizing her. "It's already spread through the village that we're a true mating pair."

She shook her head, struggling to uphold her end of the conversation when Rica thumbed her nipple. His hand then slid half an inch lower, causing his pinkie and ring finger to hover over her pussy. "What does that mean?"

"They say the frenzy seizes you when the mated pair are a true love match. As much as the romantics don't want to admit it, most of our mated pairs aren't in love when they join. If you lose yourself in your mate, it's said you're in love with them." He chuckled. "Even among our kind, the romantics run rampant."

"I didn't lose myself," she said in a sharp tone. "I was aware of them watching."

He nodded. "For all of a minute." Rica seemed pleased with himself when he said that. He obviously liked the idea of his mate being madly in love with him.

Ellie stuck out her tongue. "I'm certain you weren't lost in me either."

His sudden turn to serious surprised her. "Oh, I was, Ellie. I couldn't get enough of you." His hand slid lower to cup her pussy. He squeezed lightly while tugging on her nipple. "I barely resisted the urge to wake you up a few hours ago. I've been waiting for you to open your eyes so I could lose myself in you again."

She arched against his hand, moaning when he slipped a finger inside her lips. "I thought you'd never do that." She was pleased with her cool reply, which was such a contrast to the fire burning inside her. "Um, just like that." His finger circled her clit, coaxing the shy bud from its hiding place. Ellie tried parting her thighs, but his legs held her immobile.

"Like this?" He trailed his finger from her clit to the opening of her pussy. Rica flirted with the entrance, but didn't slide his digit inside her.

Ellie shook her head, rubbing her cheek against the softness of the pillowcase. "Deeper."

Immediately, his finger slipped a few inches inside her. She was damp with arousal, but not wet. She gasped at the friction. She was a little sore from last night, but it felt too good to ask him to stop.

She uttered a sound of protest when he withdrew his finger to cup her pussy again. Her breath came in short spurts when he squeezed her pussy, engulfing her swollen clit with her own slick folds. He moved his fingers on each side of her lips in opposite directions, causing them to rub against her clit. She went from damp to dripping in seconds.

Rica threw back the covers with his other arm. He inhaled, and his eyes darkened. "You smell so sweet, Ellie. I want to taste you."

He didn't wait for permission. She wouldn't have denied him, but she didn't have the chance to anyway. As he spoke, he slid down the bed, until his mouth was near her pussy. His legs draped over the footboard, but he didn't seem to mind the discomfort.

Just having him so near increased her arousal, making her even slicker. Now that his leg was off hers, she was free to roll onto her back and part her thighs. Rica followed her movements, and his nose hovered above her pussy. He inhaled deeply again, and she felt his breath caressing her clit when he exhaled.

She stiffened with shock when he buried his nose inside her pussy and breathed in her scent before breaking away. She wondered what she smelled like to him. Did he have the keen sense of smell of a wolf, or had his human characteristics blunted the ability? She started to make a mental note to follow up on that question, but all thought fled when his tongue surged into her.

There hadn't been any warning, and he wasn't subtle with his strokes. Rica appeared determined to devour her. His tongue squirmed inside her, seeming to be everywhere at once. He drew her clit into his mouth and sucked forcefully, causing Ellie to cry out.

She buried her fingers in his long hair, needing something to hold on to. When his tongue entered her opening, swirling around her tight walls, her cry changed to a breathless groan. She arched her hips, ignoring the dart of pain from her protesting muscles.

The way he pleasured her was fast and possessive, but he didn't lack finesse or skill. The sensations built to a fever pitch, causing Ellie to continuously buck her hips. As wonderful as his tongue felt, it wasn't enough to satisfy her. "Rica, I want your cock inside me."

That she could vocalize a coherent thought surprised her. A cacophony of confusing emotions whirled through her—pleasure, of course, but also a disturbingly intense emotional connection she felt forming with Rica. Surely, it was just because of the physical connection. She was mistaking physical attraction and sex for something deeper. She hardly knew Rica. How could she feel anything for him yet?

"Of course, Ellie." His raspy response sent shivers down her spine. Rica moved up beside her, tracing a trail with his tongue from her pussy, up her stomach, to where he paused to suckle a turgid nipple.

She arched her back. Her hands grasped his hair tighter, but he made no sound of protest. "Rica, please." Her hazy thoughts tried to focus on every moment of the experience, but she couldn't concentrate on anything except having his cock inside her. She released a handful of hair to grope blindly for his cock when he slid higher up the bed. It lay against her thigh, and she squeezed his thick shaft, pausing to stroke the mushroom-shaped head. His breath hissed between his teeth, making her smile.

His body engulfed hers as he moved fully on top of her. His cock nestled into the folds of her pussy. Rica supported his weight with his arms, locked on either side of her head. Ellie shifted restlessly, knowing there was something she had to remember. As Rica started to enter her, she blurted, "Do you have protection?"

Rica froze, staring down at her with a frown. "No."

"Shouldn't we…ah." She moaned as his head slipped inside her. "Rica, I…"

His mouth fastened over hers, cutting off the thought. His tongue surged into her mouth as his cock plunged inside her. Ellie couldn't resist responding by arching her hips. What difference did it make now? They hadn't used protection last night, and if her injection was no longer protecting her, it was too late now. Her tongue tangled with his as his cock filled her completely.

She spread her thighs and locked her legs around his hips, tightening the muscles to hold him inside her. How had she been able to go so long without a lover? Rica moved his mouth from hers, and their gazes locked. His eyes burned dark-blue, and there was a hint of barely restrained wildness in their depths. It had been easy to do without a man, because no other man had ever made her feel like this.

His eyes never wavered from hers as his hips bucked against her, alternately plunging and withdrawing his cock from her hungry depths. She cried out with each thrust, arching against him, determined to have all of him. Her cries turned to a keening moan when Rica's cock spasmed inside her, triggering her orgasm. The walls of her pussy contracted around his cock, milking him for each drop of release. She continued to arch mindlessly against him, until only a faint tremor radiated from deep in her pussy.

Ellie realized she had been holding her breath and let it out in a harsh exhalation. Rica's weight carefully settled on her, and his arms wrapped around her, holding her close. She pressed a kiss to his shoulder and snuggled closer. He was so large she might have felt overwhelmed by him, except for the way he held her. His tenderness caused her to feel safe and protected, rather than suffocated or smothered. She couldn't remember ever feeling as though she belonged in a man's arms before, until Rica.

* * * * *

She must have dozed off again in his arms. She opened her eyes sometime later in the morning to discover he was gone. She wondered what had awakened her. Was it the delicious ache between her thighs, or the all-over boneless sensation of satisfaction?

No, it was the door, she realized, when someone knocked again. Golatia or Davinia must be checking on her, to see how her first night as Rica's mate had gone. She slid from the bed and searched for something to wear as the knocking increased. Her clothes were still at Davinia's, and she hadn't come to Rica's in anything except the sash and her parka. She didn't know where Rica had put it. Her boots were probably still at the clearing. "Just a minute," she called when the knocking increased in pitch.

She went to Rica's closet and found a robe. She pulled it from the hook and slid her arms into it. She belted the tie as she rushed to the door, and hitched up the hem to keep from tripping. There was no peephole. She opened the door and froze when she saw an older woman with a teenager. Ellie self-consciously ran a hand through her messy hair. "Yes?"

"Good morning, Lupina." There was more than a hint of reverence in her tone. "We've come to welcome you."

"Oh, er, okay." Ellie stepped back and allowed them to cross the threshold. She was disconcerted by the way they both inclined their heads and stood before her. She closed the door and looked around the living room of her new home. She gestured to the sofa. "Won't you have a seat?"

They scurried across the room and took a seat. Both looked nervous. Ellie felt the same way as she took a seat in the large chair near the stone fireplace. Silence descended. They seemed to be waiting for her to say something, but she didn't know the protocol. She cleared her throat. "I'm sorry. I don't believe I caught your names."

"I am Afina. This is my daughter Carin, Lupina."

Ellie frowned. "What is Lupina?"

"You are the Alpha's mate. It is a term of respect."

She nodded. "Thank you. Please just call me Ellie."

Afina shook her head. "We couldn't, Lupina." She looked shocked by the idea. "It wouldn't be proper."

What could she do? She couldn't argue the woman into submission. Ellie wondered if her new position came with any influence. She thought about ordering the woman to call her by her given name, but decided not to. She would look like a fool if she didn't have any real authority. Not that she wanted any over these people. "I would offer you coffee or tea, but I don't know where Rica keeps anything."

Once more, Afina looked surprised. "Would you like coffee, Lupina? I will make it for you. I'm certain I can find where the Alpha keeps his supplies."

Ellie waved her hand. "No, I'm fine, but thank you."

That was about the extent of their conversation. The silence lagged. Each time Ellie managed to find a question to ask, the mother answered it quickly, without expounding, and always ending each answer with "Lupina". Her daughter never spoke. It was with relief when she saw them off a few minutes later.

She had barely closed the door behind them when there was a knock. She opened it to find a group of six women of varying ages standing on her doorstep. Some held dishes, and they all insisted on welcoming her to the Pack. She soon grew used to the title of Lupina, and the conversation lasted longer.

When the women finally left, Ellie thought she would have time to shower and find something to wear, but someone knocked again. She wasn't surprised to open the door and see another group of women. She let them in with a small sigh, wondering if the stream of visitors would ever end.

* * * * *

Late that afternoon, Davinia managed to break through the tide of women and bring her clothes. Ellie took a hot bath and dressed in her own clothes before joining her friend in the living room. "Have there been any other guests?"

"A few. I told them you were resting." Davinia grinned. "I don't believe you're regarded as an outsider any longer, Ellie."

She shrugged. "They're only doing their duty."

Davinia shook her head. "No, it isn't that. They didn't welcome me as Lupae."

"What's Lupae?"

"The Beta's wife. The women report to you, and then me, in theory, but they find their own methods of defiance if they don't want to follow the leaders' wives." Davinia smiled at her. "No, I think it must be the romantic in them. They believe you and Rica are in love, so they can overlook the fault of you being an outsider and a human."

"Maybe they've read my mind and have seen I don't plan to stay beyond the spring thaw."

Davinia arched a brow. "Werewolves aren't telekinetic or clairvoyant."

Ellie frowned. "What about Golatia?"

"Who knows? I suspect she has vampire in her lineage. Perhaps a witch or two. Werewolves aren't naturally psychic though."

She licked her lips, suddenly nervous. "What about you? Are you psychic?" Did Davinia know why she was really here? Did she care?

Her friend hesitated. "I was before marrying Viggo. Once I stopped living by the old ways—namely, drinking blood—my powers dimmed. I have an occasional flash of the future, and I can sometimes feel Viggo's emotions as my own, but that's the extent of my power." Her gaze dropped to Ylenia, sleeping on the floor in a bundle of blankets. "And I knew the moment I conceived. Within days, I knew she would be a girl."

Ellie breathed a sigh of relief. She strove for a light tone. "So, I guess you can't use your psychic powers to tell me where my new husband is?"

Davinia laughed. "I don't need clairvoyance for that. You will find Rica in the woodshop behind your home. Viggo is with him, as are several others. That's where they spend their days." Her eyes sparkled with a teasing glint. "Do you miss him, Ellie?"

She shrugged, evading a definitive answer.

"Are you happy with the outcome of the Mating Moon Ceremony?"

"I suppose. Any mate would have done, but Rica is nice."

Davinia laughed again. "You are more transparent than you would like to think." She turned serious. "I think you will not be leaving when the snow thaws."

Ellie's heart rate accelerated. "Do your powers tell you that?"

She shook her head. "No. Love will keep you here."

"I'm not in love with Rica."

Davinia chuckled. "You will be."

She made a non-committal sound, even though the lump in her throat felt as if it were choking her. Ellie wanted to loudly protest she would leave, but even she felt a hint of doubt. She knew Rica wouldn't willingly let her go, and part of her didn't want him to.

She firmed her mouth, trying to assure herself she was having a reaction to the physical attraction she felt for Rica, and nothing more. It had been an overwhelming past few days. It was no wonder she was having trouble focusing on her goals.

She reminded herself she had worked hard for the chair position. She imagined how satisfying it would be to head the department when no woman had held the post before. She had earned the job. There would be no doubt of her appointment when she published her scientifically verifiable study of the werewolves of Corsova. The prospect should have excited her, but instead, it left her feeling hollow inside.

Chapter 9

On her way home, Davinia took time to show Ellie where the shop was. She walked down the path and hovered outside the building that was larger than Rica's home. She raised her hand, poised to knock, but uncertain of her reception. What if the woodworking was some kind of men-only industry? Were the Necheans primitive enough to have superstitions about women and tools?

Before she could decide whether to knock or leave, the door opened, revealing a burly man with a long beard. He stopped in mid-step, obviously surprised. He recovered and inclined his head. "Good evening, Lupina."

"Hello."

"I'm Helgon." He nodded into the shop. "We were just finishing for the day." He stepped out of the building and held open the door for her. "The Alpha is at the back of the shop."

She gave him a smile and a quick, "Thanks," as she stepped into the woodshop. The smell of fresh cut wood, sawdust, and chemicals hit her as soon as she entered. When the door closed behind Helgon, the odors intensified. She blinked and coughed, instantly gaining the attention of the five men gathered in the shop. She had eyes only for Rica.

The three she didn't know introduced themselves before returning to their work. They weren't as friendly as the women who had stopped by to welcome her, and Ellie was under no illusion that all members of the Pack had accepted her as Rica's mate. She stood in the corner, watching as the men finished their tasks for the day and took their leave. When it was only Viggo and Rica left, she moved away from the corner to examine the works-in-progress.

Several doors lined the wall of one side of the shop. They were in various stages of completion. Even those the men had just started on showed the promise of beauty and exquisite detail. Moving on, she examined several small and medium-sized coffee tables in different stages of assembly. There seemed to be a little bit of every kind of furniture, and she looked at all of it while Rica and Viggo finished.

"Ellie?"

She looked up when Viggo called her name. "Yes?"

"Good night."

She nodded, and he left. *And then there were two,* she found herself thinking. She felt nervous for some reason when she met Rica's eyes. He stood by a large table saw, with his hip propped against a workbench. His eyes were dark, and his cock strained against his jeans, leaving no doubt he wanted her.

Her gaze moved to the table saw. "I thought you didn't have electricity."

His eyebrows rose in a high arch. Rica stood up and started walking toward her. "We have a small generator for the shop."

"Then why don't you put in power for the rest of the village?" She took a step back, although she wasn't afraid of him. Maybe she was just afraid of the intense desire she saw in his eyes. Did it mirror her own? She swallowed as he neared. "The women would have an easier time of things."

He stopped walking and reached out, bringing her close. "Do you really want to discuss electricity, Ellie, or do you want me to fuck you?"

She met his eyes again, and all hesitation fled. "I'd like you to fuck me, Rica." She arched her neck as he lowered his head. Their lips met, and she parted hers. Rica's tongue slipped inside to caress hers. His hands cupped her back, rotating in soothing circles. She pressed her body against his, reveling in the way her soft alpaca sweater molded to her curves under his hands and against his chest.

His hands left her back to travel to her breasts, but his mouth remained on hers. He sucked her lower lip into his mouth and bit gently, eliciting a moan of mixed pleasure and pain from her. Ellie gripped his shoulders, digging her nails into his skin through the flannel shirt, urging him closer. When he drew her tongue between his teeth and nipped, she tore her mouth from his. She attempted to take in a deep breath, but Rica's mouth captured hers again.

She felt lightheaded, but didn't think it was because she couldn't draw in a deep breath. His kisses and touch were definitely responsible. She shifted her lower body, searching for relief from the burning in her pussy. Her swollen clit pressed against her silk panties, which created almost unbearable friction.

Rica's mouth ventured away from her lips to trace the line of her jaw, back to her ear. He drew the lobe into his mouth and flicked his tongue around the diamond stud. She dug her fingernails deeper into him, anchoring her suddenly weak knees. When his tongue teased the opening of her ear canal, she stiffened. A gentle breath made her moan. How could her ear be so erogenous?

His warm breath segued to words. "I want to pound my cock into your tight cunt. I want to fuck you from behind, Ellie."

She tried to remember how to form words. Part of her protested the picture he painted with his words, but she responded on a deeper level. Her pussy grew slick. "You want to dominate me." She had meant her voice to emerge full of feminine outrage. Instead, it came out as a smoky whisper, with more than a trace of excitement. She didn't shy away from the realization that she wanted him to dominate her.

"Yes." His breath whispered across her cheek as he raised his head. In contrast to his words, his lips were gentle when they kissed a path from her cheekbone to her eyebrow. Rica stiffened and jerked away from her, growling low in his throat.

Ellie's passion-heavy eyes opened fully. "What's wrong?"

"Silver." He gestured to the stud in her brow. "It's poison to me."

She removed the silver spike with shaking hands, finding her concentration shot by Rica's proximity and the image of him thrusting into her from behind. It was so evocative of wolves in their natural state, and it surprised her how the idea excited her. How would she tolerate the thrill accompanying the actual position?

She didn't stop with the jewelry she slipped into her pocket. Rica's eyes were on her as she pulled the soft sweater over her head and draped it over a sawhorse. Her fingers still trembled when she struggled with the fastening of the bra. He solved the problem by stepping forward and ripping the straps. He tore open the lace and removed the ruined scrap from her. Ellie's shoulders stung where the elastic had bitten into her skin. His lips found the sensitive spot on her left shoulder, soothing it with his tongue, before doing the same to the right.

Rica was gentler with her jeans. He didn't seem to have any trouble using his hands to open the zip and snap. He definitely didn't have any trouble seeking out her pussy and stroking it through the silk. When he tried to move his fingers after a brief caress, Ellie put her hand over his. "I want more."

He grinned. "Later." His hand slipped from hers to join his other at the waistband of her jeans. He rolled them down smoothly, leaving her panties behind. He didn't ask her to remove her boots or try to take them off for her. He just left the jeans around her feet, deliberately interfering with her ability to open her legs. He put his hands on her hips.

Ellie tried to pull away so she could remove her jeans and boots. Rica's grip tightened. He didn't hurt her, but he was showing his strength exceeded hers. She gave a half-hearted glower before she relaxed. As soon as she stopped struggling, he moved one of his hands to cup her pussy. He squeezed the lips together and rubbed them against each other simultaneously. She instinctively bucked her hips.

"Mine." This was no grateful pronouncement. No, he was arrogant as hell when he said it. "Mine," he growled again, possessively.

Ellie moved her arm awkwardly to touch the front of his jeans, where his cock strained against the denim. "Mine." She mimicked his tone and knew there was the sparkle of challenge in her eyes.

"Prove it." He released her and took a step back. "Take my cock in your mouth."

She gave him a cool look, grateful he couldn't see the way her heart pounded or the way her mouth watered. She nodded. "Strip."

He lifted a brow at her tone, but his fingers moved with unerring quickness down the buttons of his shirt. It joined her sweater on the sawhorse. Her eyes stayed glued to his hands as he unsnapped his jeans. The rasp of his zipper was music to her ears, and she licked her lips when his cock sprang free. He wasn't wearing briefs.

He left his cock hanging from his opened jeans while he kicked off his boots. Then he teased her by slipping the jeans down an inch at a time, slowly revealing the firm flesh of his thighs underneath.

She had the urge to step forward and tear off his jeans with the same urgency he had displayed when removing her bra. She contented herself by untying the strings of her panties and removing them. After she draped them over the sawhorse, she started rubbing her pussy. She enjoyed the way his eyes widened and his nostrils flared. She parted her thighs as much as her restrained feet would allow and slipped two fingers inside herself. As Rica's speed at removing the jeans increased, she thrust her fingers in and out of her pussy leisurely.

"If you don't stop that, I'll fuck you this minute." His eyes glittered with suppressed desire, and his hands were rougher than he probably intended when he grasped her upper arms to drag her forward. Ellie's hand slipped from her pussy as he gently pushed her to her knees. She steadied herself by placing a hand on the back of his thigh. She stared up at him, seeing the blaze of passion darken his eyes further when she cupped his balls in her free hand.

His balls had a scant amount of hair, considering the fur that covered the rest of his body. Even on her knees, his cock was higher than her mouth, and she straightened until she could trace his sac with the tip of her tongue. She lifted his balls, trailing her tongue backward, darting into the area behind. He groaned when she teased his perineum.

He had been working all day, but he still smelled good. His scent was a mixture of wood, sweat, and his unique aroma. His skin tasted salty from his exertions, but it wasn't unpleasant. She licked his balls thoroughly before moving her tongue to the base of his thick cock and licking a trail up the underside to the head.

"Don't tease me." Rica sounded gruff, but there was a trace of desperation in his tone.

Ellie smiled before wrapping her mouth around the head of his cock. He was large enough to be satisfying, but not so large that she couldn't close her lips around him. She didn't waste time teasing the head. She lowered her mouth and relaxed her throat, taking in as much of him as she could. When she reached her limit, his hand came to rest against the back of her head to anchor her there.

To her surprise, Rica began thrusting into her mouth, rather than having her work his length. All she had to do was maintain suction and catch the steady stream of his arousal as it leaked from the tip of his head. He never tried to force his cock past the boundary she had established. She clutched his legs and varied the strength of her sucking from light to heavy, depending on the way his body jerked in response.

A cry escaped Rica, and she thought he had come, but his fluid didn't fill her mouth. Instead, he stepped back and bent down to pull her to her feet. Once she was steady, he tangled his hands in her hair and tilted her head back. His mouth claimed hers, branding her as his. He didn't shy away from his essence on her tongue. His lips and tongue devoured her, while his cock pressed into her stomach.

She broke the kiss first, gasping. A trail of fire burned from her pussy to her breasts, centering in her nipples. "I need you, Rica. I can't wait."

"Are you aching for my cock?" While asking the question, Rica spun her around. He crouched down to press his cock against her bare buttocks. The head nestled inside her cleft.

She nodded frantically. "Now, please fuck me now."

He paused only to strip off her boots and jeans before pressing her forward, bending her over the sawhorse. It pushed low into her stomach, but she didn't protest. The minor pain didn't compare to the deep ache in her pussy that only his cock could assuage. She clenched her hands around each side of the sawhorse. Rica parted her legs wide and stepped between them. He hunched low enough to fit the head of his cock against the opening of her pussy, holding her open with one hand.

He drove into her with a deep thrust, instantly easing the throbbing inside her. Rica's chest covered her back as he bent forward over her. He moved his hand from her pussy to join the other at her hips. He steadied her with his strong hold as he thrust into her rapidly. The sawhorse groaned in protest at his quick thrusts, but Ellie couldn't focus enough to be concerned about it breaking.

All she could think about was his next thrust. Each time he withdrew his cock, almost to the point of exit, she wanted to cry. That edge of frustration made each of his thrusts into her that much more pleasurable, until she was sobbing under the onslaught. She tried returning his thrusts, to keep him inside her, but his weight kept her pinned to the sawhorse. She was truly at his mercy. It notched up her excitement to another level.

"Rica." His name emerged as a long moan as he thrust into her again, hitting just the right spot with his cock. "Please…I need…" She couldn't even form the words to tell him what she needed, but he knew. His thrusts became stronger and faster, creating a burning friction in her pussy that triggered convulsions deep inside her. They radiated out from the epicenter of her G-Spot, gaining intensity, until her pussy quivered around his cock.

"Let go, Ellie. Come for me. Let me feel your cunt spasm around me."

His words, which she would have considered crude with another man, brought her to orgasm. The climax rushed through her, causing her pussy to contract around him. Rica's cry of release mingled with hers, rising almost to a howl, as he ejaculated inside her, while the walls of her pussy squeezed him for every drop of his satisfaction.

Tremors racked her body, and Ellie realized she was sobbing from the intensity of her orgasm. If she had thought last night or this morning were amazing, they now paled in comparison. Rica was a masterful lover, and he knew just how to push her beyond her limits, to satisfying results.

How could she give up this incredible passion? How could she ignore the connection between them? Heaven help her, how was she ever going to leave him?

Chapter 10

After almost a month of living among the Necheau werewolves, I find myself strangely at home among them, but still with the perspective of an outsider. Even those who accept me on the surface remain wary. I get the sense I could live here fifty years and that wouldn't change. This doesn't bother me, because that is the nature of these people. The Necheans are wary of outsiders, and with good reason. Their kind has been hunted almost to extinction. No wonder they want to keep their existence a secret.

What bothers me is the more blatant lack of welcome I've received, bordering on threatening. During the early days, it wasn't uncommon to walk out into the street and have children pelt me with snowballs. I know it was their parents' attitudes being reflected, but it bothers me to see intolerance in such young children.

Then there was the incident at the well yesterday.

She stopped writing and brought the cheap Bic to her mouth to chew on the already gnawed end, remembering yesterday. She had gone to fetch water for Golatia, who stubbornly resisted indoor plumbing. It had become Ellie's habit to get water for the older woman morning and afternoon, to save her the walk.

Lia and her mother stood near the pump, along with a few other women and Istal. Lia had stood separated from the whispering group by a few feet. When her eyes met Ellie's, she had seemed to be trying to communicate something. As soon as her mother looked at her, the girl dropped her gaze to the snow on the rim of the pump, where her hands rested.

As soon as the rest of the group caught sight of Ellie, they turned their back on her as one and walked away. Belia followed quickly, with her hand clamped around Lia's wrist.

She had paused briefly to glare at Ellie before storming by, dragging her daughter behind her.

Ellie had dismissed their reaction, having grown accustomed to it. She went to the pump and began collecting water as usual. She was halfway through filling Golatia's bucket when she looked down and saw the words written in the snow: *Watch Yourself.*

I don't doubt Lia was the perpetrator of this threat. It seems she and her mother will never accept me as Rica's wife. I'm not overly concerned with a young girl's acting-out. Her mother's group worries me. They don't seem straightforward like the rest of the Pack. My skin crawls when their eyes follow me.

Still, I'm not going to give in to their obvious hatred. I have a job to do, and I am Lupina, for now.

The most difficult problem I'm encountering centers on my mate. I'm falling in love with Rica. How will I ever be able to walk away from him?

With a sound of disgust, Ellie drew a line through the last paragraph. It was okay to record her personal observations among the hard data she had collected about the Necheans, but it crossed the line to write about her feelings for her husband in this journal.

But drawing a line through the paragraph didn't erase the truth in the words. Nor did it solve her problem. How could she have been so stupid as to allow her feelings for Rica to deepen to something more?

She tossed the pen onto the journal and rubbed her eyes. A quick glance at the clock confirmed Rica would be finished for the day any time, and she had to finish dinner. She pushed away from the small table and went to the stove to stir the rabbit stew. Her pleasure in domestic tasks had surprised her. She was amazed how satisfying it was to scrub the floor to a brilliant shine, or to have dinner waiting for her man when he came home.

She had never pictured herself as the little woman. Ellie had always been drawn to different cultures, and there hadn't been a time when her academic-oriented mother, a professor of sociology, hadn't encouraged her to attend college to prepare for an important career. Her mother was scathing about women who stayed home and did nothing, while the world moved on around them. Following her mother's example, she had naturally gravitated toward those same beliefs.

Now that she had experienced being a homemaker for herself, she had gained new appreciation for the role. It was hard work, but rewarding in a way her career had never been. Rica's never-failing appreciation for whatever she did for him gave her a bigger thrill than any kudos ever given to her by a colleague or superior.

She grinned. It was also nice to be able to stay in her pajamas until noon, if she wanted to. Of course, that would change when they had children.

Her smile disappeared, and she scolded herself for the thought. There she went again, planning a future that couldn't happen. Sure, it was fun to play Susie Homemaker, but could she do it for the rest of her life? How could she ever be content to go from a busy career to the role of wife and mother in this primitive place? Within a year, surely, she would be insane with boredom.

But Rica wouldn't be in New York when she returned. He wouldn't be there to congratulate her on her promotion. In fact, he would probably hate her by then. First for leaving him, and then for revealing the existence of werewolves to the world.

How could she expose these people? Their lives depended on secrecy. She could well-imagine what the world would do to a group of werewolves. But if she didn't publish her study, she could kiss the chair of her department goodbye. And if she wasn't going to be promoted, why bother returning to Columbia? If she didn't get tenure soon, she never would.

It was a vicious circle of doubt, and it played constantly through her mind. Ellie tried to push it aside when she heard the door open. By the time Rica entered the kitchen, she greeted him with a composed smile, seated him at the table, and served him dinner, like any good wife from the '50s. Her lack of dissatisfaction with the humble task upset her anew.

After dinner, Ellie fetched her journal and prepared to finish her day's thoughts. Rica's habit was to take a bath after eating, so she was surprised when he followed her into the living room. She curled up on the sofa, keeping the book closed tightly, watching him as he hovered near her.

"You're always scribbling in that thing. I wonder what you're putting in there." He stared at her for a long moment before sighing.

Her heart stuttered. He had always been respectful of her privacy, but had his curiosity gotten the better of him? She swallowed thickly, wondering if he had read it. She tried to keep it nearby always, but there must have been times he would have had access to the journal. She cleared her throat, preparing to speak, but without a clue of what to say.

Rica walked to the fireplace, keeping his back to her. He took something from the mantle before walking back to her. "This is for you." His tone was gruff. He thrust a wooden box at her. "I thought you could keep stuff in it, like your journal and jewelry."

Ellie released her death grip on the journal to take the box. The lump returned to her throat, but this time it came because she was overwhelmed with emotion, not with fear of discovery. She touched the cherry finish reverently, tracing the flowers etched up the sides of the small box. She caressed the lid, where Rica had carved her first name, and adorned it further with trailing vines and tiny rosebuds.

He shifted his weight. "I don't know if you like that sort of thing. Some people don't like wood. It's okay if…" He trailed off.

Ellie looked up at him with moist eyes, unable to find the words to thank him.

Rica growled low in his throat and turned away from her. "I'm going to take a bath."

She watched him go, only realizing she hadn't said a word when he disappeared from sight. She wiped at the moisture on her cheeks and gently placed the box on the end table. She opened the hinged lid and placed her journal inside, finding it almost a perfect fit. Small velvet-lined compartments in the lid offered storage for her jewelry. He must have put a lot of time and thought into this gift.

What was he trying to say? Did it mean anything? What should she say? Her eyes widened, and she got to her feet, desperate to thank him for the gift. What must he be thinking about her silence? She hoped she hadn't hurt him. Ellie rushed from the living room to the bathroom.

She didn't bother to knock on the closed door. She entered the steamy bathroom, noting the condensation on the mirror. Rica liked his baths hot.

He was in the tub, wearing a brooding expression that closed as soon as she met his eyes. Ellie moved forward and knelt on the bathmat. She reached for Rica's hand in the hot water, wincing a little at the temperature. He tried to resist, but she brought it out and to her lips. She kissed his palm and wrist. "Thank you. It's beautiful. I should have said so immediately, but you overwhelmed me."

He appeared uncomfortable. "Don't worry about it. I wasn't looking for gratitude."

She smiled at his gruffness. Rica often hid his emotions behind a scowling exterior. He might not want her gratitude, but she knew just how to thank him. He held the sponge in his other hand, and she reached for it. He surrendered it easily, and she brought it to his chest. She smoothed it over his taut muscles, pausing to tease one of his nipples with the rough surface. His breath hissed through his teeth, making her grin.

Ellie scooted closer as she brought the sponge up to his shoulder and around his back. She took her time washing the parts of him not covered by the water. By the time she brought the sponge down his stomach and hovered near his cock, Rica's breathing was ragged, and a flush tinged his cheeks.

She lowered her hand, brushing the sponge across his cock. A low moan escaped Rica when Ellie plunged her other hand into the water to lift his balls. She trailed the sponge down his cock while lightly rubbing his balls. He moaned again when she circled the sponge around the head of his cock. "Do you like that?"

"You know I do." It sounded as though it was painful for him to make the admission.

She moved the sponge away from his cock and down his leg, laughing when he tried to restrain her hand. "Let me finish the job, Rica."

"That's what I'm trying to get you to do."

She ignored him and ran the sponge across his foot before moving to the other one and working her way up that leg, until she returned to his cock. He cursed when she skipped over his cock and put the sponge on the lip of the tub. Ellie got to her feet. "I'm going to bed."

"Ellie, you can't—"

She undid the top button of her shirt. "Hurry up and join me." She turned her back and hurried from the bathroom, smiling to herself at hearing the water slosh against the tub as he got out. She could imagine how quickly he would dry himself and finished unbuttoning her shirt before reaching the bedroom. She unhooked her bra as she stepped into the room, and then tossed it and her shirt in the general direction of the hamper. Her pants and underwear soon followed, as soon as she kicked off her boots and removed her socks.

She heard Rica coming down the hall and hurried to her travel bag. She searched through the jumble of bottles until she found the massage oil Davinia had given her the day after the Mating Moon Ceremony, as a mating gift. Her friend had made the oil herself, from a special blend of flowers, including the rose bay that apparently grew rampant during summer.

As Rica entered the bedroom, Ellie walked to the bed. She patted the oak footboard. "Lie down."

His eyes narrowed. "What are you planning?"

"Please, Rica." She knew he wouldn't willingly let her take the initiative, unless she gave him proper motivation. "I want to thank you."

"There's no need—"

She frowned. "Let me take care of you. It's my turn." That was certainly the truth. Rica couldn't seem to curb his dominant tendencies, even in the bedroom. Most of the time, she didn't mind. Tonight, however, she wanted to be in charge. She wanted the loving to be slow and unhurried, rather than the frenzy that usually consumed them.

He sighed, but didn't argue. His skin glistened in the light from the lanterns on the nightstands, indicating he hadn't dried thoroughly, as he walked forward and lay on the bed. His muscles were visibly rigid, and he held himself stiffly, obviously preparing for the worst.

She bit back a smile as she walked to the bed and sat on the edge. He reached for her, and she slapped his hand lightly. His expression of shock had her biting hard on her tongue to keep from laughing. She took a deep breath to regain her calm. "Just relax. Roll onto your stomach."

He eyed the bottle in her hand distrustfully, but rolled onto his stomach, albeit with evident reluctance. If possible, his body stiffened even more.

Ellie got to her feet, and his head turned to watch her every movement. She knew when she disappeared from his sight by the way his shoulders bunched. "Relax," she said again, stopping at the foot of the bed. She swung her legs over the low footboard and perched her buttocks on it. She settled onto her knees before she opened the cap on the bottle. Rica flinched when she drizzled some of the oil across his foot.

"What are you doing?"

"Close your eyes and try to enjoy it, darling." The endearment felt strange on her tongue, but it brought warmth to the pit of her stomach. Rica's tense muscles slowly relaxed, and she waited until he was lying comfortably before she touched his foot again. She rubbed the oil into his skin with firm strokes, pressing against the arch of his foot, and pausing to carefully attend to each toe. Rica was clearly still having trouble making himself vulnerable, but she knew he was making the effort to stay relaxed.

She moved up to his ankle, working her slippery hands across the firm skin. When she moved to his calf and began working the knotted muscle, he exhaled harshly. His leg relaxed further, and she rubbed the muscle until not a hint of tension remained. Then she moved her hands up higher, to press into the back of his thigh. He moaned when she hit a sensitive area, and Ellie paid careful attention to loosening it.

As she moved higher, she felt him tense. When her hand brushed against his buttocks, he stiffened. He didn't relax until she leaned back and lifted his neglected foot. He surrendered to her orchestration, allowing her to bend his knee and bring his foot higher. She bent her head and ran her tongue across his sole, causing him to flinch.

Rica turned his head. "That's enough."

She giggled. "No, not yet. I want you completely relaxed."

"I'm relaxed." He disproved his statement by clenching his muscles when she drew his big toe into her mouth and sucked. "This is..." He trailed off, seemingly at a loss for words.

She withdrew the toe from her mouth. "Isn't it?" Ellie nipped the side of his foot, barely biting back a laugh when he cursed. She cleared her throat and lowered his foot to the bed, once more concentrating on massaging the tension from the muscles of his other leg. He seemed to relax under her touch once he realized she wasn't going to tease him again—or so he thought.

Ellie barely held in a giggle at the way Rica stiffened and shouted when she drizzled oil across his buttocks. Her giggle turned to a breathy sigh at the beauty of his glistening ass. Her hands itched to touch the skin, and she didn't deny herself. Rica clenched his cheeks when she began massaging them with firm strokes, kneading the muscles with enough force to loosen them.

He groaned when she trailed her thumb down his cleft. His tension returned when she parted his cheeks with her thumbs. She lowered her head to run her tongue down the inside of his cleft, earning a cry of outrage. She lifted her head. "Do you trust me, Rica?"

He hesitated.

She squeezed his cheeks. "Do you trust me?" she asked again. "I'm your mate. Do you trust me not to hurt or humiliate you?"

His affirmative answer was little more than a growl, but he relaxed a bit.

Ellie lowered her head again and teased his anus with the tip of her tongue. Rica shivered under her, in rhythm with her tongue. He didn't tell her to stop, but she lifted her head. She knew he'd had enough stimulation in that area. He wouldn't appreciate her delving deeper.

She allowed his cheeks to close again and didn't miss his sigh of relief. She smacked his buttocks lightly before moving her hands to his back. She paused to lift the bottle and dripped more oil onto his skin before continuing her massage. His muscles were tense and knotted, but by the time she worked her way to his shoulders, they had loosened.

Her pussy was also soaking wet. Ellie ached to feel his cock inside her, but was determined to finish what she had started. She had stretched forward to reach his shoulders, and now she leaned back, once more kneeling. "You can roll over now."

"Thank God." He moved quickly, rolling onto his back and reaching for her almost simultaneously.

Ellie shook her head. "Stay still. Hold onto the slats in the headboard if you need to."

He glared at her. "Ellie—"

She touched his lips, leaving a smear of oil on them when she withdrew her finger. "Shh. Indulge me."

He appeared disgruntled as he grasped the headboard. His breath escaped him in a harsh sigh when she drizzled oil on his chest and began to work it into his skin. "I'm going to need another bath when you've finished."

She nodded. "I'll join you." She was pleased to see that shut him up so quickly his teeth clicked when they met. Ellie bent her head and tried to focus on her task. She found it more difficult to push aside her needs with his hot gaze fixed on her, while his cock lay against his stomach, leaving no doubt he was ready for her.

She massaged his stomach with soft strokes, loving the way his abs tensed and loosened alternately under her hands. Her pussy took up the beat and began clenching in rhythm to his muscle contractions. By the time she was at his cock, perspiration beaded her face. She wanted to massage his legs, but his cock was irresistible.

She grasped it with both hands. The oil on her hands allowed her to stroke up and down his cock with a smooth, steady cadence. "I love your cock, Rica."

He grunted, thrusting his hips against her hands.

"I love how it feels inside me. So thick." She moaned, remembering how he had filled her that morning, before leaving the house. A tingle radiated from her pussy, upward. A dragging sensation pulled at her belly, seeming to be urging her to ride him.

"Let me inside." His words were barely intelligible through his gnashed teeth. He held the slats so tightly his knuckles had turned white.

She couldn't continue her plan of a slow seduction. She needed him now. Ellie scooted forward, positioning her knees on either side of his hips. She grasped his cock and maneuvered it to nudge the opening of her pussy when she lowered herself. He let go of the headboard and offered her his hands. Ellie grasped his, using them for support. Rica locked his elbows in place as she sat down on him, taking his cock inside her.

She forgot about remaining in charge, and about going slow. Rica began thrusting against her with fast, deep strokes, and she met each one eagerly. She didn't need slow and romantic with him. Things would never be that way between them. Their passion for each other was hot and intense, so why should their lovemaking be any different?

She cried out as his cock plunged deep inside her. Ellie tightened her hold on his hands, and he kept his arms taut as she leaned forward, allowing him to support most of her upper body. It was all she could do to remember to return his thrusts. Her pussy convulsed, making her cry out. Her body stiffened and released as a climax overtook her. Rica's followed within seconds, and he filled her with his satisfaction.

"I love you, Ellie."

She stiffened as he shouted the words while arching his hips against her. Her body continued to function on instinct, but her mind whirled with confusion. She tried to deny he had said the words, but knew he had. Once again, she found herself speechless, and there was no denying it hurt him when she met his eyes. The sadness she saw in his expression brought tears to her eyes. She started sobbing and broke away from him to run into the bathroom.

She was equally relieved and miffed that he didn't follow her as she gave in to the tears and confusion. Why did he have to ruin everything with his impromptu declaration? Worse yet, why did her heart have to ruin everything by urging her to respond in kind?

Chapter 11

Ellie huddled deep into her parka, hugging her arms around herself. It was strange that she hadn't noticed the coldness to this extent during the Mating Moon Ceremony, when she had been nude. Her eyes locked with Rica's as she scanned the clearing of those gathered to witness the outcome of Lia's moon-cycle claim. His closed expression seemed to harden further, and his eyes slid from hers. Perhaps the ice reflected in them caused her to feel the drop in temperature.

Since he had made his declaration two days ago, and she failed to respond, he had treated her distantly. His words were seldom, and his tone was brusque when he did speak. He was hiding his hurt behind a mask of cold indifference, but she could still see his pain.

She shifted her weight, wishing she could so easily shift her guilt to someone else. Why was she putting him through this? Not answering his expression of emotion was worse than telling him she didn't love him. The problem was, she couldn't definitively tell him she didn't love him, because she knew that was a lie. Rica had captured her heart during her time as his mate, but that was unacceptable. This life wasn't for her.

Never before had she been tempted to stay longer than required for her study. During her time in the rain forest and Africa, she had often thought of home with longing, wishing for a hot shower, a night in front of the TV, or a thousand other conveniences of modern living.

Now, those things seemed unimportant. She didn't want them to be. She wanted her life to be clear-cut, with her plans happening as she had envisioned. She should be anticipating the spring thaw, now only two months away, so she could return to the university and begin organizing her notes to publish her study. She should be looking forward to the perquisites of tenure and holding a chair. She shouldn't be longing to throw herself into Rica's arms, confess her deception, and stay with him.

The arrival of Lia, Jan, and Lasile interrupted her thoughts. She now knew the blond man was Jan, and the black-haired man was Lasile. During the past month, she had seen the three of them together many times, but like the others in the village, she didn't have a clue as to whether Lia would accept them as her mates. Ellie didn't think she would. She wouldn't be surprised if Belia were still scheming to make her daughter Lupina. Lia wanted that too, didn't she?

Tonight, Rica was officiating, since he wasn't challenging and had now mated. He had an intimidating aura as he walked over to the three, who took up position in the middle of the circle. The sash bound their hands, and all three were nude. Rica untied them with a solemn air before stepping back to look at the three of them. He held the sash at his side.

"A moon-cycle has passed. Guardian, join us."

Belia strode forward. She wore a fur over her hips, but her large breasts swung free. She took up position in front of Lia. Before Rica could ask, she said, "I reject this match."

He frowned. "The Guardian refuses to give her approval. Lia?"

When she tried to step forward, her mother blocked her steps. Lia tried to go the other way, and again, Belia stepped in front of her.

There was a definite note of anger in Rica's voice. "Do not interfere, Guardian. Allow the girl to step forward."

It was with obvious ill grace that Belia moved aside. Lia stepped forward, standing in front of Rica with her head bowed.

"You have lived with Lasile and Jan for a moon-cycle, as their mate. Will you accept a permanent union?"

"No," Belia shouted.

Rica glared at her. "Silence." His tone softened when he returned his attention to Lia. "Will you?"

The girl cast a hesitant glance at her mother, and then met Rica's eyes. "I will."

Ellie breathed a sigh of relief when Lia uttered her acceptance.

"I won't allow it." Belia's harsh tone carried around the circle. "I permitted her to participate a year sooner than customary, but it's clear she isn't mature enough to make this decision. I withdraw my consent."

Lia's shoulders straightened. "Alpha, I request to be allowed to make this judgment myself."

Rica frowned. "It is traditional that the Guardian and girl both agree to the mating. You know this, Lia."

She nodded. "There are exceptions. If I don't believe my mother is acting in my best interests, I am allowed to ask for another Guardian, aren't I?"

"You ungrateful—"

Rica snarled at Belia to quiet her before nodding. "That's correct. Do you wish to request another Guardian?"

Lia nodded, and her eyes scanned the clearing. Ellie froze when the girl's gaze settled on her. "I request the Lupina act as my Guardian."

Ellie turned her head to look at Davinia, wishing Golatia had felt up to witnessing the outcome of the moon-cycle claim. She would know how to advise Ellie on proceeding. Davinia shrugged, looking as clueless as she felt.

Rica turned to her. "Will you act as Lia's Guardian?"

She moistened her lips. "What do I do?"

"Come stand beside her. Voice your opinion of the match."

Ellie nodded and walked over to Lia. She paused. "Can I talk to her first?"

He nodded.

She drew the girl away from the two men waiting to mate with her, Rica, and her mother. "Why are you doing this?"

"Please, Lupina, support my claim." Tears sparkled in her eyes. "My mother doesn't want me to accept Lasile and Jan. She has plans…" Lia trailed off into silence before speaking again. "I want them."

She regarded the girl with narrowed eyes, searching for a hint of artifice. This didn't mesh with the threat left at the well. Her brow furrowed. "You weren't threatening me, were you?"

Lia blinked. "Lupina?"

"Your message at the well. I thought it was a threat, but it was a warning, wasn't it?"

She nodded. "I don't know what they plan, but my mother isn't content to let you remain Lupina. She wants me to have the position, or she vows Rica will not remain Alpha." Lia bowed her head, muffling her voice. "I thought I wanted that too, until the moon-cycle claim. Lasile and Jan were right. I was a spoiled child, but I've grown up." She lifted her head, and there was confidence in her stance. "I know what I want. I will not allow my mother to manipulate me."

Ellie nodded, satisfied with Lia's sincerity. She was concerned about what she had learned from the girl, but knew this wasn't the time to focus on it. She returned to her post in front of Rica, and Lia stood by her side. "As Lia's Guardian, I accept this match." She didn't know if those were the appropriate words, but they seemed to work.

Rica turned to the two men standing behind Lia. "Do you still want to claim Lia as your mate?"

Lasile nodded. "I do."

"So do I."

Rica looked satisfied. "The match is approved. Consummation will commence." He tied the sash he had been holding around Lia's waist quickly, without looking down. Then he took a step back, taking Ellie's arm and bringing her with him. His voice was for her ears only. "They require space."

She turned to tell him about Lia's warnings, but Rica's hard profile didn't invite conversation. His gaze remained focused on Lia and her mates. With a sigh, and the resolve to warn him after the mating, she turned her attention to the lovers.

Lasile held Lia in his arms, with her back against his chest. Jan had knelt in front of them, with his arms around her waist. He leaned forward to inhale her scent before his tongue slid inside her pussy. The girl's knees weakened, and only Lasile's supporting arms kept her upright. She arched against Jan's tongue as moans of pleasure escaped her.

Ellie slanted a look up at Rica from the corner of her eye. "I thought the consummation was perfunctory. Why are they drawing it out?"

He shrugged. "Perhaps they want her to enjoy it. Jan is probably ensuring her arousal before taking her. She has to accommodate both of them."

As they whispered to each other, Jan moved away from her to lie on the ground. With Lasile's help, Lia settled on top of him, taking his cock into her pussy. Lasile got onto his knees behind them and pressed his chest to Lia's back. His hands came around her to cup her breasts.

Her voice lowered another octave, so that Rica had to lean down to hear her. "Why don't they use birth control?"

"The Pack must continue. Children ensure that." His expression was brooding. "I had hoped we would have conceived by now."

She refused to look at him, for fear of him seeing the same desire reflected in her eyes. She settled for shaking her head and focusing on the three lovers.

Jan thrust into Lia, who was crying out her pleasure. Her body trembled, but Lasile was there to hold her up. As Jan thrust into her and cried out, Lasile and Lia's voice joined his in a mingled howl of pleasure. All three were visibly tremulous as Lasile got to his feet and lifted Lia before taking Jan's place on the ground. She straddled him, while Jan supported her this time.

Seconds after Lasile began thrusting into her pussy, Lia must have climaxed. Her shout echoed around the clearing, only dying down as his thrusts increased in tempo. Soon, he spent himself, and the three collapsed to the ground, with Lia between them. The two men held her with obvious tenderness, and their movements were gentle when they rose a few minutes later and helped her to her feet.

Belia had watched the union, and Ellie's gaze settled on her when she raised her voice. "You are no longer my child. I am ashamed to call myself a member of the Pack this night." She glared at her daughter before turning her back and stalking away. Several others separated themselves from the circle and followed her.

Their message seemed clear to Ellie. They were turning their back on the ways of the Pack. If they didn't acknowledge the validity of Lia's mating, what other traditions would they disregard? Would they challenge Rica face-to-face, or would they use less honorable means to try to remove him as Alpha?

* * * * *

They hadn't made love before going to sleep, as had been the pattern since Rica said he loved her, and she hadn't responded. He had turned away without speaking. Ellie couldn't help noticing Rica moved away from her each time she brushed against him. It took her a long time to fall asleep, for the weight of her thoughts, and she slept fitfully, trapped in unrelenting nightmares that never completed before morphing into the next.

When she first heard the crackling sound, she assumed it was a new nightmare. It was only when the stench of smoke reached her, causing her to cough, that she realized the house was on fire. Her eyes snapped open, and she sat up.

Rica was coughing too. He sat up beside her, and his hands skimmed over her. "You aren't injured?"

She shook her head, and then realized he wouldn't be able to see the movement from the haze of smoke in the bedroom. "I'm fine, but we have to get out. The house is on fire."

A coughing fit seized her, and she was in no shape to assist Rica when he got up and lifted her from the bed. She tried to pull away, knowing he couldn't be burdened with her weight when he was coughing as violently as she was, but his arms tightened. He held her for a brief second before releasing her.

"Get down on the floor. Less smoke there."

Stop, drop, and roll played through her mind, distant memories from grade school. Ellie got on her hands and knees, wincing at the heat in the boards. The place was an inferno.

She looked up when she heard Rica curse. "What's wrong?" She had to yell to be heard over the roar of the fire, and the action irritated her throat anew, triggering another coughing fit.

"The window has been nailed shut." He cursed again before crouching on his haunches. "This fire isn't an accident, Ellie. Someone planned this. Someone nailed shut our window while we were at the clearing last night." He stopped speaking as a paroxysm of coughing consumed him.

She nodded. "Belia."

"I'm going to break the window. I want you to get as far away from the flying glass as you can."

Ellie scurried across the room on her hands and knees. She pressed her back against the wall, but recoiled with a cry. The wood was so hot that she knew she would have blisters on her skin when she removed her cotton nightshirt.

Rica cleared the items of his nightstand and lifted the heavy oak piece. He grunted with the effort as he swung it against the window. The fire didn't drown out the tinkling of the glass as it hit the floor. The splintering of the boards in the window made a cracking sound, which intensified when he hit the window again.

He snatched the comforter from the bed and wrapped it around his arm in a thick layer before clearing the glass and broken wood from the ruined window. He gestured to her. "Hurry." Although he must have shouted the word, it was barely audible over the suddenly louder fire.

She got to her feet and bent as low as she could, while moving with as much speed as she could muster. She heard a crash behind her and paused to look, seeing the wall she had been crouching near begin to crumble. A large chunk of wood fell to the spot where she had been, bringing the flames into their bedroom. The floor ignited immediately.

She reached Rica, who picked her up less than gently and lifted her through the window. "Get away from here. The shop is a powder keg. If the flames reach it, there's sufficient wood to make the fire grow large enough to burn the village."

"Rica." She reached for him, but he pushed her away.

"Run, dammit. I'm right behind you."

She turned and ran, finding the snow a blessed relief to her bare feet that had absorbed so much heat from the floor.

She went several feet before realizing Rica wasn't behind her. Ellie turned around in time to see a section of the outer wall caving into the bedroom. It was falling in the direction of the window, where Rica's arms were visible for just a moment. They disappeared when he seemed to throw himself back, as if trying to elude the section of burning material crashing toward him. His cry of pain rent the air as the wall collapsed onto him.

She didn't think twice before turning and running back to him. The closer she got to the cabin, the harder it was to breathe. The air was hot and stifling when she reached the window.

She screamed when she looked into the bedroom and saw a section of burning log pinning Rica's leg. It was too large for him or her to lift, even if they worked together.

Tears burned in her eyes, but not from the smoke. A fragment of the wall had fallen across Rica's chest, and the skin was a horrible black in places. He must have pushed off the piece that had landed on him, but not in time to avoid those awful injuries.

She gripped his hand. "Rica, can you hear me?"

His face was blackened with ash and debris, and the sclera of his eyes was particularly bright when he opened them. "Get out," he said in a slurred voice. "Whole building's going to collapse. Tell them to douse the shop."

She shook her head. "I'm not leaving without you."

"Go." He probably meant the command to sound forceful, but it emerged as little more than a weak whisper.

She didn't hesitate to support her weight on the window frame and lift herself back into the room. Ellie brushed aside the pain from slivers of glass that embedded into her hands, legs, and feet upon her reentry. She knelt beside Rica, who seemed to be having trouble keeping his eyes open. She touched his brow, wincing at the heat. "Rica, listen to me."

"Dammit, Ellie, get out. I don't want you to die in here."

"I'm not leaving you." She shook her head for emphasis, although she doubted he saw the movement. "I can't lift the log."

"I know. Save yourself." The slur was more prominent now.

She slapped him on the cheek, as hard as she could. His eyes opened, and he looked incredulous. "Did you—"

"Focus. I need you to shift. It's the only way to get you out from under the log and out the window." She forced herself to sound confident. "I can lift you in wolf-form, but you have to transform. I can get us both out, but I need your help."

"Can't. Too injured." His eyes closed again, and she was alarmed to note his chest was barely rising and falling.

She slapped him again, this time on the other cheek. "You stay with me. I'm not going to lose you. Now change, dammit."

"I don't have the strength." The words were remarkably clear, as was the hint of defeat underlying his tone. "I don't want you to die too."

"Don't you dare give up. What kind of Alpha are you, surrendering like this?" His eyes had closed again. "Open your eyes, Rica. I love you, and I'm not going to lose you. Either we both go, or we both stay. Do you want to be responsible for my death?" If he had been more rational, the approach wouldn't have worked, but she was desperate. "Do you hear me? Change!"

He seemed to be struggling in the beginning, but then it happened quickly. With a scream of pain that turned to a howl, Rica's male form morphed into his wolf counterpart. He had obviously expended the last of his energy in the transformation, but at least he was free of the log that had pinned him.

She gritted her teeth and wrapped her arms around him. Ellie cursed and cried as she tried to lift him. Rica had slipped into unconsciousness and was no help to her, but that also meant he didn't realize she couldn't fulfill her end of the bargain.

No, she refused to let him die. Somehow, she found the strength to lift him from the floor and stagger to the window. A sob escaped her when she reached the window. How was she going to lift him high enough to clear the frame?

"Ellie, can you hear me?" Viggo was there in front of the window, as if summoned. His expression was grave as he held out his arms. "Is that Rica?"

She nodded. "He's hurt. Help him, please." Viggo leaned in the window to take him, but for some reason, didn't lift him from her. "What are you waiting for? Take him."

"Let go, Ellie. I have him now." His tone was soothing.

When she realized she held Rica in a tight clench, she loosened her arms and surrendered her mate to his brother. Her knees refused to support her, and she collapsed by the window, once more aware of the hungry flames lapping at her back, and the intense heat. She tried to stand, but her legs refused to cooperate.

With a muffled cry, she slumped forward, knowing she couldn't lift herself out. She would die here, but at least Rica was safe. That was all that mattered. Nothing else was important—not her old way of life, her goals, or her work.

Her work. Her head snapped up, and she looked in the direction of the fireplace, where the mantle had once been a resting place for the box that held her journal. Not once had she even thought of the pages of notes she had spent hours compiling. Getting Rica to safety had been her only priority.

She mourned for the destruction of the gift Rica had given her, but didn't feel even a dart of regret for the lost work. In a moment of epiphany, she knew she wouldn't have exposed the werewolves to the world. She didn't have the desire to write about them and use it to further her career. Columbia might as well be a million miles away, for all the importance it held for her now.

Hands were on her shoulders then, lifting her through the window. She recognized Eugen, who had been so clumsy with his mate the night of the Mating Moon. She was thankful for his bulging muscles as he slung her over his shoulder and rushed away from the cabin.

She looked up from her undignified position and saw many of the Pack assembled around the shop, dousing the building with water from a portable hose-and-water unit. Most of the rest of the members were using another unit to put out the fire consuming what was left of their home.

Eugen laid her on the icy ground, beside Rica, who remained in wolf-form. A fit of coughing overwhelmed her, bringing a wave of blackness with it. She was able to grasp his paw and assure herself he was alive before passing out.

Chapter 12

A sharp pain in her back woke Ellie. She opened her eyes and tried to sit up. The skin stretched taut across her back, eliciting a groan. Hands were there to assist her to a sitting position. She turned her head and saw Davinia standing beside her. She had been lying on their sofa. "Rica?" The word emerged as a harsh rasp, and her throat protested speaking.

Davinia produced a goblet containing a cold brew with a faint licorice scent. Ellie sipped cautiously, finding the taste pleasant. Her seizing throat eased when she swallowed the cooling elixir. "How is Rica?" Her voice was still hoarse, but audible.

"He's resting. I would have put you in bed with him, but I didn't want you to brush against his burns. And he was so agitated earlier, you wouldn't have gotten any rest." Davinia's hand touched her forehead. "Your skin has lost the heat it retained. You'll be fine."

She knew she would be okay. Her back was agony, and the cuts from the glass someone must have removed stung, but she didn't seem to be in life-threatening distress. "How badly was Rica hurt?"

"It's hard to say. I'm no healer, but he was able to transform twice during the night, which aided healing. His leg is still broken, and he has a nasty patch of blisters on his chest, but his next transformation should restore him to health. Once he rests and recovers his strength, he ought to be fine."

"Can I see him?"

Davinia nodded. "If you can walk. Your back is a mass of blisters. I used a poultice, but it did little more than leach the heat from your skin and heal some of the open areas."

"I think I can walk." She was weak, but needed to see Rica, to assure herself he was all right.

"Come, let me help you."

As her friend supported her arms, Ellie gingerly moved her feet to the floor. Her back spasmed, sending waves of anguish radiating up and down her spine, but she gritted her teeth and forced herself to stand. She still leaned heavily on Davinia for support as they shuffled down the hallway to the room she had used upon her arrival in Necheau.

Viggo sat with his brother. He got to his feet and came forward to bring her the rest of the way into the room. "He's sleeping, but it is restful. He's no longer thrashing." He handed her into the chair he had occupied and stepped back. "Call us when you're ready to leave, or if his condition changes."

She nodded, taking Rica's hand as Viggo and Davinia left, closing the door behind them with a soft click. She used her other hand to lift the loose pad covering his chest. She flinched when she saw the burns. They were horrible, but not even half as bad as they had been last night. Someone had washed him, removing all traces of soot and smoke from his skin. His pallor was obvious.

She lifted the sheet tucked around his waist and found him nude. His right leg bent at an odd angle, but no one had set it. Probably because it would interfere with his transformation when it was time again. "Rica?"

Her scratchy voice caused his eyes to open. They were surprisingly lucid.

She brushed a long strand of hair off his chest. The fire had singed some of his hair, leaving it choppy and of varying lengths. "How do you feel?"

"Like a house fell on me." His voice was hoarse too. "You?"

She nodded. "The same. Davinia said you will be fine in a few days. You need to transform again and rest, but you'll be on your feet soon enough."

"The hell with that." Rica made an effort to sit up, but she had no trouble holding him down with just one hand. "I have to challenge the bastards who did this, before they seize the position of Alpha. I can't appear weak."

She loosened her hold on his shoulder. "Darling, you are weak. If you face Belia now, you can't win. Please be sensible."

He growled at her, baring his teeth. "I don't want to be sensible. I want to tear her apart."

Ellie shared the same sentiment, but she had to convince him to recuperate before charging off to face them. "I want you in one piece." She winked at him. "I like being Lupina, and I want you able to defend your position, okay?"

He scowled at her, but didn't argue. Instead, he brought her hand to his lips. He frowned when he saw the bandage. "What happened?"

"Glass splinters." She frowned when he lowered her hand and began unwinding the bandage. "What are you doing, Rica?"

His hands shook with the effort, but he eventually bared her hand. Ellie's breath hissed between her teeth when she saw the gashes in her palm. Just the thought of someone having picked out the slivers made her head spin. The cuts suddenly burned.

Once more, he brought her left hand to his mouth. She expected tender kisses, and a gasp escaped her when he began licking the wounds. She tried to pull her hand away. "Stop. That's disgusting."

"My saliva will help you heal. Don't fight." He returned to his ministrations. By the time he had unwound the bandage from her other hand and started licking those wounds, the cuts on her left hand had healed.

"That's amazing." She touched her palm, finding the skin smooth and unblemished. Before her eyes, the deepest wound on her right hand closed, returning her skin to its pre-injury state. Her brow furrowed. "Will I become like you?"

He sagged against the bed. He must have spent the last of his energy on taking care of her. "You won't turn to a wolf. It takes a lot more of the enzyme in my saliva to cause a transformation. Your wounds would have to be much more extensive before the enzyme would cause transformation, because they would require more saliva." He managed a hint of a grin. "Otherwise, you would have changed already, as often as I've tasted your cunt."

"You're incorrigible." Ellie shook her head, but his teasing pleased her. It was a sign of his recovery, and she enjoyed hearing him say such decadent things. "I'll leave you to rest now." She got slowly to her feet, pausing to call for Viggo. She looked down when Rica took her hand.

"Did I dream it?"

She frowned. "Dream what?"

"Did you really say you love me?"

Somehow, she found the ability to bend down and brush a kiss across his lips. "Yes, Rica. I love you." She stood up as Viggo entered the room. Ellie squeezed his hand once before slipping her fingers from his. Viggo's arm around her shoulders lent her strength to walk slowly from the room. She paused at the door to look back and saw Rica had already closed his eyes and returned to sleep.

* * * * *

"Rica, no." Ellie's breath hissed through her teeth as sharp pain flared in her back. Two days of Davinia's poultices had gone a long way toward healing the wounds, but they were still tender. Wrestling with Rica didn't do anything to alleviate that. "You can't go. You aren't strong enough." Within seconds, she found herself in Rica's arms, and then lying on the bed where he had been sitting, while he strode to the door.

"Rica!" She scrambled to her feet, slowed by the back injury. At least she could walk properly, thanks to Rica caring for the wounds on her feet yesterday morning. "Don't be foolish. You aren't ready."

He paused to look at her. "Viggo has told me of the whisperings. Many of the Pack believe I didn't survive, and you're hiding that. They are turning to Belia and Istal for leadership. I can't allow that. My line has produced the Alpha since before we settled in Corsova."

She bit back a curse and followed him from the room. He walked past Viggo, ignoring his brother's attempts to stop him. "Do something, Viggo. He's determined to confront Belia tonight."

Viggo sighed and followed his brother.

Her mouth dropped open when Rica opened the door and Viggo followed him out, making no effort to stop him. "What are you doing? Get him back in here." She turned her head when Davinia touched her arm. "Do something."

"It's time, Ellie. He has to show he's strong enough to lead."

She gritted her teeth. "This is stupid. You have to help him."

"Viggo will stand with him, as will I. I must take Ylenia to Golatia first."

With a sound of frustration, Ellie stalked to the door, pausing only to grab her parka as she stormed through the doorway. She saw Rica and Viggo walking to the center of the square and followed.

They paused near the water pump, and Rica's voice rang out. "Face me, Belia, and your followers. Your plan has failed."

Ellie stopped walking as the doors to the cabins lining the square opened. People began streaming into the square, surrounding Rica and Viggo. Most seemed glad to see him, and several bowed their heads and spoke words she couldn't hear. She assumed they were renewing their allegiance to him.

The others formed a loose half-circle, not approaching Rica or Viggo. Their numbers were in the minority, but they still had an impressive show of strength.

She began moving again, breaking into a run to reach Rica. Her back retaliated by sending pain throughout her body, but she forced herself not to acknowledge it. She was out of breath and gasping with pain when she reached Rica's side. He didn't try to send her away. Instead, he grasped her hand in his and pulled her closer. From the corner of her eye, she saw Davinia join them, standing beside Viggo.

"I am Alpha. Does anyone wish to challenge me in an honorable fashion, rather than trying to kill me like a coward?"

The anger in Rica's voice sent shivers down her spine, and she was thankful it wasn't directed toward her. She had never seen him enraged, and she almost felt sorry for those who had opposed him. Almost.

It was no surprise when Belia and Istal stepped forward, along with a half-dozen other men and women. "I challenge you." Istal's chest puffed out as he spoke. "The Pack requires a new leader."

Rica's expression remained impassive. "Very well. We shall meet at the clearing."

Istal nodded almost imperceptibly.

Rica's posture didn't reveal a hint of weakness as he released Ellie's hand and walked toward the clearing. Her heart raced with fear. What if he didn't overcome his challengers? Would the challenge be to the death? She assumed it would. What would she do without Rica?

Viggo followed two steps behind his brother, and Davinia stood by her side. She squeezed Ellie's hands. "Pray, my sister. Pray he wins."

She turned her head from her husband's proud stance to look at her friend. "I'm frightened. He's still weak."

"I'm frightened too." Davinia was visibly shaking. "If he and Viggo lose, the new Alpha has the option of cleansing the Pack of their line." Her eyes were wide with fear when she met Ellie's gaze. "I have no doubt Istal and Belia will order our deaths." A tear clung to her lash. "I'm not so frightened for myself, but what about my baby? She has barely lived at all."

A ball of ice lodged inside her stomach. She forced her voice to emerge confidently. "Rica will prevail. He won't let them take his place."

Davinia nodded, and they joined the group making their way down to the clearing. A few feet from the top of the hill, a howl reached them, echoed by others. A cacophony of noises followed the howls, primarily among them, cries of pain and fury.

Ellie pushed through the crowd, followed closely by Davinia. They raced down the hill and skidded to a stop when they saw what was happening.

Seven men surrounded Rica and Viggo. Three of them were in wolf-form, circling the other four, who were getting closer to Rica and Viggo, also still in man-form. Blood poured from Viggo's arm, and there was a gaping wound on Rica's stomach.

"They were ambushed." Davinia's canines sharpened as she spat the words. Her gaze focused on Istal and Belia, who stood with a small group, wearing smug expressions. "This is not our way." She shouted the accusation. "You are cowards."

"You know nothing of our ways," Belia said. "You are not one of us."

"She is the Lupae, and I'm Lupina. We are the Pack, not you." Ellie wondered where the anger and courage came from that propelled her forward. "You are the ones who don't belong. You would betray your own members and traditions to seize power."

To her surprise, several members of the Pack followed her. Davinia stood at her side, having transformed into wolf-form while Ellie's attention remained focused on Belia. When she turned her head, she saw more than a dozen members had broken from the circle and stood with them. She recognized Lia, Lasile, and Jan in their wolf-form, closing in on her mother.

"End this charade. Challenge Rica the right way. The Pack will not accept you as the Alpha if you don't." The remarks were addressed to Istal, but Ellie kept her gaze on Belia as she spoke. She knew who was behind this scheme.

Growls of agreement issued from those behind her, and even from those in the circle, who had obviously decided not to intervene physically.

There was fear in Istal's eyes as he stepped away from Belia. "Leave them."

The men circling Rica and Viggo hesitated, but broke away when Istal growled at them. They didn't attempt to join the circle. Rather, they hovered away from the rest of the Pack. They must surely have realized by now that there would be no place for them in the Pack if Istal lost the challenge.

Viggo backed away from Rica, keeping his eyes on Belia as he did so.

Istal stepped into the circle, and sweat gleamed on his skin. He had discarded his fur loincloth, and Rica now shed his shirt and jeans.

Although their posture was similar to that of challengers during the Mating Moon Ceremony, Ellie could sense the different atmosphere this night. There wasn't the underlying hint of excitement and arousal in the members. Only fear and anger were revealed on those whose countenances didn't hide their emotions. Her own stomach knotted with fear. Normally, Rica would crush Istal easily, but she knew he was still weak.

As one, they changed to wolf-form. Rica leapt first, landing on Istal's back and rolling him to the ground. He howled with umbrage. His outrage turned to a yelp when Rica buried his teeth into his neck. Istal twisted and jerked, finally dislodging Rica from his back. He was quick to seize the opening by twisting onto his side and attacking Rica's exposed stomach. The transformation had healed the wound left by the men who had ambushed Rica, but Istal's teeth formed a new gash.

Rica was silent as he used his back paws to remove his enemy. He kicked out at Istal, who tumbled away, landing on his back. He scrambled up, but not quickly enough to keep Rica from landing on him and ripping into his left flank. Istal's cry resounded around the clearing, echoing up the mountain.

He bucked under Rica, and his movements were frantic. Somehow, he pushed Rica away, but didn't have a chance to attack. Rica moved with fluid grace, pinning Istal to the ground. His teeth clamped around the other man's throat, cutting off Istal's growls. His fur rose as he bit harder. Istal twitched under him, and a feeble howl escaped him. Rica cut it off ruthlessly. Soon, Istal started convulsing.

Rica loosened his hold and moved back, remaining in wolf-form. His eyes never left Istal while the other man convulsed. Even after he fell silent and his chest stopped moving, Rica remained by the body of his challenger. Finally, he threw back his head and howled. The sound echoed around the clearing, and those already in wolf-form took up the call.

As Ellie watched, those around her transformed, shedding or ripping clothes in the process. She stood in the midst of two hundred wolves, each crying out their relief at Rica's victory. The only ones who remained silent, besides herself, were those who had conspired to overthrow Rica. Their fear covered them like a shroud. All except Belia, whose deadpan expression revealed nothing.

It happened quickly. Ellie barely had time to follow with her eyes as Belia withdrew something from her fur covering and ran at Rica. She didn't transform, so she was slower than she might have been otherwise.

"Rica, behind you." Ellie's warning wasn't loud enough to carry over the howls around her, and she began running.

Rica's back was to Belia, and the other woman raised her arm, revealing a wooden-handled knife with a silver blade. Somehow, Ellie found the strength to increase her pace and interceded between Belia and Rica, just as her mate turned. He must have finally heard Belia over the howls of the Pack.

Silence descended, but Ellie wasn't more than peripherally aware of the Pack watching. All she could concentrate on was trying to keep Belia's arm from lowering and plunging the knife. The other woman had changed her aim, and was now trying to push the knife into Ellie.

Her arms trembled. She knew Rica must be changing behind her, but it wouldn't be in time. Belia's arm lowered, and the knife found its mark in her side. At least she had managed to deflect the blow from her stomach, although that didn't seem to have made much difference.

The pain was intense, and her strength fled. She fell to her knees, and Rica's paw brushed the top of her head as he leaped. He hadn't changed form after all. He hit Belia with enough force to knock her to the ground. His mouth was at her throat before she had a chance to reposition the knife or transform. There was a horrible ripping sound, and then silence returned.

Ellie slumped onto her hands and knees as the wound throbbed. She couldn't seem to focus on anything, and darkness was trying to take her. She was mildly aware of the sting of Rica's hand when he slapped her cheek. She forced her eyes open to meet his gaze. She tried to speak, but couldn't find the strength to.

"I'm going to heal your wound, but it will take a lot of saliva. Much more than we have ever exchanged. The quantity of enzyme you'll receive will cause you to change. Ellie, can you hear me?"

She nodded, finding it too difficult to mull over the ramifications of accepting the transformation. All she cared about was living, so she could be with her mate. She managed to whisper, "Do it," but lost consciousness as Rica laid her on her back.

Chapter 13

An incredible feeling of freedom filled Ellie as she ran. Never could she have imagined it would feel like this to be a wolf. She retained her own thoughts, but animal instinct definitely reigned. Her only regret was her inability to speak to Rica in wolf-form, since she didn't know any of the wolf calls yet. She wanted to call out, asking where he had disappeared.

She craned her neck, still growing accustomed to the way her new set of muscles moved. Other than a trace of the pain that had accompanied the transformation, she didn't hurt anywhere. The knife wound had closed, and her back didn't hurt at all. She should be whole again when she returned to human-form.

She was a little apprehensive about that. Changing to a wolf had happened while she was in a stupor, so she didn't know how her body had done it. Would she be able to return to her normal form? What if she were stuck in a wolf's body forever?

Her ears perked when she heard someone approaching her from behind. They were moving with stealth, but her senses had heightened during the hours she had spent as a wolf, with Rica as her guide, and she heard the telltale movements.

She stopped running and tried to stop panting, so she could hear each furtive movement. She was listening so intently that she forgot to use her eyes. She saw a blur from the side seconds before a furry body covered hers, pushing her to the ground. She recognized Rica's scent and relaxed.

Her eyes widened when he mounted her from behind, pushing her front paws harder into the ground, while keeping her rump elevated. Excitement spiraled through her when she realized he was going to mate with her in wolf-form. A disconcerting image of transforming back to her other form during the process flashed through her mind, but she dismissed the fear.

There wasn't any foreplay, but she didn't seem to need any. Her pussy accepted his cock easily, tightening around it. As Rica thrust into her, a howl broke free from Ellie. He joined in the cry, and her pussy tightened further around him.

No, that wasn't it. His cock was growing inside her. It had thickened and expanded. Ellie felt a moment of alarm, wondering what was happening. Then she was too caught up in sensation to wonder about anything except when she would climax. His hard thrusts excited her sensitive flesh, causing her pussy to convulse. Her muscles contracted, and she released another howl as an orgasm swept through her.

It wasn't the same as when she was in human-form. As a woman, the orgasm often ricocheted through her whole body. This release was more intense, centering just inside her pussy, and triggering another orgasm. The duration wasn't as long either, but she was amazed when several small orgasms ravaged her, building in intensity until her pussy was clenched so tightly around Rica's cock that she didn't know how they would ever separate.

Rica cried out when he came, pumping into her with renewed vigor. His cock spasmed with greater intensity, and for a longer period, than any other time they had made love. It was a long time before he softened inside her and withdrew his cock.

Ellie collapsed to the ground, panting. It seemed to happen naturally that she morphed into human-form again. Rica followed suit and drew her against him. She couldn't seem to catch her breath, and her heart still raced. There was a deep ache in her pussy, but it wasn't from pain…unless there was such a thing as too much pleasure.

"Was I too rough? Your scent was driving me insane. I couldn't wait another minute."

She shook her head, brushing her hair against his bare chest. "It was amazing. I never would have thought…" She trailed off with a satisfied sigh. He had been there. He didn't need a recap.

"How do you feel otherwise?"

She bit back a yawn. "Sleepy."

"I mean your wounds. Have they healed?"

"Yes." She arched her back, pressing her breasts against his stomach. "I feel wonderful. So alive."

"I love you, Ellie." His tone was gruff.

She smiled, cuddling closer. "I love you too. I was so afraid of losing you when Istal challenged you."

"I thought I'd lost you too." His voice deepened, becoming harder. "You aren't leaving when the snow thaws. You know that, don't you?"

She bit back a giggle. She could make an issue of his Alpha attitude, but why bother? She didn't want to leave. She was going to stay with him forever. "Yes, Rica," she said meekly, while laughing inside. Let him think he was taking charge. It would mollify him to believe he had made the decision for her. She knew better. She was staying because she wanted to.

* * * * *

"Leave and never come back." Rica's profile could have been etched in stone as he turned his face from her, sending a signal to those gathered in the square.

Ellie's heart stuttered with fear, but she refused to give in to it. She cast a glare at Sorin and Lucian, whose arrival had caused Rica's rage. Damn them for revealing her original purpose for coming to Corsova. Not three days after the snow melted, they had arrived to expose her.

She shifted with discomfort, knowing she couldn't place all the blame on them. She'd had months to tell Rica why she had come, but had been afraid to upset their relationship. Things had been so perfect between them that she was terrified of telling him the truth. It hadn't seemed that important. After all, the werewolves stayed to themselves. She hadn't expected the queen of Corsova to send her emissaries to inform Rica about the traitor in their midst.

She stiffened her spine. "I'm not leaving."

He turned back to her, and his fury caused her stomach to quiver. "Why? Don't you have enough information to expose us yet? Light your torches and bring your mob into our midst, Ellie. I'd think you would be eager to escape this primitive place and return to where you belong."

"I belong here." She dared to look at those assembled, finding only Golatia met her eyes. Even Davinia refused to look at her. She felt the need to throw up.

"No one wants you here. Leave while I'm allowing you to." Rica turned his back on her and began walking away. As one, the Pack turned their back on her too.

Ellie was amazed by the sympathy she saw in Lucian and Sorin's eyes. A sense of desperation filled her. She had to make them understand. "Please, Rica, don't send me away. I love you."

He stopped walking, but didn't turn. "How can I believe that? You've lied about everything else."

"Yes." Her shoulders sagged with the admission. "I did lie. I lied to all of you. I thought I had good reason for my deception, but I've realized I was selfish. I planned to use the Pack's existence to secure tenure and the chair in my department." Her words didn't do anything to soften his stance, but she continued speaking, letting the words fly from her without thought. She was speaking from her heart.

"I didn't expect any of the things that happened to me. I didn't expect to find my first real friend among your people."

Her eyes moved to Davinia, who slowly turned around. She hated the pain she saw in her eyes. "You welcomed me when no one else would, because you knew what it was to be an outsider. You've treated me like a sister, and I used you. I'm sorry."

The marginal softening she saw in Davinia's expression encouraged her. She switched her gaze to Golatia, who hadn't turned away from her. "I also found a mother among you. I've never been close to the woman who gave birth to me. I could never please her. I never measured up to her plans for me, but Golatia accepted me just as I am."

She closed her eyes, knowing the hardest part was coming. "Despite who and what I am, I have become part of the Pack. I've found a sense of belonging among you. I've found a family." She held her breath, waiting to see their reaction. She was able to breathe again when several of the Pack turned around to face her. Their expressions were closed, but at least they were looking at her. "I owe each of you an apology, and I want to make it up to you. I want to stay here and spend my life among my family."

Ellie started walking, forcing her feet to carry her to Rica, who had kept his back turned to her. She stopped within touching distance. "Don't make me leave, Rica. I do love you. You know I do, deep down. You're hurt at my deception, but you can't doubt I love you."

His shoulders moved almost imperceptibly, but he didn't turn.

She touched his arm, encouraged when he didn't flinch or try to shrug her off. "You're everything to me, Rica. I would rather die than be without you. Whatever the reasons I thought I was coming to Corsova for, you were the true purpose. I believe I was meant to find you. I'm destined to be your mate."

He turned, but his face was hard. "We mate for life. You accepted me, knowing you planned to leave. You didn't care what that would do to me."

She wished they could do this privately, but Rica seemed determined to expose her vulnerabilities to the Pack. "That's true. I intended to leave you. I didn't even think I cared whom I mated with. I thought any man would be as good as the next, for my purposes. My plan was to gather as much about your people as I could, and then leave without looking back." She swallowed the ball of moisture in her throat. "Things changed when you made love to me, Rica."

His eyes widened, and he looked at the Pack gathered. All had turned back to face her, and they were listening to every word.

She forced herself to continue. "I've never felt anything for anyone else that's close to what I feel for you. Your touch makes me burn. Your gentleness, coupled with your strength, humbles me. Every day, you remain honorable and true to your beliefs, no matter what the cost. I want you in my life, Rica. I want to have that same sort of resolve."

She bowed her head, hoping he would say something. Still, he remained silent. She wanted him to agree to let her stay because he wanted her. She didn't want to use her last option to force his hand. She had to know he loved her and could forgive her. "Please say something. Tell me you hate me, or tell me you love me. Spend the rest of our lives together punishing me with harsh words, but don't send me away."

She raised her head when she heard movement. She watched with amazement as the Pack disbursed, leaving them with the illusion of privacy. She frowned. "What's happening?"

"They're signaling they will follow my decision." Rica's mouth twisted. "They're also letting me know they won't support it in their hearts if I don't choose wisely."

Her stomach clenched. "What choice do they want you to make?"

"They want you to stay. If they didn't, they never would have turned back to you. They wouldn't have acknowledged you in any form. Don't you remember how it was when we banished Belia's followers?"

She nodded, remembering how the dozen men and women had been cast out. The Pack had turned away from them, refusing to hear their pleas to be allowed to stay. Mothers had hardened their hearts to their children, not even shedding a tear as their offspring left forever. "What decision will you make, Rica?"

"I don't know. How can I believe you, Ellie?"

She shrugged, wishing she had an answer. "I lost my notes in the fire," she whispered. "I didn't even think about them until you were safe. By then, they were destroyed. I cared more about losing the box you made me than the journal." She lifted her head to meet his eyes. "I would have died with you in that fire if you hadn't been able to transform. I would rather have perished with you than live without you." Tears streamed from her eyes.

His hands were gentle when he drew her against his chest. "I want to believe you. I want to let you stay, but how do I know you won't get bored with life here and decide to leave? How can I be sure you won't betray us to the outside world?"

His shirt muffled her voice, but she strove to speak clearly. "Because I'm one of you now. Even before you saved me by transforming me, I had decided I couldn't expose you. I don't want the world to know about us." She took a deep breath, gathering her courage. It might be the wrong time to make her revelation, but what choice did she have?

"I don't want our son or daughter spending their life running. I want him or her to grow up safe and sheltered here in Necheau." She lifted her head, daring to meet his shocked gaze. Ellie cupped his cheeks in her hands. "I want my child to learn how to be the kind of person you are."

He paled. "You're carrying?"

She nodded. "I'm having your baby. I planned to tell you tonight, but then the messengers from the queen arrived. I don't want the baby to be the reason you let me stay, but if that's the only way you'll allow it, I will spend the rest of my life trying to convince you how much I love you."

Rica sighed, and his tension relaxed. "You don't have to convince me. I know you love me. How could you not?"

A small smile curved her face at his arrogant words. "Yes, Rica."

He snorted. "Don't be meek for me. I know that isn't you." He frowned. "Unless you've been playing a part. Are you the woman I fell in love with, or was she a façade?"

She shook her head. "I've been myself with you, except the night you first summoned me, after I eavesdropped on your meeting. I found it impossible to play the useless rich girl. My love for you is real. It's more real and tangible than anything my old life could offer." She laid her head against his chest again. "Can I stay, Rica?"

"Yes. Our people need a Lupina." His gruff tone softened. "And I need you." He cleared his throat. "There are conditions."

Her heart stuttered. "What conditions?"

His expression was stern. "I expect you to tell me you love me every day. I expect you to show it too, not just mouth the words. I expect you to be my helpmate and partner. You have to honor your duties to the Pack."

She nodded eagerly. "I can do all that. I can start showing you right now, if you want?"

He seemed to be mulling it over. "That would be acceptable. You have my permission to proceed."

Epilogue

Ellie shivered as the cold wind penetrated her fur robe. She cradled Ilka closer to her, ensuring the mound of furs covering her son protected him from the night air. She heard Aurelia crying as Rica readjusted her position in his arms. She wondered how much longer the Welcoming part of the Naming Ceremony would take. Surely, by now, each of the Pack had seen the twins. She'd had enough visitors in the past week to think so. And why did they have to do this outside, in mid-winter?

Davinia stood behind her, holding Ylenia in a fur robe that nearly swallowed up the baby. She kept trying to lean forward and reach for Ilka, causing her mother to shift her position every other minute.

Ellie turned her head to smile at her friend. "She seems taken with him."

Golatia laughed, causing Ellie to turn her head to look at her.

"As she should be." A cryptic smile curved the old woman's lips.

Ellie frowned. "What do you know, Golatia?"

She smiled. "I know what I know, my dear. Some things I can tell, and some I won't."

She sighed at the familiar answer. "Fine, have your secrets."

Golatia's age-spotted hand brushed Ilka's cheek. "I'll tell you this, Lupina. Your children are special."

The Naming Ceremony lasted nearly an hour. She lost count of the number of hugs and well wishes she received. It was nice to have the Pack showing their acceptance of her and the children, but she was glad it had ended by the time they returned to their home. The construction had recently been completed, and it featured electricity, as did all the houses in Necheau of Pack members who had opted for the luxury when Rica arranged to have power put in for the village.

She gladly surrendered Ilka to Rica, who shifted Aurelia to his other arm. It was heartwarming to see his large hands cradling each tiny baby with such tenderness. "I'm exhausted."

"Go to bed. I'll join you as soon as I have the twins down."

She wasn't about to argue with him. Ellie hurried into the bathroom and washed with record speed. She brushed her hair, now falling past her shoulders, to a glossy sheen, and returned to their bedroom. By the time she heard Rica coming down the hall, she had arranged herself on the bed.

He opened the door and froze, with his eyes wide. He cleared his throat. "Did you forget your nightshirt?"

She shook her head and spread her thighs wider.

His cock swelled against his jeans, but he seemed determined to control his desire. "Aren't you cold? Wouldn't you be more comfortable under the covers?"

"No." She tilted her head. "I'd be more comfortable under you. These last few weeks have been hell."

He cleared his throat again. "It's only been a week since the twins were born. I thought you had to…you know…wait a while."

She shrugged. "If I were still human, I would. I found time to transform this morning."

His eyes widened with comprehension. "You aren't sore?"

She shook her head. "I do ache though. I need your cock. It's been too long."

His fingers seemed to fly as he shed his flannel shirt. He kicked off his boots in whatever direction they flew. The rest of his clothes followed, and he rushed to the bed.

She held out her arms, welcoming him as he covered her. "Have I told you yet today that I love you?"

"Yes, you have."

She nodded. "Good. I wouldn't want to violate any of my conditions." She grinned. "Have I shown you yet?"

Rica chuckled. "Now that you mention it, I don't think you have."

She pressed her lips to his, gently exploring his mouth with her tongue when he parted his lips. She grasped his shoulders and parted her thighs further as he settled between her legs. His cock pressed against her pussy, reminding her how long it had been since she had been able to welcome his hard length inside her.

She gasped when Rica ran his thumb across her breast. The nipple was swollen, and a trickle of milk leaked from it at the stimulation. She arched her back when he cupped the breast, rolling his palm over the engorged peak. His tongue dueled with hers, gently forcing hers back into her mouth. His followed, stroking across hers with velvet softness. He seemed to be intent on seducing her, but that wasn't what she wanted.

She broke away, turning her head to avoid his kiss. "I don't want slow and easy, Rica. I've spent the last few weeks aching for you. Just fuck me, please."

If he hadn't been so endearing, his visible swell of pride would have been irksome. "I can give you exactly what you need." His cock started to slide into her pussy, but he froze when she clenched her legs around him.

"Not without protection. I dearly love our children, and I appreciated the way you pampered me while I was pregnant, but I am not going through delivery again for a long time." Remembering the pain of the experience was almost enough to cool her ardor.

He didn't murmur a peep of protest as he sat up and leaned across her to get a condom from the nightstand. "I'm glad I ordered these," he said quietly. "I didn't think I'd need them so soon."

"I'm thankful you're prepared." Her eyes feasted on the length of his cock as he sheathed it in latex. She opened her arms again to embrace him as he returned to his position between her thighs. Rica nudged her thighs apart and cupped her pussy in his hand. He circled her clit as his tongue circled hers. She was wet and ready for him. She arched against him, but Rica refused to replace his hand with his cock.

The frustration was going to kill her. She freed her mouth. "I need you. Don't tease me."

"Yes, Lupina," he said in a mockingly servile tone. "Anything you say."

She growled at him and tried to thrust her hips upward, to seek out his cock. His fingers plunged inside her, and it brought some measure of relief. It wasn't enough though. "Rica." She had meant for her frustration to be obvious when she said his name, but it emerged as a breathy whisper when he finally parted her lips and plunged his cock inside her.

His intentions of teasing her fled, and he thrust into her in earnest. Ellie's response was equally eager. She arched against him as fast and hard as she could, taking in all of his cock before he withdrew it, only to repeat the cycle again. She dug her fingernails into his back, urging him to thrust even deeper. Her pussy was still a little swollen, providing snug passage for his cock. It ignited all of her nerve endings, causing convulsions to build in her pussy.

She tightened her thighs around him, locking Rica inside her. As his cock spasmed, her pussy clenched and released. The orgasm made her pant, but it was the look of love in his eyes that took her breath away when their gazes locked. He made no attempt to hide the intensity of his emotions for her. He exposed his soul to her, and she embraced the gift, holding him tightly against her. As soon as she could breathe, she would certainly remind him how much she loved him.

BLOOD BOND

Dedication

For Starr R. She wasn't the inspiration for this character, but she is always inspiring.

Chapter 1

The scent of incense filled the small tower room, making Starr's head spin with its intoxicating aroma. She kept her eyes closed as she shifted on the thick pillow cushioning her buttocks. A hint of a vision played at the back of her mind, but the more she tried to focus, the more elusive it became.

She took a cleansing breath and tried again to focus. She sensed two—no, three—people in the vision, but couldn't make out what they were doing. Slowly, the first one's visage clarified, and she recognized Lucian, with his boyish smile and carefree attitude. A smile lit up her face in response to his.

Sorin solidified next, crouched in front of a third person, whom he had his arms protectively around, as Lucian knelt on the floor beside them. Starr struggled to make out their location, moaning quietly when she realized it was her bedroom. As Sorin shifted, pushing back his longish hair as he rose to his knees, her face emerged.

A blush tinged her cheeks in real life when she realized she was nude, as were the two men. When Lucian's hand cupped her breast in the revelation, Starr's nipple beaded in real life, pressing against the soft linen of her blood-red robe.

As Lucian pressed closer to her, Sorin pulled her into his arms, resting her back against his chest. His thick body hair crackled against her bare skin, and she rubbed herself against him, moaning. Lucian's hands moved to cup both her breasts, and Starr parted her thighs, instinctively inviting him to nestle between them. She was conscious of Sorin's cock pressing into the curve of her hip, and she reached a hand behind her to caress its head.

Starr shifted with discomfort on the cushion, alarmed, yet also aroused, by the swell of moisture between her thighs. She knew she could open her eyes to end the vision, but couldn't tear herself away just yet.

Lucian slid up onto the bed, settling between her thighs when she parted them. He lifted his head to suckle at her breast. One of Sorin's hands moved from her waist to stroke the thatch of curls between her thighs. Starr parted her legs wider, moaning in the vision and real life as Sorin stroked her pussy lips, spreading her dew through the damp curls as he parted her.

She threw back her head and bit her lip as his large thumb glided across her swollen clit, igniting feelings she hadn't expected. Starr arched her hips, allowing Sorin freer access, as Lucian's teeth grazed her nipple. "Oh, God, I want you."

Her eyes snapped open, and she blinked, straining to dispel the vision. Having spoken aloud had ruined the sensual trance, and she took a deep breath, finding the incense cloying now, rather than soothing.

Her pussy ached with need, and Starr clenched her thighs. Her body hungered for release, and she pushed away from the cushion, pausing only to extinguish the candles and incense before she left the chamber.

Each step down the twisting staircase inflamed her clit to the point where she could barely stand. With a moan of frustration, she rushed to her chambers, pushing against the door with one shoulder, even as she struggled to raise the hem of her robe. She kicked the door closed with her foot and collapsed on the stone floor, unable to make it to the bed.

Her fingers buried themselves inside her pussy, seeking out the sensitive nub. Starr circled her clit with her thumb and finger, shivering as sensations coursed through her. These weren't nearly as vivid as those she had experienced when Sorin touched her in the vision, but her body welcomed the pleasure.

She increased her pace while picturing Sorin and Lucian's nude bodies. She imagined Lucian sliding his cock inside her as she took Sorin's into her mouth. She moaned and began rubbing her breast with her free hand. She writhed against her fingers, flirting with the opening of her pussy before withdrawing.

She imagined Sorin's tongue sweeping across her swollen clit, and a flood of moisture accompanied the thought. Small convulsions built deep inside her womb, extending outwards, until her pussy clenched. Starr stopped caressing her clit as the waves pulsed through her. Tears streamed down her cheeks, and her heart raced.

It was a long moment before she found strength to drag herself to the bed. She lay back, letting the cool air in the room caress her pussy, leaving the robe pushed up to her hips. She licked her lips, imagining Lucian's mouth against hers. She wondered how he would taste. Despite the recent rash of vivid visions, she had never even kissed Lucian or Sorin, except in a friendly way, when they were younger.

She rolled onto her side, cuddling the pillow against her. She never would either. As the spiritual leader of Corsova, she had to remain chaste. Her mentor, Ylenia, had told her impurity could interfere with interpreting the visions she received. She choked back tears, knowing they wouldn't change anything. It was her responsibility to follow the traditions of her people. Even pleasuring herself was taboo. Making love when she held such a position could spell the ruination of their way of life. She might incorrectly interpret a vital vision if her thoughts remained centered around love instead of duty.

But how was she supposed to do her duty when the only visions she had received recently revolved around the two men she loved? How could she see what was best for her country when she couldn't see past her own heart's desires?

Chapter 2

"You look like hell."

Lucian's teasing tone caused Starr to jerk with surprise and spill the potion she had been mixing for Petru's migraines. She looked up to see Lucian and Sorin standing in the doorway of the circular room of the tower, where she now spent most of her days.

"I didn't sleep well." She gave them a small smile, praying her eyes didn't mirror the thoughts dancing through her head. Their blood-bond with her was probably strong enough to allow them to read her thoughts if they chose, but she was almost confident her mind was stronger. After all, psychic abilities came naturally to vampires, while werewolves only received them by ingesting vampire blood.

She straightened to her full height, just two inches shorter than Lucian, who stood five-ten. Sorin still towered over the both of them, even slumped against the doorway. Her eyes traced the way the thin cotton shirt clung to his muscles. The white material didn't have a prayer of hiding the thick growth of black hair covering his body. She could place her hand on his chest and feel the crispness of his hair underneath…

She blinked when Lucian chuckled. Her cheeks felt warm as she turned to him, wondering if her expression had betrayed her thoughts. She swallowed a thick ball in her throat, worried they could smell her arousal. "What?" Her voice sounded normal. If only her hands would stop trembling, she might be able to project an aura of cool indifference.

"You're a million miles away. You didn't answer me."

She frowned. "What was the question?"

"We're going to the lake for a swim." Sorin shrugged. "You are coming with us."

She shook her head. "I can't. I have to finish this—"

"We'll wait." Lucian's tone lacked the steely thread of command that had been present in Sorin's, but his expression was firm.

"You used to come with us all the time." A twinkle appeared in Sorin's eyes. "*Sans* suit, usually."

A full blush bloomed on her cheeks at the memory. In those days, she had enjoyed the innocent sensuality of swimming naked with the two men now in front of her. She couldn't deny she had been aware of an undercurrent between the three of them, but she had felt no rush to explore it. Nor had she felt any discomfort being nude in front of them back then. Now, she couldn't imagine doing such a thing. At some point in the last two years, she had lost her youthful innocence under the weight of her current responsibilities.

"Really, Lucian, Sorin, I can't go today."

Sorin stood up to his full height, six-and-a-half feet, and strode into the room. He took the goblet from her numb fingers and placed it on the long wooden table. "This will be here when you return. I saw Petru this morning, and he appeared fine. He even commented that your daily dram helped keep his migraines at bay."

"I like to have this on hand..." She trailed off as Sorin's hand engulfed hers. She stopped resisting when he tugged her gently toward the door. The thought of swimming appealed immensely. It was a hot day, and the moisture in the air clung to her hair and caused the red robe covering her body to stick to her skin. "All right, but I can't stay long."

Whom was she kidding? It was almost an hour to the lake, at a full run. It would be evening before she returned to the castle. Starr thought she should probably feel a dart of guilt for shirking her duties for the afternoon, but couldn't muster any remorse. For two years, her life had revolved around trying to live up to her mentor Ylenia's teachings, while she stumbled through completing the training on her own. Surely, there was no harm in stealing a few hours for herself, spent in the company of the two men she loved?

Although the day was too hot, causing the sluggish air to hang heavily against her fur, Starr reveled in the freedom of running. How long had it been since she had indulged in a run, just for the sake of running? For that matter, how long had it been since she slipped into wolf-form, a state where she used to spend most of her time?

Most importantly, it had been much too long since she spent any time with Sorin and Lucian. She was usually too busy, as were they. Since becoming emissaries for the Protector, matters of state often occupied their time. Now she found herself dodging the men she loved, just to avoid having to face the intensity of her desire for them.

As Bulgain Lake came into sight, Starr slowed her pace. The men bracketed her, and she could sense the coiled tension in Sorin and Luican's frames. She knew they had held back for her sake. She wasn't capable of keeping up with them now, having gotten soft from lack of physical exercise.

She was determined not to change to human-form, to avoid revealing her nudity, but had no control over Lucian and Sorin doing so. Even as she vowed not to drink in the sight of their nude bodies, her eyes eagerly devoured them.

They were such a contrast, on the surface. Sorin's black hair curled wildly and was barely restrained by the short ponytail at the back of his neck, while Lucian's brown hair was smooth and sleek, falling precisely to collar-length. Both men were in excellent shape, but Lucian's frame was lithe and lean, while Sorin's muscular physique rippled each time he moved. Lucian's body was nearly hair-free, despite his wolf heritage. Both were tanned, but Lucian's skin was the fairer of the two.

But there was one area where they were very similar. Their cocks, both erect, were long and thick, beckoning to her with promises of fulfillment. She couldn't imagine anything more exciting than to have both of them fill her at the same time. Although a nest of dark fur obscured Sorin's balls, she could plainly see Lucian's, barely concealed by scant amounts of brown hair.

Almost without conscious thought, Starr's wolf-form melted away, revealing her in the state she knew she shouldn't be in, what with the thoughts consuming her more each day. Without looking down, she knew her nipples were hard. The areolas were dusky-pink with her arousal. Her full breasts probably heaved from heavy breathing, caused by a combination of exertion and excitement.

She didn't think she imagined the way their eyes traveled over her body, pausing at her concave tummy to eye the ruby stud there, just above her belly button, before slipping lower. Some compulsion she couldn't fight caused her to shift positions and part her thighs, to better reveal her pussy. Would they be surprised to find only a thatch of neatly trimmed blonde curls at the start of her pussy that gave way to smooth skin? Were either of them longing to taste her?

The moment seemed frozen in time, as though they were all locked in a sensual haze. She wondered fuzzily how they could ever have been naked around each other before and not have been aware of each other sexually. How could she have taken those carefree days for granted, even in her naiveté of how difficult it would be to forgo pleasures of the flesh and assume Ylenia's role?

Starr finally forced herself to move. She got to her feet and walked to the water, certain she could feel their eyes practically caressing her naked flesh. Feminine instinct took over, making her roll her hips and flex her buttocks as she walked. She paused just before stepping into the cold water, barely resisting the urge to look back and measure the effect of her show on the men who she knew stood as still as statues.

She dipped her foot into the lake, hissed, and then sighed at the coldness. She kept walking, slowly getting deeper into the water, allowing its chilliness to leach some of the sexual heat from her body. She turned in the water, conscious of the way the gentle waves lapped just under her plainly visible breasts. "Well, aren't you coming?"

On one level, Starr recognized the danger of teasing Sorin and Lucian, and that's exactly what she was doing. She wanted a response from them, even as she feared where it would take them. If she were smart, she would rein in the impulse and head back to the castle right now, before she broke a basic tenant of her position.

Instead, she swam backwards, distancing herself from the shore by a few more feet. Lucian and Sorin moved as one to enter the water. She could sense their tension and excitement as they followed her. No, as they tracked her, hunting her like prey. What would they do when they caught her? She knew the answer to that, and her pussy clenched. Would she try to stop them, as she knew she should?

Starr suddenly plunged under the water, soaking her light-brown hair in the process. She paid no attention to the wet mass as she swam several more feet from them before letting her body sink to the bottom of the lake. She held her breath and waited for them to follow.

After what seemed like minutes, she finally got a glimpse of one of them swimming very near her. By that time, her lungs felt close to exploding, and she kicked off from the sandy bottom of the lake and rose to the top. As soon as her head broke from the water, she dragged in a lungful of air.

Their hands were there abruptly, pinning her between them. Before she could even think, Starr was trapped, with her back pressed against Sorin's stomach, while Lucian's chest pressed against her breasts, made exquisitely sensitive by the slippery water, icy temperature, and arousal. She licked her lips, watching Lucian's brown eyes darken with desire.

"We were worried about you." Sorin's breath was a caress against her neck as he dipped his head. "You shouldn't have stayed under so long."

Starr nodded, finding herself incapable of speech. Her faculties were further impaired when Lucian's hands settled just under her breasts. She caught her breath when his thumb swiped one of her nipples. She was aware of Sorin's cock pressing into her thigh. When Lucian shifted positions, moving closer to her, she felt his cock against her stomach. Her pussy responded to the stimuli with a flood of moisture.

Time stood still as Lucian's head dipped, bringing his mouth ever closer to hers. Starr closed her eyes when Sorin's tongue traced across her shoulder. As Lucian's lips settled on hers, Sorin's teeth grazed the bend of her neck where it met her shoulder. A moan escaped her, swallowed up by Lucian's lips as they parted hers.

Of their own accord, her arms wrapped around Lucian's waist. Sorin moved closer, pinning her more tightly between them. One of his hands settled on top of Lucian's, bringing it up to cup her breast. Together, they rubbed her nipple in slow, alternating strokes. Starr couldn't stop her hips from pumping, bringing her pussy closer to Lucian's cock.

His tongue slipped inside her mouth, sliding gently across hers. His lips moved with gentle pressure, while Sorin's nips contrasted to the almost-lazy sensuality of Lucian's kiss. Starr opened her mouth wider, inviting deeper access. She dug her nails into Lucian's skin as they squeezed her breast in concert.

She couldn't hold back another muffled groan as Sorin's thick finger sought out her pussy, gliding easily inside her lips with the aid of her arousal and the water. She whimpered at his first light caress across her clit. Lucian's mouth was now more urgent, and his tongue darted deeper inside her mouth. He cupped her other breast in his hand, rolling the nipple in concert with his strokes of her other breast.

She could die right then, just from the pleasure coursing through her. Instead, Starr opened her eyes and tried to focus as Sorin's finger penetrated her folds to flirt with the entrance of her pussy. When he encountered the barrier of her virginity, he withdrew, tracing a path up the inside of her lips, to circle her clit.

This was wrong. It didn't matter how right it felt. She knew she couldn't allow things to go any further. Her first duty was to Corsova, and though it might hurt her to do so, she had to do what must be done.

She pushed against Lucian and slipped beneath the waves before either could think to hold on to her. She swam several feet away before resurfacing. She didn't pause to look back as she made her way to shore. Once out of the water, she turned back to them. She couldn't find any words.

"Starr, come back."

Lucian's coaxing tone was nearly her undoing. Tears gathered at the corners of her eyes before falling free, as she somehow found the strength to shake her head. "I can't."

"You complete us." Sorin's rough tone hinted at his frustration and pain. "We need you."

Once more, she shook her head. "You know I can't do this." Without conscious thought, she assumed her wolf-form and turned away from them, running at full-sprint. They could easily catch up with her, but apparently decided she needed space. She didn't know whether to be grateful or annoyed about that as she gave in to the urge to run back to the sanctuary of her tower room.

* * * * *

She stood in the shadows, watching them. How she came to be there, she didn't know. She couldn't spare the energy to focus on that question when she couldn't tear her eyes away from the two of them, lying on the bed together.

She knew they were lovers, but it had never mattered. They had never made her feel like she wasn't an essential part of their relationship. She had never felt like they were a couple, and she was just the fifth-wheel. In truth, Starr had often thought they were merely waiting for someone.

How could she not think about it when they were spread so temptingly before her? Such a glorious sight. The depths of her own arousal surprised her as she watched them writhe together. Her dripping pussy spasmed, begging for release. Her mouth watered as Lucian pleasured Sorin. She ached to be the one drawing Sorin's cock between her lips as she watched Sorin pump his cock into Lucian's mouth.

What would it be like to cross the distance separating her from the bed and join them? She had no doubt they would welcome her. They would lavish her with pleasure and shower her with love.

Her nipples beaded to the point of pain as a summer breeze blew in through the open balcony doors and caressed her breasts. The air brushed against her inflamed pussy, making her squirm.

She should leave, but she couldn't turn away. She had decided to go forward. Starr took a step toward them, and they became aware of her. Neither Sorin nor Lucian made any attempt to hide what they were doing. Lucian continued pleasuring Sorin, who raised his hand as she drew nearer. Her feet carried her without conscious thought.

As she neared the bed, Starr reached out, intent on burying her fingers in Sorin's hair and drawing him to her for a long kiss. She touched his hair, but it felt like cotton, not the soft texture she had expected. She frowned.

And woke up. Starr's eyes snapped open, and she was conscious of clenching the light sheet covering her from the waist down in a death grip. Her mind had made the dream so real that it took her a moment to realize she was in her own bed, and that she had not been in Lucian and Sorin's chamber, watching them make love.

A groan escaped her as she loosened her hold on the sheet and tried to relax her stiff muscles. Starr's pussy ached, deep down inside, where she couldn't reach. It was an accustomed ache, but that made it no easier to bear. Her body craved Sorin and Lucian. Even her dreams reflected her desires.

She sat up, shaking her head to dispel the mental fog lingering from the dream. Instead of fading, the images sharpened, eliciting a moan. Her pussy spasmed, reminding her yet again how aroused she had been from seeing them together. She longed to slide out of bed and go to the floor below hers, where she would make the dream a reality.

What would Sorin and Lucian think of her if they knew she fantasized about watching them together? Would they be embarrassed, or would they show her what she longed to see?

She knew one thing. If she went to them, things might start out with Sorin and Lucian making love, but she would inevitably join them. By the morning, her virginity would be gone, along with that deep ache inside. But she would have betrayed the trust of the people and the Protector.

"Damn." Starr rarely cursed, but she felt the urge to let fly a few more expletives. The frustration she felt had stretched her nerves taut and sharpened her senses. The cotton she lay on was too rough against her skin.

She knew she wouldn't be able to dismiss these thoughts unless she sought release, but pleasuring herself was only a temporary solution. She had to find a way to deal with her desires, to banish them, so she could return to the state of mind she should be in as spiritual leader of Corsova.

She leaned back against the pillow and closed her eyes. Starr kept her breathing even, determined to reach a state of meditation. Perhaps she could soothe her tightly strung nerves and get a few more hours of sleep before the dawn.

Starr focused on relaxing, but sleep refused to come. She tossed and turned a long time before admitting defeat and rising from bed. As she slid her arms into the oversized robe, she cursed her body for its refusal to accept it couldn't have what it craved. Waves of desire still pulsed through her, bringing a sensation that bordered on pain. Her hands trembled, and she stuffed them in the pockets of the robe as she left her bedchamber and walked through the east wing of the castle.

She made her way to the kitchen, seeking solace in a cup of cocoa laced with brandy. It was a sleep remedy she found herself turning to increasingly these days. The last few months, her hormones seemed to be in a constant state of hyperactivity. No matter how she tried, she couldn't rein them in. Instinct and her own heart propelled her to Lucian and Sorin. Only her mind resisted, knowing she couldn't indulge in the forbidden relationship.

Once she had prepared the cocoa mix and brandy in a mug, Starr took milk from one of the refrigerators and poured it into a copper pot. She could have sent one of the servants to prepare her drink, but she liked the simple act of doing for herself. She still hadn't adjusted to the reverent treatment afforded her by the citizens. She wondered if she ever would.

She watched the milk without really seeing it. Her thoughts returned to the previous afternoon, when she had so nearly given in to temptation. Part of her cursed her sense of responsibility—the part of her thrumming with need. Her nipples chafed against the terry of the robe, giving a low, constant reminder of how sensitive the buds could be to her lovers' touch.

The scrape of a shoe in the doorway broke Starr's thoughts. She turned quickly and froze. She bowed her head. "Your Highness." She sounded hoarse and felt guilty for her erotic thoughts. She had no reason to think Anca would probe her thoughts, but still made an effort to shield them as she straightened.

"Starr." The queen wore a sated expression. Her hair was mussed, and her lids drooped lazily over her eyes. It was easy to infer what she had recently been doing. "I didn't expect anyone down here this time of night. Demi and I normally have the castle to ourselves during the wee hours."

She cleared her throat. "I, um, couldn't sleep." She gestured to the boiling milk, realizing it was about to burn. She lifted the pot from the burner. "I was making cocoa. Would you care for some, Highness?"

Anca shook her head. "No. I just came for a midnight snack." Instead of going to the fridge, she walked over to Starr, standing a few feet away.

Her hands shook as the queen watched her every movement. Anca intimidated Starr, although she didn't know why. The queen was always friendly, but she couldn't relax around her. Perhaps it was a product of her upbringing and training under Ylenia. It had been drilled into her from an early age to respect and revere the Protector of Corsova, to honor their sacrifice for the people with diligence to her duty.

With clumsy fingers, she poured the milk into the mug. She placed the pot in the sink, and it clattered against the basin as her fingers released it prematurely. She felt tears pricking the back of her eyes and didn't know why. Her emotions had been in a heightened state the last few months too. Could that be attributed to sexual frustration, or was it a side effect of the more pervasive soul-deep emotional deprivation she felt?

She almost yelped when Anca touched her arm. Starr jerked away and took a step back. Shallow pants escaped her, and she made a conscious effort to control her breathing as the queen watched her with an expression of concern. "I'm sorry, Your Highness. I don't know what got into me." She tried to laugh, but it emerged as a high-pitched choking sound. "I'm—"

"What's wrong, Starr? And don't tell me 'nothing.' You haven't been yourself for the past few months."

Starr forgot how to breathe. Was it so obvious? "Your Highness, I'm fine—"

"You aren't."

The soft counterstatement, said so gently, caused Starr's control to slip. "The visions, Highness. I can't sort them out. The more I try, the more I—" She clamped her mouth close, realizing she was too close to revealing where her thoughts led her while meditating. "It gets blurry," she settled for saying. She tensed, wondering what Anca's reaction would be. In the history of Corsova, she didn't know of any other spiritual leader having failed in her duties. Would she be banished?

"You need a break. When I used to struggle through Algebra—and that was quite a struggle, believe me—my mother would tell me to take a walk. She was right. Physical exertion always cleared my cerebral block." Anca grinned. "You need to do something that's just physical and stop thinking. Have a little fun, Starr. You certainly deserve it."

If only the queen knew what thoughts her words inspired, she would probably order Starr segregated from Sorin and Lucian for the rest of her life. A flush of heat swept up her neck, and only sheer willpower kept it from invading her cheeks. "I don't think that's a good idea, Highness."

"Sure it is. I want you to take a vacation. Go into the mountains or visit one of the cities."

"I can't abandon my duties."

Anca waved her hand. "What is there to see to? Helena's Pledging Ceremony to Jon isn't until next month."

"What if Ezru's baby comes early?"

"The midwives handle the delivery. The Welcoming Ceremony for the baby can take place up to three months after its birth, so don't use that as an excuse either." Anca touched her again, lightly patting her arm. "You know she isn't due for several weeks. I insist you spend some time away from here. Forget about your duties for a short time and just enjoy yourself."

"I can't go, Your Highness." Starr tried to be firm, but it was difficult to retain her resolve to stay when the idea was much too tempting.

"You can't go alone, that's certain." Anca shook her head, no longer listening to Starr. "What fun would that be? No, you must take Sorin and Lucian with you."

"I couldn't!" When she blurted that half-hysterically, Starr choked. Once she caught her breath, she shook her head. "They have duties."

"If anything comes up, we will cope. I'm certain they would appreciate some time alone with you. Demi tells me you're their blood-link. It must be difficult to be away from them."

"I do miss them." *I ache for them so much I hurt.* She quickly blocked the thought, lest it be transmitted to Anca.

"Good, then it's settled. You'll leave as soon as you've packed."

"No! I—" Was this really happening? Was the queen sending her away with Sorin and Lucian, giving her *carte blanche* to have fun, without thinking about her duties? Maybe she was still upstairs and had fallen back to sleep without realizing it. She would awaken to learn this was a dream.

"Of course, you'll need to let us know where you're going. Unless there's an emergency, we won't bother you. You will return by Helena's Pledging Ceremony, won't you?"

Starr nodded numbly, surprised she was capable of moving. "Yes."

"Do you know where you'll go?"

She didn't have to think about it. Memories of lazy days spent in the mountains came back to Starr. "Yes. My parents have a cabin in the mountains. No one has stayed there for years, not since they moved to Bulgainia, but it should be fine, with a little effort."

"Don't spend too much time working. I want you to enjoy yourself."

A shiver seized Starr. She didn't doubt she would enjoy herself if she gave in to her desires, and it seemed unlikely that she could resist Sorin and Lucian for an entire month. That was the reason she had no intention of letting them accompany her on her imposed sabbatical, regardless of what the queen said. Having them close would be more temptation than she could resist and would defeat the purpose of taking time to gain perspective and control her desire.

Chapter 3

The cabin had definitely needed some work. Starr lay in the canvas hammock she had strung up between two gârnita trees—similar to the smaller white oaks around the side of the property, but with scaly bark—just hours after she finished cleaning the cabin and restoring it to habitable conditions. It had taken most of the day to complete everything, and during that time, she had been so physically drained that her brain hadn't found the time to obsess over her raging hormones.

She turned her attention to the stars twinkling in the twilight sky. Complete darkness would come in less than an hour, bringing with it a nearly full moon. She didn't know why, but the knowledge that it was the last night before the full moon caused her a vague sense of restlessness, spurring her to finish restoring the cabin by tonight. The air felt heavy with anticipation.

She almost thought Sorin and Lucian were up to something, but refused to invade the privacy of their minds for answers, even if she had been in close enough proximity to do so. Since they were back at the castle, and she was here, she couldn't reach them anyway. Still, she couldn't shake the notion that something was coming. Did they have something planned? Her stomach clenched with nervous excitement. She trailed her fingers lightly across the taut flesh, wishing her hand belonged to one of them.

She slid her hand lower to explore the flesh under the waistband of the skimpy shorts she wore, before bringing her hand higher. Starr skimmed over her stomach again and stopped her hand just under her breasts. She cupped one of her breasts, rubbing the nipple through the blue cotton tank top she wore, *sans* bra. She had forgotten how good casual clothes could feel, having spent the last two years wearing the red robe that symbolized her position.

Right then, she wanted to be out of all clothes, to let the soft breeze blow across her hot skin, heated more by the thoughts flowing through her mind than the exertion of the day.

She closed her eyes and allowed her hand to slide lower, once more to the waistband of her shorts. She flicked open the button and lowered the zipper with stealth, not certain why she was being so discreet, since she was alone. Her pussy ached, and she couldn't help but trace the outline of her swollen lips through her panties. She moved her hand lower, encountering moisture leaking into her panties.

Starr squirmed in the hammock, spread her thighs wider, and slipped her fingers under the crotch of her underwear. She recalled a mental image of being with Lucian and Sorin, and it stoked her desire while she pleasured herself.

Sexual release had become an addiction. She was convinced of that. Her pussy pulsed as she pushed a finger inside her tight opening, stopping only when she encountered a barrier. She arched her hips, causing the hammock to sway. A moan slipped from her, and she bit hard on her tongue to keep further sounds of pleasure from escaping. Hiding her pleasure had become so innate that she didn't even think about the fact she was alone and could shout about her gratification if she wished.

She should stop, but couldn't. Her body needed fulfillment too much, even though she knew her orgasm would only give her empty satisfaction. She needed something more than her own hands to be truly fulfilled.

When Sorin cursed and took a step toward the door, Lucian touched his arm, attempting to restrain him. "She can't know we're watching."

"I can't stand this. My cock is about to explode. Look at her, touching herself. I think she senses our presence. She couldn't really think we would stay at the castle and wait for her to return after she slipped away in so cowardly a fashion. She had to know we would come after her. She must have planned for us to discover her in the act." The last part emerged as a growl, as Sorin's eyes darkened and took on a wolf-like appearance.

Lucian knew Sorin was close to losing control, but who could blame him? He was barely holding onto self-control himself. Only the knowledge of what they had planned kept him from tearing through the door and claiming Starr that minute. "Patience, *dragostia.* She will be ours tonight."

"What if she can withstand her desires? This is our only chance to consummate our relationship." Sorin ran a hand through his shaggy hair, not bound by the leather thong right now.

The possibility worried Lucian too, but he placed his faith in the belief that her desire for them was as strong as theirs was for her. Their need for each other was building in intensity. Once she got over the shock of having them show up and the surprise they planned, she would have to give in. Surely, she wouldn't be able to resist giving in. He clung to the hope, and had done so for the last month, since he and Sorin concocted the plan to lure Starr away from the castle and her constant duties.

It had taken some finesse to get Anca to suggest the vacation without openly requesting she do so, but she had, much to their relief. Now the only obstacle standing in their way was Starr's sense of duty. He couldn't fault her for that, because his loyalty to Corsova and the Protector ran deep. However, his need for Starr outweighed his strong sense of obligation. It was the same for Sorin, and Lucian knew the self-perceived weakness angered his lover.

Sorin stiffened and leaned closer to the window. Lucian did the same, and his breath caught in his throat as Starr lifted her shirt above her breasts and began rubbing one of her nipples. Her other hand matched the rhythm as she pumped it in and out of her pussy. His cock jerked against the fly of the worn jeans, and Lucian shifted his weight to relieve the pressure.

His voice emerged as a husky croak. "Come on, Sorin. Let's wash up in the stream and prepare our surprise."

It was a long second before Sorin tore his attention from the view outside the window and turned to the back door of the cabin. Lucian followed him, but couldn't resist one last peek over his shoulder. He groaned as a low sound of pleasure reached his ears. Starr's body convulsed, and she slowly relaxed into the hammock. Obviously, she had climaxed. He hoped she had only whet her appetite, rather than curbed it. Otherwise, the night's events would do little to entice her, and their plans would be for naught.

It took Starr almost an hour to compose herself after her impromptu orgasm. As darkness consumed the sky, save for the ripe beauty of the moon, she finally propelled herself from the hammock and to the stream running behind the cabin.

She cast a glance over her shoulder, scanning the area for predators or any of the Pack out for a run, before throwing off her clothes and wading in. The stream, fed from a mountain spring, was chilly, and she shivered at the contrast of the cold water and warm night air. It was just cold enough to cause her to hurry through bathing.

When she finished, she left the water and crouched by the stream, letting drops of moisture slide down her body. She hadn't washed her hair, but the ends were wet. She finger-combed the strands and stood up, shaking off the droplets in much the same way she would have in wolf-form. She was still damp when finished, but not so much that she couldn't put on her clothes and return to the cabin.

She was aware of the way the ribbed cotton clung to her damp breasts. In the light, she imagined the areolas were plainly visible, as were her hard nipples. The denim of her shorts chafed against her damp legs as she walked to the back door of the cabin and let herself in.

Silence greeted her, only to be broken by low moans. Starr froze for half a minute, listening. She felt the urge to turn around and leave the cabin without discovering the source of the sounds, but deeper instinct propelled her through the small kitchen and into the living area of the cabin.

It was a studio design, with no room breaks. An old couch was against one wall. A large stone fireplace dominated another wall, but the bed drew her gaze. Rather, what was happening on the bed caught her attention. Her lips parted in a gasp. It was her fantasy, brought to life.

Sorin and Lucian lay on the bed, embracing. Lucian's hand stroked up and down Sorin's thick cock, eliciting the moans she had heard. Starr clapped a hand over her mouth as she watched Sorin receive pleasure. His hair was wild about his face. The column of his throat was plainly visible from the way he had thrown back his head. His lips had skinned back from his teeth, and it was clear he was close to climaxing.

Lucian's soft voice reached her ears, speaking endearments and words of encouragement to his lover. He didn't appear to care that Sorin's hands weren't stroking him. It seemed to be enough for his lover to hold him.

Lucian thumbed just under Sorin's thick head, causing the other man to cry out. Starr couldn't restrain her own cry as spurts of satisfaction exploded from Sorin's cock. She tried to melt into the shadows, but their eyes moved up to settle on her, freezing her to the spot. She couldn't tear her gaze away from the sight of Sorin's fulfillment streaming from his still-rigid cock.

"Starr."

At the sound of her name on Lucian's lips, she finally wrenched her gaze up to look at them. "What are you doing here? You shouldn't—" She couldn't go on. The tenderness evident in their embrace brought a lump to her throat. She felt tears at the back of her eyes and yearned to join them.

Sorin extended his hand, making no apologies for showing up unexpectedly, nor for the scene she had walked in on. "Come to us."

She shook her head, even as her feet obeyed him. Was she really surprised to see them? She had to admit she wasn't. In the back of her mind, she had expected they would follow her. When she left the castle, she had acknowledged this was a likely outcome of leaving the sanctuary of her tower room and watchful eyes of those in the castle. She had anticipated this moment since her arrival, which was why she had worked feverishly to have everything finished. She was ready for this to happen.

A flicker of doubt shadowed her eyes when she reached the bed, but it faded when Sorin and Lucian each took one of her hands to pull her down beside them on the bed. The last bit of internal resistance disappeared when Sorin pulled her against his chest. Lucian draped his arm across Sorin's waist to squeeze her hip. "This is what you wanted, what you needed," he said.

It felt right. She lay on the bed without speaking, relishing the feelings sweeping through her. There was desire, as she had expected, but also warmth, and the sensation that a void inside was slowly filling. Why had she fought this for so long, she wondered, as all else slipped from her mind.

She rested her head against Sorin's chest, wondering what would happen next. She knew they would be lovers by the morning, but didn't have the courage to initiate the next step.

She lifted her head when the bed moved and Lucian sat up. She frowned, thinking he was leaving. She wanted to protest. She wanted to make love with both of them, not separately.

She didn't have to worry. As she kept her eyes glued to Lucian's nude form, he walked around the bed and dropped down on the other side, pressing himself against her back. His breath caressed the back of her neck, and a sharp surge of desire accompanied his hand when it settled on her breast, through the tank top.

Before she could speak or move, Sorin's hand was between her thighs, lightly brushing against her pussy through the denim. She closed her eyes when Lucian's hand slid lower, to the hem of her shirt, slowly lifting it. Her breath hissed through her teeth when he splayed his hand across her bare side and trailed it higher.

He cupped her breast, as Sorin's hand moved higher to unzip her shorts. "We love you."

She didn't need Lucian's whispered assurance. She knew how they felt. She had felt the same since becoming their blood-link at seventeen. Six years had only strengthened her emotions. "I know," she whispered in return, breathlessly. A gasp issued from her when Lucian tugged gently on her swollen nipple.

Seconds later, Sorin's finger slipped past the barrier of her panties and stroked her pussy lips. Another gasp escaped her when his finger plunged inside to flirt with her clit. Starr arched her hips, and Lucian followed the movement, thrusting his cock against her buttocks, keeping her pressed against the light pressure Sorin exerted. She whimpered as he circled the sensitive bud. Lucian mimicked the movement on her nipple.

Starr writhed under the pleasure. She was conscious of Lucian's cock pressed into her buttocks, while Sorin's pressed into her stomach. She slipped an arm behind her to grasp Lucian's cock. She imitated the motion she had seen him use on Sorin, and he responded by thrusting against her buttocks, pressing her even closer to Sorin's finger, inflaming her clit further.

Her other hand was trapped between her and Sorin. She freed it and reached down, searching for his cock. When her hand closed around it, she felt traces of his ejaculate, released earlier. Starr ran her thumb through the sticky substance, pleased when Sorin's cock spasmed.

She was curious of the taste and released Sorin's cock. She brought her thumb to her lips and licked away his cream. Both men moaned in concert, and it felt as though their cocks suddenly swelled even larger. It seemed to happen quickly that she was in a sitting position, with Lucian stripping off her shirt. Seconds after that, he lifted her by the waist to allow Sorin to strip off her shorts and panties.

Her pussy flooded with arousal as their eyes caressed every inch of her. Starr didn't resist when they lowered her onto her back and leaned over her on each side. She reached out and rested her palms on their upper backs.

Sorin's head lowered first, to press a kiss to her neck. Starr turned her head to allow his lips freer access. Lucian's head dipped lower, and he traced his tongue across her abdomen. She moaned when Sorin nipped her, while Lucian flicked his tongue across her stomach, inching slowly upward.

Sorin's lips seemed to be moving south, and she knew they would meet at her breasts. Starr opened her eyes and moved her hands from their backs. She felt behind her for a pillow to prop up her head. Her stomach quivered, and she held her breath when their heads got closer together. A shudder moved through her when Sorin's mouth fastened on her left breast at the same time Lucian's lips took possession of her right nipple.

She arched her back, offering them more. Sorin's tongue was rough and raspy over her swollen nipple, while Lucian's was more gentle. The sensations made her quiver, and moans tore from her. When Lucian's soothing tongue turned to a provocative nip, a cry escaped her. "Please..." She didn't know what she was asking for, except that they relieve the ache deep inside her womb.

They were in no hurry though. They continued to feast on her breasts, causing her body to clench with excitement. Her pussy spasmed, and she tightened her thighs, seeking relief. It seemed like ages since she had masturbated in the hammock. Her pussy ached as though it had never known release. "Sorin…" She tangled her hand in his hair and raised his head. "Please, I need…" She squirmed, unable to voice what she needed.

Lucian lifted his head and chuckled. "In time, Starr. We've waited too long for you to rush through this."

She bit back her protests and released Sorin's hair, allowing his head to return to her breast. She returned her hands to their backs and dug her nails lightly into their skin, seeking the strength to withstand the passionate torture they were inflicting on her.

It seemed as though they spent years on her breasts, exploring each plump inch, savoring the taste. By the time their heads drifted lower, she was close to screaming with frustration. She felt a wave of relief as their tongues blazed a trail down her stomach, where one of them briefly licked around the jeweled stud. They shifted away from her, and she let her hands fall to the bed. Her breasts ached with the pleasure they had given her, and she balled her hands into fists, mentally repeating to herself that they would soon fulfill her.

She was pliant as Sorin lifted her into a sitting position and draped her against his chest. She held her breath with anticipation as his large hands moved to her thighs, parted them widely, and then moved to open her pussy. Lucian was now kneeling on the floor, with his upper body still on the bed. His breath was hot against her lips as he blew gently against her clit. Starr tensed, waiting for him to taste her.

He moved forward with what seemed like deliberate slowness, but finally, his tongue swept down her slit, licking away the juices that had collected there. Starr shifted impatiently, finding the rough texture of Sorin's hair against her back only further inflamed her senses.

Lucian's tongue darted inside her, swirling around her clit. A small scream managed to free itself, and Starr gripped Sorin's forearms, not certain if she would survive the pleasure. She had never imagined a tongue could be so soft, or that her clit could be so responsive. Why didn't it feel like that when she touched herself?

"How does she taste?" Sorin's tone was so gruff with passion that the words were barely distinguishable.

She moaned when Lucian pulled away to answer.

"Like Heaven." He sighed. "She's sweet and tangy at the same time. She's so wet."

Her pussy spasmed as he described what she tasted like. It was amazing how his words could turn her on and make her long to taste herself on his tongue. "Kiss me." She uttered the words without thought, giving her impulses free rein.

Lucian nodded and rose to his feet. He settled on the bed on his knees between her opened legs and leaned forward. His mouth was gentle when it settled on hers, but Starr didn't allow that. She brought up a hand and buried it in his hair, bringing him closer. She thrust her tongue into his mouth and flicked it across his. Her taste lingered on his tongue, as she had expected. It was different from the taste of Sorin's arousal.

He leaned closer, pressing her into Sorin's chest, as his tongue tangled with hers, stroking eagerly. Starr's heart raced, and she opened her mouth wider, allowing his tongue deeper into her mouth. Sorin cupped her breasts and squeezed gently, reminding her he was watching.

She released Lucian's hair and turned her head slightly to break the kiss. Starr leaned back against Sorin's chest, with her face upturned, watching Sorin. "Now kiss him." She leaned back a bit to allow Lucian to get closer to Sorin. She held her breath as their lips met. Her heart pounded as Sorin's tongue darted into Lucian's mouth to taste her essence on his tongue. The kiss they shared was no less hungry than the one she had experienced with Lucian, and it made her anxious to taste Sorin.

When they broke apart, Lucian rested his forehead against Sorin's chest, while his hand sought out hers, which lay on Sorin's thigh, squeezing gently. Starr leaned closer, and she could hear their hearts racing as quickly as hers. Slowly, she raised her head and brought her mouth near Sorin's. She didn't want to push Lucian away, and he seemed to realize this. He shifted enough to nuzzle her neck as she tilted her head. Sorin's mouth came down on hers. His kiss was urgent and possessive.

She responded enthusiastically, opening her mouth to let his tongue sweep inside. She moaned as Lucian's fingers sought out her pussy and began stroking her clit. She was vaguely aware of Sorin leaning back, bringing her with him. Lucian lay across her, but balanced most of his weight on his free arm. Once again, his mouth slid lower, pausing to suckle her nipple, before continuing down. He flicked his tongue around the ruby stud in her belly before drifting even lower.

She bit down on Sorin's tongue when Lucian's tongue slipped inside her pussy again. As he probed her entrance, she pushed her tongue into Sorin's mouth, branding him with her touch. Almost imperceptibly, he shifted her onto her back once again on the bed, only then disentangling his mouth from hers.

Starr panted for breath as Sorin kissed her cheek before shifting positions. Now he was kneeling and slowly sliding his mouth down her body. She parted her thighs further as he neared her pussy, where Lucian's tongue continued to explore.

"Oh!" She was surprised the sound was at all intelligible when Sorin's tongue joined Lucian's in her pussy. One swirled around her clit, and the other probed at her opening, seeking entrance. She arched her hips without control, unable to stop the instinct. Their strokes increased in tempo, and with her last conscious thought, she lifted her head to look. The sight of their heads pressed together, between her thighs, triggered a wave of spasms deep in her pussy.

Her body convulsed as her pussy contracted and released, bringing an intensity of release she had never experienced before. She sobbed out their names and grasped the coverlet on the bed in her fists, trying to weather the storm of pleasure without passing out.

Her heart seemed to stutter before slowing gradually. Starr could almost breathe normally again when they turned her on her side. Lucian's tongue resumed caressing her clit, making her cry out. "I can't do that again." How did she manage to speak at all?

"You can." Sorin's tone brooked no argument. He didn't speak again as his lips skimmed her buttocks, and his tongue darted into her cleft.

She stiffened when Sorin's hand parted her cheeks and one of his thumbs pressed lightly against her anus. She stiffened further when something thin penetrated her, followed by something warm and slippery filling her anus. Her eyes widened with alarm. "What is that?"

Lucian's lips left her throbbing pussy long enough to answer. "Anal lube. We came prepared."

She tried to relax as Sorin's finger penetrated her anus. It wasn't that difficult, as Lucian's expert touch reduced her to a pile of sensation. It didn't take long for her sphincter to relax and for Sorin's ministrations to become pleasurable. She closed her eyes and surrendered her body to the thrust of Sorin's fingers and the velvety exploration of Lucian's tongue.

"Is she ready?"

Starr's eyes snapped open when Lucian's tongue left her pussy again.

"Almost. I can feel her pussy convulsing."

"What's going on?" There was a thread of panic in her tone. She knew they wouldn't hurt her, but couldn't help feeling apprehensive about what might come next.

Sorin was the one to answer. "We want to make love to you in every way imaginable. Together, separately... Do you want us to take you at the same time?"

She didn't have to think about her answer. "Oh, yes."

Sorin stretched her anus as another finger joined the first. "We want to possess you here, but you need to be prepared. Do you trust us?"

Again, she didn't need time to think about her answer. "With my life."

Sorin sounded hoarse when he answered. "Then relax, *dragostia*. Let us pleasure you."

Starr obeyed him and focused on relaxing. Soon, Lucian's tongue and Sorin's fingers once again induced a passionate trance, and she was helpless to keep her body from responding, even if she had wanted to.

She could feel her orgasm building, and Lucian must have realized, because his strokes increased in pace. Abruptly, her pussy convulsed, and she cried out. As she reached the summit of her orgasm, something entered her anus. She stiffened at the intrusion, but more from surprise than pain. Her orgasm continued, making it impossible to ask what Sorin had slipped inside her for several long seconds.

When her body slowly relaxed and her heart rate slowed, Starr realized whatever he had put in her was still in her anus. She opened her eyes and lifted her head, straining to see.

Sorin caressed her hip. "Shh, *dragostia*, it's just a plug to stretch you. After a short time of having it in there, you will be ready for me." He chuckled. "But first, are you ready for Lucian? His cock is begging to have you."

She shivered with mingled anticipation and anxiety. She wasn't afraid of the pain—well, maybe a little. Rather, it was what their joining meant that truly frightened her. Once Lucian took her virginity, there was no going back. Even as she had the thought, she knew it was already too late. There had been no going back from the moment she formed a blood-bond with these two. They were her destiny.

Chapter 4

"Are you ready for me, Starr?" Lucian's voice was gentle and hesitant, with an underlying note of need he couldn't mask.

She nodded, feeling incapable of speech. It was only a sudden dart of worry that caused her frozen tongue to thaw. "What if I get pregnant?"

"You won't." Sorin sounded confident.

"I could—"

"No. We've planned everything carefully, *dragostia,*" Lucian said. "For the past month, Sorin and I have been taking a contraceptive potion." He laughed. "We found the mixture in one of your books while you were busy with other matters."

Then she had nothing else to worry about. She nodded. "I'm ready."

Sorin settled against the headboard and drew her against him. Her head rested against his stomach. Starr licked her lips as Lucian shifted positions and knelt between her thighs. She looked up at Sorin. "Why Lucian?"

"Would you rather have Sorin?" Lucian asked.

"I want you both at the same time, but I can't do that my first time." She shrugged, conscious of Sorin's crisp body hair brushing against her shoulders. "I just wondered why you two decided on Lucian going first?"

"Sorin is…" Lucian cleared his throat. "Well, his cock is larger than mine. We thought I would be easier on you."

She groaned. "If that's going to be easy…" Starr trailed off as Lucian scooted closer. She locked her thighs around his waist as he leaned forward.

"Just relax." Sorin caressed one of her nipples. "Don't think about the pain. Focus on the pleasure, *dragostia*."

It was good advice, but her stomach insisted on fluttering with nerves as the head of Lucian's cock paused at the entrance of her pussy. She grasped Sorin's thighs and took a deep breath. Her pussy still throbbed with arousal, and she was wet. Physically, at least, she was ready for Lucian's possession. She nodded again.

His cock entered her with one deep thrust. Starr closed her eyes, but the flash of pain had faded almost before she realized it had hurt. She let out a deep breath and was aware of the tension in her muscles easing. She hadn't even known she was tense.

"How does it feel?" Lucian asked, looking down at her intently.

She parted her thighs and shifted her buttocks to accommodate his length. "It's wonderful."

That was before he began thrusting. The first time he withdrew and entered again, it hurt a little. Starr breathed through the pain and resisted the urge to tense up. By the time he entered her again, only pleasure remained. She hadn't expected to feel so different just from having a cock inside her. There had been a persistent ache in her pussy the past few years, but it was now fading away. Each time he surged inside her, the ache slowly changed to a nagging pull that triggered minor contractions deep inside her womb.

She could feel the tug of desire in her belly. Her entire body ached, and Sorin's rough thumbs on her nipples served only to heighten her need. She thrashed in his arms, as her hips instinctively rose to meet each of Lucian's thrusts. Breathless moans escaped her, but she was powerless to rein them in. Starr dug her nails into Sorin's flesh, searching for an anchor as Lucian filled her.

Small convulsions began inside her pussy and radiated outward. Lucian must have felt them, because he slipped a hand between their bodies to stroke her clit. Starr tightened her thighs around him, trying to keep him in. As he thrust into her, his fingers worked her clit in small circles, mimicking Sorin's actions on her nipples.

She cried out as Sorin tugged on her nipples, while Lucian thrust deeply into her. He pushed lightly against her clit, and spasms overtook her. Starr could feel all of her body shaking as her pussy clenched and released around Lucian's cock. She cried out from the release as intense pleasure washed over her. She was vaguely aware of Lucian coming inside her, but the intensity of her orgasm consumed her, making it impossible to take much joy in the knowledge she had pleased him. Later, she would be able to reflect on that.

Lucian collapsed on top of her, but supported his weight on his arms. Starr opened her eyes, not even realizing she had closed them, when he pressed light kisses to her brow. Sweat beaded his forehead, and his face was flushed. He was breathing as heavily as she was, and their pants filled the room.

Starr tilted her head and looked up at Sorin. His eyes glittered with need, and a flush filled his cheeks too. She could feel his cock poking into her back and was ready for him, just like that. She loosened one of her clenched hands from his thigh and brought it up to caress his hair. She smiled. "Your turn."

To her surprise, Sorin shook his head. "Not tonight, Starr. You might not feel it now, but you'll be sore in the morning. I don't want to hurt you."

"I want you, Sorin."

He brushed his hand across her forehead. "Tomorrow, we'll see how you feel."

She frowned. "But it's not fair to you."

"I can survive some frustration, *dragostia*. Lucian saw to my needs earlier, knowing this would be the outcome tonight."

She shook her head, refusing to deny Sorin release. Yes, Lucian had pleasured him earlier, but he was hard and ready again. "I want to do something for you. What can I do?"

Sorin and Lucian traded looks before he answered. "I don't want to overwhelm—"

"You won't. What do I do?" Would he want to penetrate her backside? She swallowed a hint of apprehension, determined to do whatever he asked. He had been so generous with her tonight that she couldn't do any less.

"Well, if you don't mind…" He seemed hesitant. "I know you haven't before. If you don't want to—"

Lucian must have realized Sorin was having a hard time uttering his request. "He wants you to suck his cock, Starr."

She nodded eagerly. "Okay."

Lucian rolled to the side, allowing Starr to roll over onto her stomach. She scooted down until her mouth was at his cock, and then looked up at Sorin. "What should I do?"

Lucian touched Sorin's shoulder, and he propped his back against the headboard, while still sitting. His eyes remained wide, obviously preparing to absorb every detail of the first touch of her mouth on his cock.

She turned her head as Lucian settled beside her. He rested his head on her back. "Put your mouth around him, Starr. Just relax your jaw."

She opened her mouth and tentatively took the head of Sorin's cock into her mouth. It barely fit, and she was momentarily thankful Lucian had been the one to take her virginity. As she supported the base, she swirled her tongue around the head of the cock. Sorin groaned, and she took that as a sign of pleasure. Once again, Starr flicked her tongue around his cock, pausing to trace the tip.

"Feel the V with your tongue? Lick him there." Lucian interspaced his instructions with a string of kisses across her back and shoulders.

Starr found the spot and flicked her tongue across it. Immediately, liquid dripped from Sorin's tip and flooded her mouth. She paused to swallow before resuming her ministrations.

"Apply suction. Just enough for him to feel it." As he continued, Lucian's hand slid under her to grasp her breast. He thumbed her nipple, while sucking gently on her shoulder. How could that one spot be so sensitive? Darts of pleasure spread from the epicenter of her shoulder, making it difficult to focus on Sorin. She tried to clear her mind and return to the task at hand.

Once again, Starr followed Lucian's instructions. She was soon sucking Sorin and moving her mouth up and down the length of him, as far as she could go. Lucian continued to caress her nipple, causing the little bud to ache with desire. She pressed her pussy against the bed when her need increased again.

Reassured by Sorin's sounds of pleasure, she found her own rhythm. She stopped sucking to trace her tongue down the vein throbbing in Sorin's cock. She heard a low growl escape Sorin, and his cock spasmed. Instinctively, she put her mouth around him and resumed sucking, enjoying the way his cock convulsed in her mouth. She could feel his muscles bunch and swore his cock hardened further, as he neared climax. In seconds, he was coming, sending hot spurts of satisfaction into her mouth. She swallowed as quickly as possible, but some trailed down her chin.

She kept her mouth around him until his cock began to soften. Finally, Starr lifted her head and shot a glance at Sorin, to gage his pleasure. He had his eyes closed and was breathing heavily.

She turned her head when Lucian stopped kissing her shoulder.

Sorin's tone was gruff when he said, "You're a natural, Starr."

She smiled at Lucian. "I had a good teacher." Starr discreetly wiped her mouth and flexed her jaw muscles. Sorin was more than a mouthful. As Sorin turned onto his side and patted the bed, she scooted up and cuddled against him. She was aware of Lucian removing the plug from her buttocks before he nestled behind her. He put his arm around her, and his hand rested on Sorin's hip.

Starr draped her arm across Sorin's waist and placed her hand on Lucian's. Her body still thrummed with desire, but pleasant exhaustion was flooding her. She found it impossible to keep her eyes open. A yawn escaped her, and she cuddled just a bit closer to Sorin. Lucian followed the movement.

Curled together, they slept.

Starr couldn't remember sleeping better in her life, which made the nightmare particularly horrifying.

She was lying in bed, but not the one she shared with Sorin and Lucian. In the vision, she was bound somehow to the bed, but not by any physical means. As she watched with wide-eyed terror, a glint of silver flashed above her. As the silver descended, the moon shining through the window reflected off something sharp…

She awoke with a scream trapped in her throat, and her heart racing in her ears. It took Starr a second to realize she was no longer in the dream, but back safely in the cabin. She frowned, wondering if the nightmare had just been a dream, or if it was actually a vision. She had always required an herbal concoction, incense, and meditation to induce visions in the past.

Could it be that her powers were increasing? She knew Ylenia had been adept at tuning into visions without the aids Starr used, and had often received messages in her dreams.

But what did it mean? Was it a message, heralding someone was going to stab her, or was it allegorical? Did it symbolize her betraying Corsova, in effect stabbing the Protector in the back?

Starr's attention wavered from the dream when the bed dipped. She turned her head to find Sorin watching her. She curled closer, while grasping Lucian's hand. She couldn't hide her anxiety, but they must have misinterpreted the cause of it, not being privy to her vision.

"Please don't regret what happened," said Lucian, sounding mournful.

"We have done nothing wrong," Sorin said quickly. "This was meant to be."

"Everything will be fine. It will work out. You must believe that, *dragostia*," Lucian added.

She shook her head and tried to hide the lingering disquiet from the nightmare. It didn't seem like the right time to burden them with the vision, especially since it was probably nothing more than a manifestation of her anxiety over having given in to her needs.

It was difficult to meet their eyes. Shyness welled inside her, and she looked down. Memories of the night they had spent together flooded her mind, reminding her of just how uninhibited she had been. She wondered what they thought of her this morning. "It *was* meant to be, and I don't regret what we did," she whispered. It was true she didn't regret making love with them, but she couldn't help dreading the consequences.

Lucian stroked her hip, while Sorin's fingers gently turned her face up to meet him. Before Starr could feel disconcerted by his gaze, he brushed his lips against hers, giving her no time to speak. As he lifted his mouth, Lucian's lips traced across her neck, eliciting a groan from her.

Her discomfort melted away, replaced by a surge of desire. Starr ached for them again, with an unnerving intensity. It was even stronger than the need she'd had for them before they made love to her. She cupped her hand around Sorin's cock, and then made a sound of surprise as he pulled away. Didn't he want to make love to her, as Lucian had? She stared at him with confusion.

He gave her a tender smile. "I want you, Starr."

She leaned forward, wetting her lips, but withdrew at his next words.

"But not today."

She made a sound of distress, and then bit hard on her tongue. She didn't want him to see the pain his rejection caused. She resisted the urge to turn her head away when Sorin caressed her cheek. "You need your rest for tonight, *dragostia*."

Starr's brow furrowed, and she forgot her ire. "What happens tonight, Sorin?"

Lucian laughed, low in his throat. "It's a surprise."

Sorin also laughed. "That's not the only surprise. We have one more for you, so hurry and dress." The note of huskiness in his voice and the gleam in his eyes led Starr to believe the surprise was of the carnal sort. A shiver of anticipation went through her. She couldn't help imagining what sorts of things they had in mind for her. She didn't doubt each one would be a sensual delight.

Chapter 5

The first surprise turned out to be a trip to the natural hot springs a few miles up the mountain. When Starr asked why they were going there, Lucian had replied, "To loosen your sore muscles. You must be ready for tonight."

She felt a stir of frustration at their cryptic attitude, but bit down the urge to demand an answer. Anticipation had already heightened her senses. She could just imagine what state she would be in by the time they unveiled the surprise.

It felt wonderful to sink into the hot water. Muscles she hadn't been aware of until last night ached with low-grade persistence. Almost as soon as she settled in the waist-deep pool, the water soothed her tense areas.

Lucian and Sorin slid in on either side of her, but made no move to touch her. Starr looked up at them through the veil of her lashes, waiting for one or both to reach for her. Her mouth settled into a frown when all they did was lean back and close their eyes. The water bubbled around her with gentle whispers, but it couldn't calm her racing thoughts and taut nerves.

As the silence settled between them and lengthened, she sighed. Finally, it was too quiet. The water was too relaxing, and she was too anxious to rest. "Well?"

Lucian opened one of his eyes and gave her a lazy look. "Well, what?"

"What are we doing here?"

"I told you…relaxing."

She sighed again. "I'm relaxed."

Sorin chuckled, but didn't open his eyes. "No, you aren't. We can feel your mind thrumming with thoughts."

Her mouth dropped open. "*What*? What do you mean, you can feel my mind?"

He finally opened his eyes and looked at her. "Today, your mind is so strong, I can't block mine from yours. There's a constant," he paused, frowning with concentration, "hum coming from you. Not all of your thoughts are flowing to me, but I can feel your emotions."

"I can sense them too," Lucian added. "If it had been this easy before, it wouldn't have taken so long to figure out what you needed."

"I don't—" Starr broke off, turning a puzzled gaze on Lucian. "What do you mean?"

Color had warmed his cheeks, and he shared a long look with Sorin, who seemed annoyed with him. Lucian cleared his throat. "We, uh, we deliberately eavesdropped on your thoughts whenever we sensed you were aroused. We were trying to discern what you wanted, so we could give it to you." His blush deepened. "We hoped that fulfilling your fantasies would convince you to join with us."

She felt a stir of anger, remembering how she had always respected the barriers in place between them. Being a vampire, it would have been easy to tune in to their thoughts, especially in the early days of their bonding, when their minds hadn't acquired any psychic abilities. How dare they not give her the same respect?

"We felt bad about it," Sorin said. "We knew it was wrong, but we never, *ever* listened in when you were doing other things. It was only when we sensed your arousal. You have to understand that it was desperation driving us, *dragostia*. We've been aching for you since we were seventeen and formed the blood-bond with you.

"When we joined with you, we didn't think about not being able to have you in every way. When we realized what your future position meant for all of us, we tried to deny our feelings for you, but the time passing has only increased our need, not diminished it, as we had hoped it would." He gave a small, forced laugh. "Your being forbidden made you all the more tantalizing."

She remained motionless when Lucian touched her thigh. She refused to look at him, but couldn't pretend that her heart didn't race at the light touch.

"Hasn't it been the same for you? Knowing you can't be with us, but longing for it. Haven't you been tempted to do things you thought you shouldn't?"

She turned her head to meet his eyes. She winced at the mingled shame and desire she saw there. Slowly, she nodded, remembering the hours she had spent masturbating while fantasizing about the two of them.

"We planned to tell you that we had seen your fantasies," Sorin said. He glared at Lucian. "We just hadn't planned to today."

Heat blossomed in her cheeks, and it wasn't from the temperature of the hot springs. "You know what I fantasized about. Was last night staged?"

There was a hesitation, before Sorin spoke again. "We did arrange for you to walk in on us. We'd hoped you seeing what you desired would crumble the last of your resistance—because we are all lovers, *dragostia*."

Should she be angry for their manipulation, or grateful that their plan had finally overruled her sense of duty? Starr couldn't decide. She had known coming to the cabin with them would lead to lovemaking, but had expected it to occur naturally. She hadn't imagined it would happen because they had orchestrated it.

Would she have been brave enough to make the first move? Even last night, she had been powerless to act on her wants for a long time. If she were honest with herself, she had needed that extra push provided by Sorin and Lucian.

She fixed a frown on her face. "I expect you to stay out of my mind now that you've gotten what you want."

"We will," Sorin said.

"What we all wanted," Lucian added simultaneously.

The last bit of anger faded away, and Starr relaxed. "Yes, that's true." She leaned back and closed her eyes. Sorin and Lucian moved closer to her, but neither reached out to touch her. They seemed content to relax without speaking.

It was a while before she broke the silence. By then, her muscles had relaxed, and apparently, her tongue had loosened too. "We're very near Necheau. Perhaps you should visit your families." She was instantly aware of the way they tensed and could have kicked herself. She knew they didn't like talking about their past, but still couldn't resist trying to get them to reconcile with the Pack at least once or twice a year.

She opened her eyes when Sorin shifted away from her. The bleak expression he wore made her frown. She looked at Lucian and saw it mirrored on his face. This was different from their usual brusque reaction to any mention of the life they had turned away from when they were seventeen. "What is it?"

It was a long moment before Sorin answered. He sounded reluctant, and there was no disguising the trace of pain in his eyes. "My mother is dead, Starr. She died a year ago, last winter, challenging Rica. Lucian's father was killed too. They tried to steal leadership of the Pack. Rica did what was necessary."

She gasped. "Why didn't you tell me?"

Lucian wasn't looking at her when he answered the question she had asked Sorin. "It wasn't that important."

Starr shook her head. "How can you say that? They were your family. You didn't get a chance to reconcile with them before their deaths."

Lucian turned to look at her. "They didn't act like our family, Starr. My father and Belia turned their backs on us when they discovered our relationship and intent to seek out a vampire to form a blood-bond. We did our mourning when we left Necheau. We've been dead to our families the last six years, so what does it matter if they are now dead to us?"

She turned to look at Sorin, searching his face for signs that he held a different sentiment. His expression bordered on glacier. "Sorin, surely—"

He frowned. "You should understand how it is. Look how your parents reacted when you formed a blood-bond with us."

Starr flinched at the reminder of how narrow-minded her own parents were. Rather, her mother. Her father had just followed his wife's lead. Starr's mother was one of the few vampires who believed in maintaining pure bloodlines. She saw no advantage in gaining the ability to transform into a wolf by bonding with a werewolf. To her, that merely weakened pure vampire blood.

When Starr refused to break the bond forming with Sorin and Lucian, her parents had moved from the castle and turned their backs on her. Their only contact these days was through stiff letters and an occasional meeting when Starr ventured into Bulgainia. The separation bothered Starr, but she knew there was no way to bridge the gap. Like Sorin and Lucian, she had made her choice long ago and must live with it. Still, she didn't think she could be so blasé about either of her parents dying.

The reality of how short time was, even for a vampire, hit her. She reached for Sorin, touching his arm. "What about your sister? Don't you want to get to know her again?"

He shrugged. "I never really knew her at all, and from what I remember, she allowed Mother to rule her life. She was twelve when I was banished. I doubt she remembers anything of me at all. When we returned to Necheau eighteen months ago to deal with the anthropologist, Lia didn't even look at me."

She could see the way they were withdrawing from her and knew it was time to drop the subject. She wouldn't give up trying to get Lucian and Sorin to approach the Pack again, since things had changed in the werewolf community with the arrival of the anthropologist who became Lupina, but now wasn't the time. She didn't want to spend a moment of their short month together wasted on angry words or bitter feelings.

* * * * *

To her frustration, Sorin and Lucian refused to give her even a hint of what they had planned for later as the day wore on. They kept her in a constant state of suspense, and it was with a feeling of aggravation that she stood by the fireplace later that night, watching Sorin and Lucian disrobe. She had already removed her clothing and now walked to the bed.

"No," Sorin said. "Not there."

She looked up at him, posed to question his words, but her eyes fell on something Lucian held. It was thin and red. "What's that?"

He tossed it to her, nodding when she caught it nimbly. "Tie that around your hips and come outside. Don't wear anything else."

"Not even shoes," Sorin added, as he walked to the door and opened it. Before exiting, he winked at her. "Don't keep us waiting too long. The moon won't be full forever."

Lucian followed him out before she had a chance to question either of them. Starr stared down at the scrap of silk in her hands and slowly stretched it out. It was a scarlet sash. She frowned, realizing there was something significant about the garment, but unable to recall what. It was something Ylenia had mentioned long ago, but she couldn't remember to what it related.

With a sense of hesitation, she draped the sash around her hips and tied it in a knot on one side. Was she wearing it properly? She didn't know, and they weren't here to ask.

She had spent the day wondering what they had planned, but now, she was almost too worried to step outside and find out. There was something different about their moods. Excitement, yes, but also apprehension. Were they as uncertain about whatever was coming as she was? That thought did nothing to bolster her confidence.

She took a deep breath and exited the cabin. Starr frowned when she saw Lucian lighting a small bonfire. It was much too hot to need a fire. Before she could query him, he rejoined Sorin, who beckoned her forward. Her feet obeyed, as her mind questioned their intentions.

She stopped walking when she stood before them, waiting to see what happened next.

Sorin was the first to speak. "The moon is perfect tonight."

"For what?" Neither of them answered.

"Perfect," Lucian echoed.

Sorin cleared his throat. He appeared uncomfortable. "It can't be official, of course, but it's the best we could do, with just the two of us."

She frowned. "What are you talking about?"

"Welcome to your Mating Moon Ceremony," said Lucian, flashing white teeth in a feral grin. "There will be no challengers, save us."

Her frown deepened. "What is a Mating Moon Ceremony?" As she asked the question, her memory stirred. She knew she had heard the term before. Even if she hadn't, she had a pretty good idea of what was happening. "Sorin, Lucian, I—"

"This is our wedding ceremony, Starr."

She shook her head at Sorin, denying his words. "I can't do this."

Lucian's grin faded. "You won't accept us?"

She sighed. "You know I can't. Our time together is finite. Once we return to the castle—"

"You are our wife." Sorin spoke the words with quiet conviction. "You have been emotionally since the day we bonded, if not physically. Last night, you accepted our claim on you. Tonight, you will accept both of us as your mates."

"I can't!" Her voice echoed through the forest.

Sorin and Lucian stepped forward, as one. "We would rather die than deny what is in our hearts," Sorin said.

She trembled as they reached for her, drawing her into their embrace. She could feel her resolve weakening as Lucian stroked her back, while Sorin caressed her stomach, just above the sash. "Please don't make me do this."

"We don't want to force you," Lucian whispered in her ear. "We want you to accept us."

"You want to accept us," Sorin said firmly. "Do not worry so much about the future. Seize the moment, *dragostia*."

She closed her eyes, trying to fight the seductive pull of their words and her own heart's cravings. She opened her mouth to refuse, but Sorin's lips settled over hers, sealing off her protest. She whimpered as Lucian's mouth drifted lower, to kiss her neck. She should step away, but it was so difficult to fight them and herself.

"Will you accept us as your mates, Starr?" There was a note of formality in Sorin's voice.

"Accept us," Lucian whispered, and his breath tickled her skin.

Starr took a deep breath and made herself step away from them. With obvious reluctance, they let her go. "I can't accept you. We will all end up hurt if I do."

"No more hurt than we'll be without you." Lucian made no attempt to hide his suffering, and it hit her in the stomach like a physical blow. "Now that we know how it can be—"

"—how it should be—" Sorin interjected.

"—we can't go back to the way it was. We need you. You need us. Don't fight it."

She took a step back, hoping that putting distance between them and her would let her think more clearly. "It's impossible. I can't mate with you."

Sorin and Lucian shared a look. What passed between them was inscrutable, but a quiver of disquiet worked its way up Starr's spine. She resisted the urge to prod their minds for more information. "What?"

Sorin straightened to his full height. "By rights, we now invoke a claim on you. We have one moon-cycle to convince you to accept us as your mates."

Her eyes widened. "What? You can't do that."

"It's our way. The Pack has followed this tradition for hundreds of years."

She glowered at Sorin, who sounded so arrogant. "You have turned your back on the Pack and their ways."

"Not in this," Lucian said. He crooked his finger. "Come to us, so we can complete the ceremony."

Her feet propelled her forward. Common sense tried to reassert itself, but the force of her desire muted its sensible urgings. Starr stopped within inches of them and waited, wondering what would come next. She didn't expect Sorin to untie the sash from her waist, nor for Lucian to hold out her arm and place his hand atop hers. When Sorin put his hand under hers, she watched with fascination as the two men worked together to bind the sash around their hands, joining them.

"At the next full moon, you will have to give us an answer, Starr."

"I have my answer—"

Lucian put his finger to her lips. "You didn't let Sorin finish. You can accept us before the moon-cycle ends, but you can't reject us for the duration of the claim."

She glowered at him. "Who makes these rules?"

"Men," Lucian said, and then laughed. "Our ancestors, I suppose, who liked being able to claim the women they had their sights on."

"Things were simpler once," Sorin said softly, with a gleam in his eyes. "A man saw the woman he wanted and claimed her."

She frowned at him, feeling a tad disgruntled. "How have things changed?"

He grinned a long moment before answering. "She couldn't reject him back then."

"Lucky times have changed," she said sarcastically.

They both laughed. Lucian drew her back into his arms. "They haven't changed that much, *dragostia*. You won't refuse us."

She nodded to emphasize her resolve. "I will."

A throaty chuckle escaped Sorin. "No, you won't. By the time we've finished with you, you won't want to."

She held her tongue, knowing she couldn't refute his statement. She already knew she didn't want to refuse to accept them as mates. It was only because she was duty-bound to do so that she had summoned enough willpower not to agree as soon as they presented the Mating Moon Ceremony. How would she maintain her determination for a month, with the two of them doing everything in their power to weaken her resolve?

Chapter 6

She was still in a state of bemusement when they brought her inside and led her to the bed. She stood passively as they untied the sash and dropped it on the floor. Starr let Lucian lay her back, as she stared up at Sorin, enjoying the heat of desire in his eyes. Tonight, he would be her lover too. She shivered with anticipation, but wondered at the change of scenery. She started to ask, but her voice emerged as a husky croak. She had to clear her throat before she could speak. "You told me earlier that we wouldn't be using the bed."

"We were optimistic," Sorin said. "If you had accepted us, we would have had the Consummation Ceremony. Since we had to invoke the claim, we will not make love under the light of the full moon this month."

"Instead, we'll spend the next four weeks seducing you senseless," said Lucian, before lifting her leg around the calf and bringing her foot to his mouth. He kissed her ankle gently before lowering her limb to the bed.

When they rose, Starr tried to sit up. Sorin pushed her carefully back against the pillows. "Lie here and wait for us to return."

With a long-suffering sigh, Starr slowly relaxed and watched them walk into the kitchen. What were they planning now? Her aching pussy hoped it involved something sensual and satisfying.

As Lucian filled a porcelain basin with warm water, Sorin poured oil into a small glass bowl. The scent of rose bay caused his nostrils to twitch, reminding him of nights spent running through the mountains as a wolf, in the days before responsibility weighed so heavily on all of them. Perhaps they had all been naïve, assuming the queen would be able to easily assume Valdemeer's role in ruling Corsova. She had slowly adjusted, but not without a lot of help from those closest and most loyal to her.

Thinking of loyalty, he swallowed thickly, wondering how the Protector would feel about their blatant disregard of the tenants of Starr's position. They couldn't claim ignorance. Both he and Lucian had full knowledge of what they were doing. Would it matter to Anca if she knew love drove their desperate actions, leading them to break tradition and possibly risk all their lives?

In his optimistic moments, he assumed she would. After all, her deep love for Demi was obvious in every glance. How could she fail to understand their need for Starr, and her need for them?

In his grimmer moments, he imagined her taking a more pragmatic view if she ever found out. As the leader of the country, she would surely point out that only tradition and following the old ways had allowed their way of life to continue for centuries. She would certainly mention that the three of them were too insignificant to assume they could be allowed to change anything.

How would she deal with them if she ever found out Starr was no longer pure? Would she sentence them all to death, or order they be banished? Would she blame he and Lucian, or would Starr be punished as well?

He felt a moment of doubt at continuing with their plan, but it faded. As of last night, it was too late to restore Starr's purity, and call him a selfish bastard, but he ached to have her as Lucian had done. He felt empty inside. Damn the consequences, but he had to join with Starr. Six years of aching frustration was too much for any man to bear and still be reasonable.

Starr had grown impatient by the time they returned. She watched as Lucian set a basin on the small table near the bed. Her gaze wandered to Sorin as Lucian got onto the bed and settled on one side of her. She saw a small bowl in his large hand and wondered what it contained. When Sorin set it carefully on the bed beside her, within easy reach for Lucian, she craned her neck to see what the liquid was. The scent of rose bay reached her nose.

"What's that?" She tried to think of mixtures that called for rose bay, but her ability to concentrate disappeared when Lucian caressed her lips.

"Close your eyes."

It was no trouble to comply. Her lids closed, and Starr concentrated on relaxing. She was tense with anticipation, so the first brush of Sorin's fingers across her foot made her stiffen. He had coated his fingers with something slick and slippery. She recognized the mysterious liquid as massage oil and relaxed before either of them could chide her to.

She squirmed when Sorin pressed lightly against the sole of her foot and traced a line from heel to toe. Lucian traced his fingers across her forehead and down her nose. He had also dipped his hand into the oil, and it left a slick residue behind. An involuntary gasp escaped her when Sorin pressed two of his fingers into the ball of her foot, while Lucian's fingers probed gently at the area behind her left ear.

Tingles ran from her head to her feet, and each little movement from them caused the sensation to intensify. They were just touching her foot and head. How would she survive when they moved on to more sensitive areas?

She opened her eyes when Sorin shifted positions to grasp her foot between his hands. As she watched with heavy lids, he massaged her foot, alternately applying pressure and light strokes. Lucian now had both hands on her, and his fingers were working the tension from her shoulders. The process was a bit awkward since he was massaging from the front, but it still served to ease her stiff muscles.

That wasn't all their slow massage did. Starr's pussy wept, and her nipples had beaded to hard points that begged for attention. She squirmed, but they ignored her movements.

As good as their loving touches felt, Starr wasn't certain she could withstand the tender torture. She had the urge to scream out her frustration and demand they stop teasing her. She had spent all day in a state of arousal, responding to the slightest caress, but neither man had made an effort to go beyond casual flirtation. Her body cried out for them.

Only knowing they had put a great deal of thought into their seduction helped her bite her tongue and keep from voicing a protest. She felt a dart of hope when Sorin placed her foot on the bed, but it faded when he picked up the other one, to give it the same careful attention.

Lucian's hands moved outward from her neck, to squeeze her upper arms. Starr closed her eyes again and tried to let his touch lull her into a state of relaxation. Her body refused to cooperate as Sorin's hands slid up her calf, while Lucian's slid down her arms. Silently, she pleaded for their hands to meet in the middle and focus on her aching pussy.

Her breathing became ragged as Lucian's hands moved from her wrists and slid across her chest. She held her breath as his hands skimmed over her breasts, but released it with a harsh exhalation when he skipped over her nipples and settled his hands on her abdomen. She gave a small, disgruntled sigh when he began rotating two fingers from each hand in tiny, firm circles.

Sorin was in no more hurry than Lucian was, apparently. He had worked his way up to her thigh, but it seemed to be taking him forever to reach the crux, where her swollen clit awaited attention. Once more, she held her breath as he kneaded her thigh with steady pressure, while moving his hands higher. Yes, he was so close…now his fingers would slip inside her pussy…yes…

No. She had tensed with longing, but let her muscles relax as Sorin dropped his hands before touching the spot she really ached for him to explore. She gave a low moan of frustration when he returned to the neglected leg and began working his way up from the calf.

And how was it that Lucian found her stomach so engrossing? He had surely massaged every inch of her abs, sides, hips, and waist at least twice now, but still hadn't managed to reach her pussy. They must be coordinating their movements, to draw out her frustration as long as possible. On one level, she was annoyed with their machinations, but also heartened to know they cared so much about her pleasure, at the expense of their own. They couldn't receive much gratification from massaging her.

Lucian unexpectedly brushed his palm against her pussy, causing it to spasm, and making Starr jump with surprise. A cry tore from her, and she realized how silent the cabin was. The only sounds were her occasional moans and sighs, and Sorin and Lucian's heavy breathing. "Please," she whispered, as more of a breath than a sound.

She tensed as Lucian's hand cupped her stomach, while Sorin's made its way up the last few inches of her thigh. She didn't doubt they would finally touch her this time. There was nothing else for them to massage, besides the areas they had carefully avoided. Her nipples screamed for consideration just as fervently as her convulsing pussy.

She opened her eyes when Sorin released his hold and climbed off the bed. She gave him a baleful glare as he walked away. She watched with a blend of anger, interest, and frustration as he lifted the basin from the table and brought it back to the bed. "What are you going to do?" Was that husky tone her voice? She sounded almost alien in her need.

"Wash you," Lucian said. "You don't want that oil on your skin, and we don't want it to seep into the bedding when we turn you over."

"I guess not…" She frowned. "What do you mean?"

Sorin laughed. "You'll see."

She subsided into silence, mentally cursing their deviousness, while reveling in the slightly rough texture of the cloths they used to wipe the oil from her skin. It was the perfect stimulus for the heightened sensitivity of her skin, and she moaned with pleasure as the warm water trickled down her skin. Maybe they were on to something, with this slow seduction of her senses.

"Sit up, Starr," Lucian whispered in her ear, as he finished wiping the oil from her face.

She briefly questioned her passivity in their lovemaking, but dismissed the thought. She would have plenty of time to take a more active role later, and it felt decadent to let them direct everything. All that she had to do at the moment was enjoy whatever was coming next.

She let them turn her onto her stomach. Starr cradled a pillow in her arms and laid her head on it, finding it a poor substitute for either man's embrace. She felt a trickle of oil down her back and sighed. Seconds later, Lucian began sliding his hands over her flesh, working the tense muscles of her lower back. She waited for Sorin to begin massaging the backs of her legs, but he didn't.

A finger feathered down her cleft before pushing between her buttocks. Starr gasped when Lucian hit a sensitive spot with his probing fingers, while another probing finger lightly caressed her anus. She tensed when something hard probed at the opening, but Sorin's hand smoothed over her buttocks, while he shushed her.

"It's just the lube. Relax, *dragostia*."

She took a deep breath and forced her muscles to loosen. The applicator slipped easily into her sphincter, and the thick lube filled her quickly. Lucian was now focusing his attention on her shoulders, while Sorin squeezed one of her cheeks lightly in his hand. The other was apparently occupied with the lube. When he withdrew the tube, she wondered what would come next. Would it be the plug again?

Her question was answered when Sorin parted her cheeks with one hand, while his finger entered her anus to his knuckle. She squirmed when he wiggled it, surprised by the jolt of pleasure that accompanied the slight burning sensation. As Sorin entered her with another finger, she tensed. Lucian responded by decreasing the pressure he applied to her back and changing his touch to slow, soothing circles.

Before she had much of a chance to adjust to Sorin's fingers, he removed them. She arched her hips to signal she wanted more. It had felt surprisingly good, for the brief time he was inside her anus.

Either he complied with her unspoken request, or he was already planning to, because his hand continued to hold her cheeks parted, while the bulbous head of the anal plug pressed against her sphincter.

Starr closed her eyes, balled her fists, and bit down on a mouthful of pillow to stay relaxed as the plug entered her completely. There was the same burning/stretching sensation as last night, but it soon faded. For a moment, she felt neither pleasure nor pain—only pressure.

And then they were rolling her onto her back again. They hadn't even bothered to wipe off the oil. She could feel it seeping into the sheet under her, almost gluing her to the bed.

She turned her head as Lucian scooted up beside her. He was propped up on his side, with his arm across his side. He was smiling at her. "What now?" she managed to ask breathlessly.

"Now, we make love."

The whispered words served to inflame her desire further, rather than soothing her, as he had perhaps intended. A flare of pleasure radiating from her stretched anus shot through her pussy, bringing a fresh wave of moisture. She cried out as Lucian cupped her breast and finally tugged lightly on the hard nipple.

She lifted her head to see what Sorin was doing. He had moved from the bed to wash his hands, but was now back. Rather than straddling her as she had expected, he knelt between her spread legs, with his hands on her upper thighs. A sob escaped her when he moved one hand higher to touch her pussy. She almost thought she could have come just from the light brush of his palm against her swollen lips. When he pushed his palm deeper into her soft flesh and rotated it slightly, she arched upward.

The plug in her anus seemed to settle deeper inside her as she did so, causing a moment of discomfort before it changed to heated pleasure. Starr spread her legs farther, and in her impatience for Sorin to touch her properly, she had almost forgotten Lucian was playing with her breasts.

She remembered as he pinched one forcefully, as if to get her attention. She turned to look at him and the blaze of desire in his eyes swept her away. He was always the calm one, and always in control of his emotions. Sorin was the unpredictable one, with a hint of wildness that couldn't be tamed. She would have expected the expression she saw to be on Sorin's face, not Lucian's.

Out of curiosity, she lifted her head again and assessed Sorin's expression. It was difficult to concentrate when Lucian bent his head to lave one of her nipples. She groaned and lowered her head, but not before seeing deep hunger and need in Sorin's eyes. She didn't doubt she wore a similar expression, but maybe they needed to hear how much she wanted them. Maybe if they did, they would finally do more than tease her.

"If you don't take me soon, I'm going to die." That sounded silly, but it was how she felt. There was a pressure building inside her—and not from the anal plug—that threatened to boil over and explode. She didn't know what would happen when it did. She only knew she had to release the pressure, and the only way to do so was by submitting to the pleasure Sorin and Lucian were creating.

That seemed to be all Sorin needed, because he stopped lightly stroking her lips. Two of his fingers surged inside her, making her cry out. There wasn't even a hint of soreness as he finger-fucked her. The hot springs had certainly loosened her.

Lucian drew her nipple into his mouth, sucking forcefully, while his hand squeezed her other breast. His thumb ran across the rigid nipple repeatedly, applying enough pressure to make her want to scream.

Almost by sixth-sense, Starr realized Sorin had switched positions. His fingers withdrew from her pussy, and before she could utter a protest, his cock surged inside her. Her eyes widened at the fullness she felt from his cock and the anal plug. If she had ached to be filled, her wish was granted. It was almost more than she could accept. As Sorin withdrew and thrust into her for the first time, the pressure increased, and she wondered how her body would accommodate both of their cocks.

His hips driving his cock deeper into her drove the thought from her mind. Starr could hear Lucian moaning and knew she had neglected him. She reached forward, searching for his cock. When she found it, she cupped her hand around the hard shaft and gave in to instinct, which urged her to grip his cock firmly and move her hand up and down. His cries of pleasure rewarded her.

Sorin's groans mingled with Lucian's as he thrust faster and faster inside her. Starr's lower body tensed as her pleasure grew, and she knew no amount of massage could relax her this time. As Sorin's cock hardened inside her before beginning to spasm, waves of pleasure crashed over her. Her pussy convulsed around him, triggering his release. Lucian's ejaculate dripped down her fingers as she came. The convulsions shaking her caused her anus to clench around the plug, which heightened her sense of release.

As Sorin withdrew from her pussy, Starr struggled to catch her breath. To her surprise, the pressure was still building inside her. Her orgasm hadn't been sufficient to stifle it. "More."

"Yes," Lucian said as he lifted his mouth from her tingling breast. His cock grew hard again in her hand, seconds after his orgasm. Wasn't that supposed to be impossible?

As Sorin brushed against her leg, his hard cock poked into her flesh. Starr wondered if they felt the same nameless need she did. Apparently, they hadn't been completely satisfied either.

Lucian disengaged her hold on his cock and scooted backward before turning her on her side. Sorin settled on his side beside her, pressing his chest against her breasts. Starr put her arm over his waist and squeezed his muscled buttock.

Lucian pulled the plug from her anus, and Starr knew what would happen next. She felt a flutter of alarm, remembering how Sorin and the plug had stretched her, but her longing was stronger than her fear. They were meant to fit together—three parts of the whole.

Sorin just held her as Lucian lay against her, pulling her cheeks apart with his hand. Starr met Sorin's gaze as the head of Lucian's cock pressed against her anus. She moved her head forward to kiss him as the cock pressed inside her. It was a snug fit, and she felt a moment of pain, but it faded as Lucian stayed in her without moving. Sorin's tongue darted into her mouth, mimicking the motion his hips would make soon.

She draped her thigh over Sorin's as his lower body pressed against hers. He slipped a hand between their bodies and parted her pussy. She broke the kiss and buried her face in his hairy chest as his cock probed her opening. She took a deep breath as he sheathed his cock in her pussy, and her body responded to their presence with a moment of pain. Her breathing sounded like an explosion when she exhaled, while concentrating on keeping her body relaxed.

It was almost like meditation, as she pictured their cocks surging in and out of her. Somehow, just visualizing the act helped her expand to accommodate them, although she was still tight around their cocks.

"Starr? Can we thrust?"

She nodded, and then realized Lucian probably couldn't see the motion of her head. "Yes, please." Sorin's hair tickled her lips as she spoke, while his hard chest muffled her voice. Lucian must have heard her answer anyway, because he began to thrust in and out of her, in concert with Sorin, so that they both entered her simultaneously.

There wasn't any pain as they moved. Starr thought that was significant, while she was still able to think. Within minutes, their thrusts had driven any logical thoughts from her mind. Their movements reduced her to a creature of sensation, whose voice's only purpose was to give life to sounds of her pleasure.

The intensity was building inside her. It was a sensation washing over her, going deeper than her convulsing pussy and clenched anus, begging for release. This was something different. It felt like white heat burning her from the inside out, and colors exploded behind her eyes, like fireworks.

As Sorin surged deep inside her, with Lucian following suit, Starr's orgasm swept through her. She screamed with the pleasure, but also with the surge of heat that flooded her. The colors grew more intense, and she opened her eyes, hoping to drive them away. She could still see them and realized it wasn't something she was imagining. She was undergoing a physical reaction to their lovemaking, and it wasn't just from the pleasure she felt.

Her climax reached its zenith when Lucian and Sorin came inside her. As their cocks spasmed, filling her with their satisfaction, it was as though a vortex opened in her mind. She could feel it drawing her in, but was powerless to stop the wave of blackness that overwhelmed her, stealing consciousness from her.

The vision from the previous night consumed her immediately, and it was clearer now. She was no longer viewing it from the perspective of the person on the bed. Rather, she watched from a shadowed corner of the bedchamber as a figure that was clearly feminine lifted a silver dagger high over her head. With a harsh laugh, she plunged it down with all her might.

Starr gasped when the dagger penetrated the heart of the queen, tethered to the bed, as was Demi. This time, she could see faint bands of purple energy holding Anca and the king in place and recognized it as true magic—not like the form practiced by their people, which relied heavily on natural herbs, tradition, and ceremony.

A cloud shadowing the moon shifted, illuminating the window near the bed. The attacker's face almost came into view as she turned to advance on Demi, who struggled to cry out, but couldn't get his voice to cooperate. She shouted a cry of warning when the woman raised the dagger higher, but could effect no change on the outcome of the vision. She watched helplessly as the attacker dispatched Demi with equal ruthlessness.

She jerked with surprise when someone called her name with desperation. At first, she thought it was someone entering the queen's bedchamber, and braced herself for attack. The voices became distinguishable, and she recognized Sorin and Lucian calling to her. Immediately, she realized she was in a vision. She struggled to open her eyes, to return to reality. With one last look at the bloody dagger the woman was wiping on Anca's white robe, she wrenched her eyelids up and returned to the cabin.

Sorin and Lucian hovered over her, both wearing identical expressions of concern. She blinked and struggled to remember what had happened. They seemed to sense her confusion, because they began speaking in a rush, talking over each other.

"You passed out—"

"—couldn't wake you—"

"—are you all right, Starr?" Sorin asked.

Slowly, she nodded, almost surprised to find her body responded to her brain's command. She still felt sluggish and disoriented. She attempted to sit up, and they both supported her. She touched a hand to her pounding head. "I...I passed out?" she asked in a husky voice.

"Right when you came. You scared the hell out of us," Sorin said with anger, but with an underlying thread of concern he couldn't mask.

"Your eyes rolled back, you started shaking, and we couldn't rouse you," Lucian added, sounding slightly calmer now than he had seconds ago.

"I was having a vision." Her brow furrowed. "I was seeing the future, but I can't say when. It could be tonight or next week." Starr's eyes widened. "We have to return to the castle."

Sorin nodded. "You need a healer—"

"No," she said, cutting him off, "I must warn the queen that she is in danger. In my vision, a woman murdered Anca and Demi. I didn't see her face, but she seemed familiar...." A sense of urgency seized her. "We must go now."

"Now?" Lucian sounded doubtful. "It's only about midnight. Surely, we have time..." He trailed off at Starr's vigorous head shaking.

"I'm sorry, but we have to return to the castle. I can feel it." The sense of urgency had increased. She couldn't be certain, but Starr thought the queen was in pressing danger. Tonight felt like the night the Protector would come under attack.

Sorin sighed. "If you think it is necessary, we will return, *dragostia*."

She could see their disappointment, and it mirrored her own, but Starr couldn't remain in the cabin, indulging her every sensual whim, while their Protector's life was at risk. As she rose from the bed and washed, she tried to console herself with the thought that surely the queen or king had foreseen the danger. It brought little solace, because she knew Ylenia had often had visions long before anyone else.

She should have known about this threat weeks ago. If only her own wants hadn't so consumed her, she would have known about the assassin's plan and could have warned everyone, so they could formulate a plan. What if the queen died because she had been here with Sorin and Lucian?

Starr paused in the process of transforming to wolf-form. The realization came to her that making love with Sorin and Lucian had somehow increased her powers. If she hadn't given in to what her heart and body longed for, she wouldn't have known the queen's life was in peril. She cast a glance at Sorin and Lucian as they transformed, hoping she would have the chance to tell Anca that, in support of allowing them to mate. She couldn't hide her love for Sorin and Lucian any longer, and she refused to live a lie.

But now wasn't the time to fret about that. They had to hurry. Starr could taste danger in the air, and instinct warned her there were more foes than the one she had seen in her vision to worry about, as they left the cabin. If she had remained longer in her vision, she might know from where to expect danger. Since she hadn't, they were running blind as they rushed through the forest, relying on their senses to warn them of jeopardy in advance.

They ran steadily for the better part of an hour, but Starr's head began buzzing. Pressure filled her ears, and her eyes scanned the forest around them constantly. The thought came to her that they weren't going to make it to the castle.

Sorin had been running slightly ahead of them, and her eyes focused on him. *Stop,* she shouted into his mind. *Stop, Sorin. There's something up ahead.*

He stopped so quickly that his paws skidded into the mossy carpet of the woods as he spun sideways to look back at her. Lucian must have heard her too, because he was now facing the other way, sniffing deeply, while his eyes slowly examined every inch of forest.

Starr closed her eyes and tried to concentrate on the feeling of danger overwhelming her. There seemed to be an invisible cord pulling her attention off to her left. She turned her head and opened her eyes, howling with shock when her gaze locked with narrowed eyes of indeterminate color, looking down the stock of a crossbow. A gleam of silver on the tip of the arrow caught her eye, just as the person holding the weapon released it.

Sorin, move! While warning him, Starr shifted to human-form. Before he could move or react to her words of caution, the arrow had penetrated his side, eliciting a howl of rage and pain. In the time it took Starr to watch the arrow enter his flesh, the man or woman with the crossbow must have moved, because she couldn't see them when she looked up again.

Lucian's howl morphed into a cry of rage as he transformed to human-form and rushed to Sorin, who remained in wolf-form. Starr cautiously approached, while scanning the forest for the hunter. The sense of pressure in her head was easing, leading her to think the immediate danger had passed. The person had probably gone deeper into the forests, hoping to catch them from a different vantage point.

"What happened?" Lucian was staring with horror at the arrow sticking out from Sorin's side. "Sorin?"

"It was a man, I think, but it could have been a woman. They had their face shrouded, and I couldn't make out any other details. I saw him in the woods," Starr said. "He was using a crossbow."

Sorin's lids remained closed over his eyes, but they could see the pupils moving rapidly underneath. His furry sides heaved with each breath, and his shallow exhalations caused them to exchange worried looks. His eyes didn't so much as flicker when Lucian called his name again.

"I don't understand why he won't respond. This injury shouldn't have affected him this badly so quickly."

"I think the arrow was tipped with silver. It gleamed in the moonlight."

Lucian's eyes flashed, and he started to get to his feet.

Starr touched his arm. "Where are you going?"

"To catch the man who did this. I'll kill him." There was no mistaking the air of wild recklessness surrounding Lucian.

"We can't leave Sorin. The hunter will have to wait. We have to get Sorin to the castle." She tentatively touched the smooth shaft of the arrow. "If we pulled out the arrow and had him transform, he would heal himself, wouldn't he?"

Lucian shook his head. His brief flash of uncontrolled rage seemed to have faded, leaving him pale with concern. "Silver is poisonous to us, as you know. It requires special treatment. Having him change would only expend energy he needs right now to survive."

She bit her lip, feeling inadequate. She could deal with any of the few vampire afflictions, but had only scant knowledge of werewolf care, even after these last six years. Neither Sorin nor Lucian had ever been more than mildly ill and always recovered without the assistance of a healer. How could she help Sorin?

Her training as a vampire healer did nothing to prepare her for saving her lover. There had never been any need before to heal a vampire in wolf-form. They simply transformed back to their original state before treatment for the few ailments that might affect their race. "What do we do?"

Lucian hesitated before shrugging. "I don't know."

"We'll get him back to the castle—"

"No." Lucian heaved a sigh. "There's only one place he can find the right help, and they're closer than the castle."

She knew what it cost him to make the suggestion, and she kept her tone carefully neutral when she asked, "Necheau?"

He nodded, but didn't speak. There was a look of grim determination on his face as he knelt down and lifted Sorin into his arms. He grunted with the effort of carrying the large wolf, but looked as though he planned to reach the Pack by sheer strength of will.

Starr touched his shoulder. "You can't carry him that far. You'll have to go to them and bring them back."

Lucian shook his head. "I won't leave you out here with someone trying to kill us."

"You'll be in as much danger as I, but we have to separate. I'll stay with Sorin until you bring back help." She could hear an invisible clock ticking in her mind, warning her that every second was precious. She had to get to the castle to warn the queen. If only telepathy reached across vast distances, instead of requiring close proximity.

Lucian hesitated, appearing to be conjuring another argument.

"You're wasting time with arguing. You have to go, Lucian." Starr kept her voice firm, and tried to sound confident. "I can handle anyone who might attack. I *am* a vampire."

He still looked dubious as he transformed into wolf-form. He cast a look at her over his shoulder as he began running, and then turned to face the trail in front of him, seemingly running as fast as he could.

Starr watched him go and fought back a feeling of vulnerability. Having Lucian with her was no guarantee they wouldn't be attacked. No one had expected Sorin to be shot, but it had happened. She was alone, but she also knew she could handle the average foe. A human wouldn't have much of a chance against her strength. She ignored the quiver of doubt that hit her stomach as she sank to her knees beside

Sorin, assuming a protective posture. She mustn't forget that silver could poison vampires too.

* * * * *

He knew he had made good time, but it still seemed to take forever for Necheau to come into sight. Lucian almost stumbled when he saw the warm glow of electric lights, having forgotten Rica had allowed the village that luxury after the spring thaw. He hadn't been back in two years, since the change, and it had been daytime during his last visit.

It was a vastly different community from the one he had left six years ago, also in the middle of the night. During the brief visits he had made here in Anca's service, he had made a concentrated effort to block out unpleasant memories.

Sorin had also been with him, providing silent support, although his wounds ran just as deep, or deeper, than Lucian's. At least he had only received a beating from his father when their relationship came to light. His grandmother had cared enough about him to take him into the forest and hide him while he recovered, lest Istal change his mind and decide to kill Lucian. Of course, she hadn't cared quite enough to turn her back on tradition and accept him for what he was.

For Sorin, there had been no one to assist him. After Lucian's father—Belia's lover—finished with his own son, he turned to Sorin, beating him even more savagely than he had Lucian. Lucian had thought at the time, and still did, that Istal believed Sorin had seduced him, although that wasn't the truth. They had always been drawn to one another.

When Istal finally finished with him, Belia had cut the word "Abomination" into Sorin's chest and chained him to the well in the center of the square, leaving him subject to ridicule by all who passed. It had taken weeks and several transformations for the scar to fade completely, because she had carved so deeply.

He swallowed down the memory of that incident, and the subsequent escape they made via stealth, when Lucian was recovered enough to leave the forest three nights later and free Sorin from the chains, so they could flee together, knowing there was no future left for them in Necheau. He didn't have time to think about that now. He had come to Necheau to save his lover's life, not to win the approval of these people. That was something he knew they could never do. The Pack was too old-fashioned in their views.

He ran into the square and searched for signs of anyone awake. It was after midnight, but many werewolves were nocturnal by nature. To his misfortune, none were loitering in the square.

He scanned the street, seeking out the leader's house. He spotted the one he thought it was, and then saw the workshop in the back. It wasn't the same house the leader used to occupy, but he knew there had been a fire that destroyed Rica's home two winters ago. This house still had an almost-new look about the wood and fence surrounding it, and it must be the one that was under construction the last time he came to Necheau.

He didn't hesitate to turn in that direction and run to the house. He felt a pressing sense of urgency, knowing Sorin and Starr were alone in the woods and vulnerable to attack.

He had reached the porch before remembering he was still in wolf-form. The Necheans weren't telepathic, so he would have no way to communicate with them in his present form. He took time to assume his human appearance again before slamming the mouth of the howling wolf knocker against the wood of the door. He didn't spare a thought for what the person answering the door would think when they saw him standing there naked. Nudity was an everyday fact-of-life among the Pack.

But the woman answering the door obviously hadn't become accustomed to it. Or perhaps she wasn't used to seeing strangers standing nude on her doorstep. The anthropologist, who was now Rica's mate, wore an expression of disbelief.

Lucian didn't wait for her to speak. He forgot about his discomfort in regards to approaching the Pack for assistance. All he could think of was Starr and Sorin, alone together and vulnerable. It didn't matter any longer what the Pack thought of him, as long as he could persuade them to help. The words flew from his tongue as Rica appeared in the doorway behind his mate, looking stern and unwelcoming. "I need your help. Sorin has been shot, and the queen's life is in danger."

* * * * *

Starr divided her attention between the woods around her and Sorin. He had grown progressively paler, and he was losing more blood than he should be from the wound. Out of desperation, she ripped open her wrist and pressed it against his mouth, letting her blood flow into him. His ability to swallow encouraged her, but she couldn't help wondering if it was more of an automatic response than a conscious act on his part.

The wound continued to weep rivulets, and Starr began alternating applying pressure with her hands, careful not to press the arrowhead deeper into his flesh, while still scanning the forest. When she looked down again to check on Sorin and the gash, she saw the bleeding around the protruding arrow had slowed just a bit. She realized blood from her wrist was trickling into the injury. Were the healing agents in her blood slowing down the loss of blood?

Starr opened her wrist anew, to allow more blood to dribble into Sorin's wound. She watched, starting to feel light-headed, as the blood flowing slowed to a trickle. She withdrew her wrist and pressed it against her robes until the slash closed.

The sound of someone approaching tore her attention from Sorin. She turned in the direction from where she'd heard the sound emanate and knelt stiffly on the ground, in a semicrouch, preparing to pounce on whomever emerged from the underbrush.

She could have wept with relief when Lucian came into sight, rather than the individual with the crossbow. Her eyes widened with surprise when she saw ten werewolves emerging behind him. She was surprised to see the group included the Alpha and Lupina when they resumed human-form. She had been afraid they would turn their backs on Lucian. She had dared to hope maybe a few—including Sorin's sister—would come to their aid, but she hadn't imagined the leaders of the Pack would lend them aid.

Lucian rushed to her side, dropping onto his knees beside Sorin. "How is he?"

"I'm not sure. The wound continues to bleed. My blood seemed to help a little, but he's still unconscious."

Starr looked up from Sorin as two muscular men knelt beside them. When they made to lift Sorin, she put out a hand to stop them.

Lucian touched her hand. "It's all right. They're going to carry Sorin back to the village."

She bit her lip when Sorin whimpered as they lifted his large form. "Can they help?" she whispered to Lucian.

He hesitated, and there was a haunted look in his eyes when he finally answered. "I don't know, but they're going to try."

She nodded and rose to her feet, suddenly conscious of her nudity in front of the Pack. She crossed her arms over her breasts before realizing the gesture betrayed her unease. She dropped her arms at her side and tried to pretend she didn't feel vulnerable before them. "Are we returning to Necheau?"

To her surprise, the Lupina stepped forward. "No. Rica and I will take you on to the castle. Lucian tells us the queen is in danger."

Her eyes widened. They were going to help her? She looked at Lucian, allowing her confusion to show. His shrug didn't reassure her. "Will you come with us?" she asked in low tones.

He shook his head. "I'll accompany Sorin." He embraced her quickly, whispering in her ear, "I believe we can trust them, but watch yourself. I hate to leave you, but he is in a weakened state. He needs someone with him."

She knew he was right, but couldn't deny the dart of fear she felt at proceeding with only the company of werewolves she didn't know, except by sight. Lucian's presence at her side would have reassured her, but she knew Sorin needed him more than she did.

She pressed a quick kiss to Lucian's mouth and brushed her hand against Sorin's muzzle as the men holding him passed. She hoped Sorin would be healed the next time she saw him, and she hoped she made it to the castle in time to warn Anca. The pressure that had propelled her earlier was returning with greater force, now that she could concentrate on something besides Sorin's safety, and she had to resist the urge to tell Rica and Ellie to hurry as she transformed into wolf-form. They must have sensed her urgency, because they transformed and kept pace with her as she plunged into the forest.

Behind them, three other wolves ran, while scanning the forest around them. They must be looking for the hunter. Starr allowed her focus to shift from the danger in the forest to the jeopardy in the castle. They had to hurry. She knew that instinctively.

Chapter 7

Lucian watched anxiously as Golatia bent over Sorin, still in wolf-form, to examine his wound. He was barely aware of the presence of the others in the room. The Lupae hovered near the doorway of the cabin where they had brought Sorin, alongside Sorin's sister, Lia. Her mates had accompanied Starr to the castle to warn Anca, and he wondered why she hadn't gone with them. Did she still harbor some sort of familial emotion for her estranged sibling?

He tensed when the old woman picked up a straight razor and waved it at a girl he didn't recognize, but appeared to be assisting her. His hackles rose, and he braced himself to intercept any attempts to cut Sorin. To his surprise, the woman handed the razor to the girl and looked up at him, as if reading his thoughts.

She gave him a small smile. "We must be able to see the wound, so the fur around it has to be removed. My eyesight is not what it once was. I don't want to knick the boy while shaving around the area."

He relaxed slightly, but remained alert as the girl scraped away the thick fur obscuring the wound. He tensed with Sorin when she worked some of the matted pelt out of the bloody mess. That must have hurt, as evidenced by his lover's brief bout of thrashing, which quickly subsided once the girl moved away.

Sorin groaned as Golatia probed the wound, making Lucian tense. He battled with the urge to protect Sorin from those gathered around him, knowing they wouldn't have come to their aid if the Pack meant to do them harm.

Still, old habits and emotions were difficult to overcome, and he remained rigid as Golatia took a bowl from the girl and dipped a clean cloth in it, before cleansing the wound. Sorin flinched, and Lucian bit down the reflex to gag when the smell of the thick green mixture wafted to his nose.

"Should you remove the arrow?" he asked gruffly.

The old woman shook her head. "Not yet. The bleeding must finish before I take the arrow, because it will surely begin again, when the silver comes out. I want to heal as much of the surrounding area as possible first."

Lucian stood sentry as Golatia continued to daub the wound with the foul-smelling brew, continuously turning the cloth to reveal a clean section as Sorin's blood stained the rest of the cloth. Halfway through the process, she took another cloth from her assistant to begin the procedure anew. Sorin's groans subsided to occasional grunts of pain, allowing Lucian to slowly relax.

Golatia nodded her head and folded the white cloth before placing it in the mixture. "The wound has healed, except for the area around the silver arrowhead. I am surprised the mixture worked so quickly, as silver poisoning generally requires many hours of tending…with mixed results." A hint of sadness flashed across her wrinkled face, and she gently patted Sorin's slack paw.

"The vampire with them put some of her blood in the wound," Lia said, as she stepped closer.

"Clever," Golatia said. She looked up at Lucian. "You will have to remove the arrow. My hands aren't strong or nimble enough to pull it out quickly, and I do not want to cause Sorin unnecessary pain."

He nodded, feeling nauseated at the prospect, as he grasped the broken shaft of the arrow and waited for Golatia's signal. He swallowed down his queasiness and tried not to think about the pain Sorin would feel when the arrow came out. His hands felt slippery, and he tightened his grasp. The old woman lifted the cloth and placed it under the wound. When he saw her nod, he wrenched the arrow free from Sorin's side with one tug.

The amount of blood pouring from the wound horrified him, and he turned away under the auspices of disposing of the silver arrowhead safely, so that none in the Pack would accidentally be injured by it. By the time he turned back, after wrapping the silver in a soiled cloth and placing it in a wooden box it would be burned in, Golatia had covered the wound with a new cloth, soaked in the healing potion.

He could read her apprehension by the set of her shoulders and the expression on her face. It was obvious she was worried, and he didn't miss her sound of distress when she replaced the cloth with another from the stack held by the girl. She didn't look at Lucian as Sorin's wound soaked two more cloths in five minutes, but finally met his eyes when her assistant handed her the last cloth before going to fetch more.

"He's losing a lot of blood, Lucian."

He swallowed and struggled to sound calm, but his voice broke. "Can you save him?" The fear in the old woman's eyes shook him.

"I do not know. Sorin's mother was the healer, not I." Golatia turned her gaze to Lia, beckoning her forward. There was no hesitation in the younger woman as she hurried forward. "Lia, did you ever learn anything of healing? What would your mother have done?"

Lia's mouth twisted. "My mother would have let Sorin die."

Lucian flinched. He prepared himself to force Sorin's sister to assist him, but she spoke again before he could move.

"Mother was a fool and let her stupid pride cost her many things." Lia's tone changed from bitter to confident. "I believe she would have used an infusion of rose bay, knapweed, and Echinacea. To that, she would add the blood of a family member." She spoke matter-of-factly, but there was an expression of doubt on her face. "I can try to make it."

Lucian's eyes widened. "You would do that for him?"

She frowned at him. "He is my brother." She blinked. "I do not know if I can make this mixture correctly. Mother did not write down her potions, so all I have is vague memories of her treatments."

The girl assisting Golatia returned with a fresh stack of cloths. The older woman looked up from replacing the soaked cloth to say, "You must try, Lia. It is better to attempt to save him than do nothing."

Lia nodded and hurried from the cabin, appearing as anxious as Lucian felt while he watched the blood soaking through the cloth once again.

He began to pace around the confines of the small room, avoiding eye contact with Davinia, Golatia, and the girl he heard them call Clara. From time to time, he paused in his pacing to check Sorin's wound. It still bled freely. He was certain he was going quietly mad as the time passed without Lia reappearing.

His thoughts turned to Starr and how she needed him with her, but he found those thoughts distressing too. In truth, he felt useless. He couldn't do anything to help Sorin, but he didn't want to leave him alone in Necheau. He could offer no assistance to Starr, being so far away from her. He had to place trust in her safety with members of the Pack. It was a bitter pill to swallow, as he had spent the last six years hating the Pack and everything to do with it.

His morose thoughts scattered when Lia finally returned carrying a large wooden bowl. When she placed it on the small table beside the bed where Sorin lay, Lucian saw a cloth wrapped around her wrist. Some of her blood had stained the bright white strip. When she dipped a fresh cloth in the infusion she had brought, he saw it was a scarlet color, indicating a generous amount of her blood was in the mix.

Golatia removed the soiled cloth soaked with Sorin's blood, and Lia pressed the one she held against the wound. To Lucian's surprise, Sorin's body relaxed. He felt a moment of fear as his eyes closed, thinking his lover had died, but was reassured when Sorin twitched. Lia removed the cloth to dip it back into the mixture, and Lucian's eyes widened when he saw the wound had begun healing already.

It didn't take long for the wound to stop weeping blood and scab over with the infusion Lia dabbed on it continuously. He felt almost lightheaded with relief when she wrung out the cloth over the wound, replaced it in the wooden bowl, and said, "The potion is working. The wound won't completely disappear until he is able to transform a few times, but he will live."

Lucian didn't doubt it. Already, Sorin's ragged breathing had eased, suggesting peaceful sleep, rather than unconsciousness. As relief filled him, Lucian's thoughts turned from concern for Sorin to revenge. Whoever had injured Sorin would pay for what they had done. He would not stand by uselessly even a moment longer.

No one tried to talk him out of leaving Necheau to investigate the forest for signs of whoever had been tracking them. Lucian didn't know if it was because they thought he should search, or if perhaps his air of raw rage made them shy away from trying to reason with him. He didn't care which it was right then. All he could focus on was punishing the hunter who had injured his lover and forced Starr to face unknown danger without her mates by her side.

* * * * *

Starr and the werewolves accompanying her reached the castle a little more than an hour after setting off together. The werewolves had set a frantic pace that left her breathless, though they seemed barely affected.

She kept her eyes focused on the tower where Anca and Demi slept as they rushed across the courtyard. They encountered no one as they entered the castle, but it was the middle of the night. She tried not to worry about the lack of activity as she led the others up the winding staircases, through the wings of the castle, and up to the tower room of the queen and king.

Starr hesitated at the doorway of their room, wondering how she should proceed. If her sense of timing were off, she would be bursting in and needlessly putting them in a panic. One didn't simply push open the door to the queen's chamber and rush inside, shouting dire warnings.

Undecided, Starr transformed to human-form, barely aware of her lack of clothing, and knocked on the door. Her senses urged her to dispense with politeness, but she knocked again, waiting a few seconds for a response. She knocked louder, but again, no one answered the door.

She closed her eyes and placed her palm flat against the wood worn smooth with the passage of time. Starr tuned out the presence of the wolves behind her, who were in various states of assuming their human forms. She closed her eyes and tried to concentrate on what was happening behind the door.

She searched with her mind, seeking the reassuring presence of either the Protector or her lifemate. Any sort of response—even anger at an unwarranted probing of their minds—would have been a relief.

She strained mentally, but couldn't receive a vision, nor connect with either Anca or Demi. She struggled to relax and allowed her thoughts to turn to the erotic moments she had spent in Sorin and Lucian's arms, hoping the rush of sexual energy would increase her mental abilities, as it had done exponentially earlier that night.

Her lips parted with a soft gasp as she imagined Lucian cupping her breast in his hand, while thumbing the hardened nipple. Sorin's phantom fingers toyed with her swollen clit, causing moisture to leak down her thighs. Her breathing grew ragged, and her eyes moved rapidly under her lids.

As she remembered the sensation of having both cocks penetrate her simultaneously, an image formed in her mind. It was dark, and someone stood over a bed. At first, she thought it was a memory of being at the cabin, but as her body recalled the way Lucian and Sorin had made love to her, the vision crystallized.

A woman stood over the bed of Anca and Demi, who were bound by some invisible force. It was the same image Starr had seen earlier, but now clarified. She gasped when she realized who the assailant was, as she opened her eyes to look at the door. It couldn't be, but it was. How had she escaped the little-known prison in the Ukraine and made her way back to Corsova? How had she entered the country? More importantly, was Nikia with her? Was that who had shot Sorin in the forest?

Sian held a dagger in her hand and wore an expression of concern as she eyed the door. She must know Starr was on the other side, and her hand suddenly shot up, grasping the dagger firmly, and preparing to plunge it into Anca's heart.

Starr cried out as the dagger started to lower, and she began to push frantically against the locked door. Rica and the other two men pushed her aside and threw their weight against the wooden door. Even as it splintered against the force and formed a hole large enough to allow Rica to reach inside to unbolt the door, Starr knew they wouldn't make it in time to prevent Sian from stabbing Anca.

* * * * *

The pain in his side awakened Sorin. It radiated up into his chest with a hot, pulsing rhythm that had him gritting his teeth. At least his head was clear, and he immediately recognized where he was when he opened his eyes. A rush of conflicting emotion assailed him when he saw the familiar interior of his mother's home. No, not Belia's home now, because she was dead, killed with her lover during their bid to seize power.

He turned his head when he caught the scent of another in the room with him. His eyes widened when he recognized his sister. He had seen her briefly during his return to Necheau to warn the Pack about the anthropologist, but had not truly looked at her. He was amazed how mature she looked, but her eyes were the same ones he remembered from her childhood. Only now, they held concern and weariness that hadn't been reflected there the last time he saw them, right before his relationship with Lucian was discovered.

She smiled at him, and some of the grimness left her expression. "You are awake. How do you feel?"

He grunted a response, uncertain how he should respond. "What am I doing here?"

"The Pack brought you. Lucian came to ask for help." Lia frowned. "At first, Rica seemed like he would refuse, but the Lupina didn't let him. She insisted we help, and those of us willing to do so accompanied Lucian through the forest, to where your mate waited with you."

The knowledge they had come to his aid was unsettling. Even more so was knowing he would probably be dead by now if the anthropologist he and Lucian had tried to keep out of Corsova hadn't forced the issue. He cleared his throat and attempted to dismiss the foreign emotion of gratitude to anyone in the Pack. "Where are Lucian and Starr?"

"Starr has gone on to the castle to warn your queen of danger." Lia grimaced. "Lucian has left to find the hunter lurking in our forests. Shortly after he left, other members realized we could all be in danger if there is a hunter using silver, and many left to aid in the search."

Sorin sat up, wincing at the fiery sensation in his side. "I must get to Starr. She'll need me."

Lia touched his arm, trying to ease him back to a prone position. "A werewolf escort accompanied her. Your mate will be fine."

He shook his head. He wasn't the kind of man to lie around while others faced danger. When his sister again tried to ease him down, he shoved her away. "Get out of my way."

Her eyes sparkled with a hint of anger. "Stop being so stubborn. You can't help anyone in your current state. You need to rest, to gain your strength for transforming, to speed healing."

Sorin ignored Lia's words and tried to stand up. He grunted when her weight hit him from the side, and he fell back into the bed. He stared up at her with wide eyes, recognizing the glint of determination in her eyes. It was one he often saw in his own, when glancing in a mirror. He was startled to note other similarities in their facial shape, and something indefinable that instantly pointed to them being related.

With an almost vicious jab, she touched his wound, causing him to draw in a breath. "How far do you think you could get, brother? You're staying right here. You will cause those who care about you needless worry if you go traipsing off into the forest in your weakened state."

He allowed his tense muscles to relax. An unbidden question escaped him, before he could call it back. "Are you among those who would care, sister?"

She frowned. "Of course. You are my brother."

He felt a lump forming in his throat and tried to ignore it. "Do you still consider me so?"

Her eyes softened, and she brushed back his hair with a motherly gesture. "There is no way to undo the last six years, Sorin. I followed Mother's lead when she ostracized you. The Pack made no attempt to intercede, and when you went to the vampires, you were considered dead to many." Her voice broke. "I shouldn't have been one. If I had been older and wiser—"

"It doesn't matter." It truly didn't. A void inside him had already begun to fill with her words, and he realized his anger had never been with her for not acknowledging him as her brother or defying their mother. His anger was more general, aimed at all members of the Pack who had allowed his mother's lover to beat him, and then hadn't said a word when his mother left him naked and bleeding, with the word *Abomination* carved on his chest. None had come to his assistance, causing the anger to increase.

Six years had turned the rage to a dull, bitter emotion he carried around without thought. He could feel it fading away as he met the teary eyes of his sister. His own eyes blurred, and he closed them, pretending he was close to sleep in an attempt to hide his sudden vulnerability. The process of forgiveness might have begun, but he wasn't ready to announce it to anyone else, even the sister who seemed to want to know him.

* * * * *

Lucian's wolf eyes scanned the forest in front of him when he lifted his head from sniffing a footprint. The man—and he knew it was a man from the smell he left—was probably a skilled hunter. It had taken Lucian almost an hour to find any trace of him, but a mile back, his prey had grown careless and left a footprint. Now, a mile later, there was a partial imprint of the heel of his boot. The man's scent lingered heavier in the air, letting Lucian know he was close.

He increased his pace, allowing his nose and instincts to guide him. He sent his mental powers out ahead of him, searching for the presence of another. During the hunt, he had occasionally sensed the essence of other wolves and assumed they must have joined the hunt. His focus remained on the man who had tried to kill Sorin, and he filtered out the odor of any other werewolf in the vicinity.

He jerked when his mental tentacles collided with a human presence. He was pleased to note the underlying scent of fear in the man's stink when he breathed in deeply. He could sense the other's flagging energy and once more increased his pace, knowing his prey would tire much sooner than he would.

His extra burst of speed brought him to the top of a hill, where there was a partial clearing, ringed by fallen logs. A form crouched low near an overturned tree. Lucian saw the glint of silver as the man shot his crossbow. Instinct made him twist away, and the arrow whistled by him with several inches to spare. He didn't allow the hunter to make another shot as he jumped from an awkward angle.

Lucian righted his gait in mid-leap and landed on the back of the hunter, knocking the man to the ground and pinning him there. He transformed into human-form and resisted the urge to tear out the man's throat without getting answers to the questions he should ask. "Who are you?" There was still a heavy growl in his tone, making the question animalistic in sound. The man seemed disinclined to answer, so Lucian cupped his throat and tightened his grip. "Answer me."

"A-abel Schneider," the man managed to push out breathlessly, with a thick German accent. He had little volume, because Lucian hadn't eased his grip.

"What are you doing in our forest, human?" Schneider's blue eyes looked close to popping onto his cheeks. The stench of urine filled the air, and Lucian growled with disgust. He did loosen his grip slightly, in case the man's wide eyes were caused by strangulation, rather than fear.

"I am a hunter." The answer was a thin squeak.

Lucian roared, "Who were you hunting when you shot my mate?"

Schneider seemed reluctant to answer, but apparently, the rage in Lucian's eyes convinced him remaining silent would be even worse for him than imparting the truth. "I came to Corsova to hunt werewolves."

He had already guessed that, from where the man had been hunting, his choice of targets, and the weapon he was using. "How did you find out about werewolves in Corsova?" He shook the man, finding a bit of his rage lessened when the man squealed with pain.

"I met a woman in Belarus. After time in her company, I admitted to her that I had come to Belarus to kill a wolf."

"Why?"

"This wolf is legend. His pack terrorizes small villages, preying on livestock and fools who stray across their path." Schneider paused to swallow, and Lucian tightened his grip again. When he spoke once more, his voice was thin with the struggle to speak and breathe at the same time. "No hunter has been able to slaughter the alpha wolf, and I was determined to do so."

Lucian curled his lip. "And did you?"

"No. The woman persuaded me to pursue bigger game. She showed me something amazing…transformed into a wolf. Told me about this country…told me about the Alpha of the Pack." A glint of excitement gleamed in Schneider's eyes. "I knew I had to kill the one called Rica."

"How did you get into the country?"

"The woman acted as my guide. She said she couldn't openly enter the country and had me hide her in a trunk, after she drank something she said would keep anyone from detecting her presence. She needed my essence to shield her own, and I needed her to show me where to find the Pack."

Unease stirred in Lucian. "Who is this woman?"

"Her name is Sian."

Lucian jumped when he heard the name, inadvertently tightening his grip. Schneider's gasping made him realize what he was doing, and he looked down dispassionately. The hunter's eyes bulged again, and his skin had taken on a blue cast.

He was debating about whether to tighten his grip or just render the hunter unconscious when he heard a movement. Lucian looked up and saw at least a dozen wolves emerging from the forest. As they formed a ring around him and the hunter, Schneider's eyes shone with fear.

He released his grip and stood up. He met the eyes of a midnight-black wolf and nodded. "He came here to kill Rica. I'll leave him to you, shall I?" He had business at the castle, if only it weren't too late. Lucian didn't spare another glance for the hunter as he morphed into wolf-form and set off at a run, hoping to reach the castle in time to assist Starr. Warning her had taken precedence over avenging his mate, but Lucian knew Sorin would have made the same decision.

Besides, what did it matter? Whether by his hand or not, the hunter would be just as dead by morning.

Chapter 8

A soundless cry escaped Anca as the dagger tore into her shoulder, just inches away from her heart, which surely had been Sian's target. Starr froze for a second when she realized they had been granted an extra moment to act due to Sian's careless aim. Sian's howl of rage as she wrenched the dagger free and raised it again broke Starr's paralysis.

Somehow, though Rica was the closest, Starr reached Sian first. She gave no thought to transforming to wolf-form as she rushed the other woman and knocked her to the stone floor. Sian's head connected with a dull thud, and her fingers loosened their hold on the dagger.

Starr held her down as one of the men—either Lasile or Jan—wrested the knife from Sian and tossed it across the room. She kept her full weight on the woman until each man took one of Sian's wrists and lifted her to her feet, holding her straining body between them.

Starr turned away from them, but couldn't block out the sound of Sian's vile insults. She rushed to Anca and bent to examine the wound. It was already healing, thanks to Anca's heritage, but she reached out to push back the section of pajama, to see how deeply the dagger had plunged, to rule out any damage that wasn't obvious. An inch from Anca, she hissed with pain when she encountered what felt like a field of electricity and withdrew her hand. She whirled back to Sian. "What magic is this?"

Sian's eyes glittered. "A binding spell I learned from Nikia's mother's people, while I was in Belarus. Only I can penetrate or release the spell."

"Then release it."

The other woman laughed, but gave no other answer.

Starr's anger built inside her as the mad laugh echoed around the chamber. "Undo the spell, and you might live through this."

A strange expression crossed Sian's face, but it wasn't one of fear. Rather, it was joy. "That enticement holds no promise for me. A death is necessary to complete the spell." Her mouth twisted as she glared at Anca, who was attempting to break free from the nearly invisible light-purple bands binding her, but having no luck. "Now that the original sacrifice is thwarted, I know what must be done."

Starr eyed her with confusion. "What are you talking about? What spell? The binding spell?"

It happened in seconds, even before Starr finished questioning her. Sian slammed her booted foot onto one of the men's bare feet. He howled with pain and released his hold on her at the unexpected assault. Before the other man holding her could get a better grasp, Sian raked her nails down his cheek and kicked his knee. She broke free in the process and ran to the window.

Starr saw it all happening and tried to stop her, as did Rica and Ellie. None reached Sian in time, and she paused for only a second to look directly at Anca. "Nikia will avenge me." Then she plunged through the stain-glass window and seemed to hang suspended in mid-air for a long second, before gravity re-exerted its control, and she fell from sight. She uttered no sound, and there was a stunned silence in the room, making it impossible to miss the sickening thud of Sian's body against the cobblestone several stories below.

Colors whirled behind Starr's eyes, and she felt light-headed. The room spun around her, and she barely noticed Anca and Demi were free from the binding spell as she fell to the floor and the vision consumed her.

A cinnamon-haired woman—once voluptuous, but now gaunt—lay in a hospital bed. Her eyes blinked under her lids, and the monitors measuring her heart and brain activity beeped rapidly. Her eyes snapped open, and she sat up in bed, seeming to be looking straight at Starr, although Starr couldn't see where her body was in the vision.

Before she could learn anything else, consciousness returned to her in the form of smelling salts. She gasped for air and sat up so quickly her head spun again. The Protector was crouched before her, holding a vial. The words formed of their own accord, as though put into her mind. She couldn't seem to hold them in, to find a way to prepare Anca for the news. "Nikia is awake. Somehow, Sian found a way to revive her."

* * * * *

Lucian had made good time, but not so much so that he arrived in time to assist. By the time he made it to the royal chambers, the excitement had passed. Servants had already removed Sian's body from the courtyard and hidden it away. It was destined for a funeral pyre without ceremony in an undisclosed location.

Starr was in the sitting room of the queen and king's chamber, sipping tea, when he came in, and she was so relieved to see him that she nearly got up and ran to him. She appeared outwardly calm, but her heart still raced. Although nearly an hour had passed since Sian plunged through the window, she still felt shaky. Having Lucian hold her would take away the last of her anxiety, but that was impossible, with the Protector in the room.

The queen and king were in pajamas. The werewolves who had accompanied Starr sat on a large couch, and all wore robes bearing the symbol of Corsova—two cupped hands around a red orb. It represented the Protector guarding the life source of the people, which was blood. They had grudgingly accepted the garments pressed on them by Helena, personal maid to Anca.

He seemed to have no thought of restraint for convention's sake. Lucian went to Starr without even greeting the king and queen. He dropped to his knees beside the chair she occupied and leaned forward to kiss her. At the last moment, she turned her head, and it became an awkward hug. She hated the flash of pain in his eyes, but knew they couldn't reveal their betrayal of Corsovan tradition in so blunt a way.

He cleared his throat and regained his feet, pausing to bow to Anca and Demi, before turning back to Starr. "When I left Sorin, his sister assured me he would recover."

Starr breathed a sigh of relief. She stared down into the cup of tea she held and tried to make out a pattern in the tea leaves, but saw none. She had never been able to see the future from reading the dregs, and apparently, her new surge in power didn't make her any more adept with the skill.

Anca cleared her throat, and every eye shifted in her direction. She wore a soft smile. "I am pleased to hear of Sorin's recovery and thankful to have such loyal subjects." She looked at Rica and Ellie, dipping her head. "I also extend my gratitude to the Pack. I hope this will lead to a new…understanding between our people."

Rica made a non-committal sound, but there was no missing Ellie's quick nod and the look of censure she threw her mate when he didn't elaborate on his grunt.

"I'd like to speak privately with Starr for a moment," Anca said.

As though she had waved a magic wand, the others seemed to disappear, they left the room so quickly. Only the swish of the door closing revealed they had left by less-than-supernatural means. Starr tried to hide her apprehension when she looked at the queen, fearful of the gleam of knowledge in her brown eyes.

Anca wasn't intimidating on the surface, but there was a quiet strength in her demeanor, and Starr knew she cared deeply for the homeland she had come to just two years ago. No matter if it might hurt her, Anca would do what was best for the people. That was programmed into her by thousands of ancestors. It had become habit. No, more than habit. It had become instinct.

Starr knew the queen could order their deaths—and would do so—if she decided that was the best way to protect Corsova. She didn't know why she was so certain Anca knew about them, but she could sense it. She waited for the queen to begin, determined not to betray herself by inadvertently saying the wrong thing, if she was mistaken about the queen's perception.

"Have you mated with them?" Anca posed the question in a soft voice, with just a hint of curiosity.

Starr couldn't detect an underlying thread of anger, but the muscles she had thought were completely tense tautened further. She couldn't bring herself to meet the Protector's eyes. "Not in an official ceremony."

Anca waved her hand. "That's paper. You know what I mean."

Starr nodded, feeling sick. "Yes. I've betrayed my position and the people of Corsova. I've betrayed you." When the queen remained silent, Starr dared to look up. She hadn't known what to expect, but the amusement she saw in Anca's expression shocked her.

"I don't feel betrayed. I have done some research and spoke with Demi. Neither of us could find a reason why the spiritual leader is required to remain chaste. Nor could we find any hint of dire consequences associated with her taking a lover…or two, in this case." She grinned.

Starr frowned, puzzled by the queen's jocularity. "I don't understand…"

Anca grinned. "You aren't the first spiritual leader to give in to desire, Starr. There have been a few others, all documented in our records."

She shook her head. "That can't be. I would know—"

"These records are viewed only by the Protectors. They document everything that has ever happened in our country, and some pre-date even the gathering of all the groups of vampires to form a society together."

"What happened to the others?"

Anca paused to sip tea before answering. "A few were executed. One retired early, and her acolyte assumed her position. Three were granted dispensation by their Protectors to have mates." She gave Starr an assessing look. "It's interesting to note that those who were allowed the pleasures of a mate were among the most powerful spiritual leaders of our people."

Starr's eyes widened at the information. Remembering how her power had swelled when she finally joined with Sorin and Lucian as one made her realize that was how it was supposed to be. Just as the Protector was destined to have a lifemate, so was the spiritual leader of the people destined to have one who was complementary—or sometimes two, she thought with a small smile—who would augment her powers.

"It's an archaic tradition, and I can find no practical reason to enforce it," Anca said casually. "I suspect Sian's assassination would have succeeded if you *hadn't* been with Lucian and Sorin, and had an increase to your power."

Starr nodded, and then met Anca's eyes directly. It was uncomfortable to do so, because she held the other woman in such high esteem. "There is one thing I do not understand. Why would you research this, Highness?"

Anca winked. "It was obvious what was happening between the three of you, and I was determined to find a way to allow it. At times, life is lonely enough, even with a mate. It's ridiculous to require one to be alone, especially when there is such great love waiting."

A lump formed in Starr's throat, and she found it difficult to speak. "We have your permission to mate?"

"I expect to be in attendance at the Pledging Ceremony," Anca said, as answer. She set aside her teacup and cleared her throat. "I believe you have Lucian waiting to take you back to

Sorin, and I want to seize this chance to speak with Rica, to see if we can amend the original treaty between our people, to allow our groups to function more cooperatively." She looked down at her pajamas, glancing at the hole where the dagger had passed through. The wound had healed. "But first, maybe I'd better change."

Starr got to her feet and walked to the doorway, pausing to turn back when she reached for the knob. "Highness?"

"Yes?"

"What will you do about Nikia?"

Anca sighed, and it was a long moment before she answered. "What I must."

Chapter 9

Starr glanced up at the moon that was still nearly full, but had waned somewhat from the way it had been last night, when she had stood under it while Sorin and Lucian tried to convince her to officially accept them as mates. Had it been just last night? So much had happened in such a short time that it felt like weeks had passed since they registered a moon-cycle claim.

It was strange to have members of the Pack standing around her, watching her. She felt self-conscious in her nudity, with so many unfamiliar eyes upon her, but tried to hide her unease. She knew how important it was to Lucian and Sorin, who had begun the long task of reconciling with the Pack, to have the Mating Moon Ceremony concluded in the tradition accepted by the Pack.

Sorin had arranged it, before asking either she or Lucian. Rica had agreed to allow them to have a Consummation Ceremony, to end the moon-cycle claim. All that was left now was to go through with it, with everyone watching.

She took a deep breath as Rica stepped forward to ask if she would accept these men. "Yes," she said in a clear voice. She had no one to act as Guardian, because there had been no time to contact her parents, and she knew they would have refused her request anyway. The ceremony wouldn't quite be official without all the steps completed, but it was only "paper," as Anca had said.

Besides, this ceremony was for Sorin and Lucian, to acknowledge their culture. The Pledging Ceremony happening tomorrow at moonrise would be for Starr, and would have the added bonus of making their union official to the people of Corsova.

Rica turned to Lucian, repeating the question. After Lucian's acceptance, and then Sorin's, he removed the sash they had tied on their hands before the ceremony. "The match is approved. Consummation will commence." Then he stepped back into the circle of Pack members around them.

Starr knew it was time to begin, and she tried to quell her nerves when Sorin put his arms around her. She made a conscious effort to relax as he drew her against him. She held out her arms as Lucian stepped in front of her. He dipped his head to brush his lips against hers, while Sorin bent his head to nibble on her neck.

Her nervousness faded as their lips played on her skin. When Sorin cupped one of her breasts and drew his thumb across the nipple, it hardened immediately. She groaned and closed her eyes when Lucian took possession of her other breast and caressed the hardened peak. He parted her lips and slid his tongue inside to duel languorously with hers.

The last remnants of tension left her, and she forgot about the members of the Pack surrounding them. Sorin and Lucian must have picked up on her relaxation, because they chose that moment to lower her to the ground. Sorin lay underneath her with her legs spread on either side of his, and Lucian knelt in front of her. Starr's eyes fluttered open when Lucian's mouth once again claimed her flesh, this time concentrating on her breasts rather than her lips.

Sorin held her around the waist, balancing her atop him. His cock pushed against her buttocks, and she squirmed, anxious to feel him inside her. She gasped when he moved one hand from her hips and cupped her buttocks. He parted the cheeks and slid his fingers down the cleft, probing at her sphincter with one thick finger.

Her eyes flew open when Lucian's tongue sought out the heat of her pussy. His tongue twirled circles around her swollen clit, and she drenched his mouth. A cry escaped her when his tongue swept lower, to probe her opening. She stiffened when it darted inside her, and her hips had a mind of their own as they thrust upwards to encourage him to go deeper.

He responded to her unspoken invitation by going lower. He trailed his tongue down her pussy and parted her with one hand. Sorin's finger slid aside to allow room for Lucian's tongue, and he dipped inside, exploring the puckered opening. Starr cried out at the invasion, from mingled shock and pleasure.

As Lucian's tongue swirled inside her tight anus, he brought a hand between her thighs and stroked her clit. A new wave of moisture greeted him when he brought his hand lower and entered her pussy with two fingers. Starr writhed helplessly against the stimulation, still not certain if she wanted to avoid his tongue or urge it deeper.

Lucian made the decision for her. He withdrew his fingers and tongue before leaning back on his knees. Starr watched him through heavy lids as he grasped her hips and shifted her slightly. Sorin's cock pressed against her anus in the new position, and she took a deep breath to prepare herself as he slowly thrust into her. She forced her lower body to relax and accept all of him.

When Sorin's cock was finally nestled in her anus, she barely had time to catch her breath before Lucian's cock probed the entrance of her pussy. She wasn't frightened, because they had done this before, but her muscles still felt stiff. She wondered if she could take them both as he sank into her. She gasped at the twinge of pain, but it faded quickly to pleasure.

Starr wrapped her arms around Lucian's neck when he lay down carefully on top of her. As he thrust into her, Sorin thrust into her, forcing her hips upward to meet Lucian's cock.

"Oh, my loves," she said softly, for their ears only. They stretched her to her limits, but it felt so wonderful to share her body with them, at the same time. Even the occasional protesting muscle or section of throbbing flesh didn't detract from her pleasure. She surrendered to the pace of their thrusts, closed her eyes, and savored the sensations coursing through her.

Their rhythm and the harmony of their movements were so perfect that Starr could feel Sorin and Lucian's cocks spasm with approaching release at the same time. Her pussy contracted in response, and the orgasm came quickly, coinciding with the hot spurts Sorin and Lucian spilled inside her. The climaxes sealed their union by tradition of the Pack. Only the Pledging Ceremony remained before she would belong completely to them, and they to her.

* * * * *

The solemn formality of the Pledging Ceremony was a direct contrast to the Mating Moon Ceremony of the Pack. Starr wore a black velvet robe and stood between Sorin and Lucian, who wore white robes, below a dais where the queen stood. The tight knot holding her hair was giving her a headache, and she mentally urged Anca through the words she needed to say.

Because Starr couldn't officiate her own Pledging, the Protector had stepped into the role. If only Starr had selected an acolyte already, the ceremony probably would have been finished by now. She made a note to begin the search once the Isolation Phase of the Pledging passed in two weeks. Until then, all she had to focus on was time spent in the company of her mates, with no duties.

The tradition had begun a long time ago, in the days of arranged marriages, to allow the newly pledged pair time for acquaintance. Since she was already intimately familiar with her mates, they would put their time to more erotic use.

She blinked when she realized Anca had just said her name. She had been so impatient, and the process seemed to be going so slowly, that she was surprised to find them nearing the end. She knelt on one knee as Sorin and Lucian did the same. Starr held her hand in front of her, and they both covered it with theirs.

Anca asked, "Do you accept a union with this man…" She cleared her throat and appeared flustered when she looked up briefly from the scroll from which she was reading. "…these men? Will you embrace them with your body and soul? Will you share your mind and heart with Sorin and Lucian until death parts you?"

Starr raised her head and looked at Sorin, then Lucian. The careful visual measuring was part of the ceremony, giving the bride a last chance to refuse. She did it by rote, having no heart to reevaluate her decision. "I will."

Anca nodded, and then turned to Sorin, asking, "Do you accept a union with this man and woman? Will you embrace them with your body and soul? Will you share your mind and heart with Starr and Lucian until death parts you?"

Sorin's voice was husky when he said, "I will."

She turned to Lucian, asking, "Do you accept a union with this man and woman? Will you embrace them with your body and soul? Will you share your mind and heart with Starr and Sorin until death parts you?"

There wasn't any hesitation in Lucian's answer. "I will."

Anca stepped off the dais after lifting a knife with an ornately carved ivory handle from the altar beside her. She knelt in front of the three of them, and her blood-red robes spread out around her. She touched their joined hands, and each released their hold, allowing their palms to show.

She began with Starr, making a deep gash with the sharp blade across Starr's heart line on her palm. Starr's breath hissed through her teeth, but she held her hand steady as blood flowed down her palm and into the sleeve of her robe. She watched as Sorin stoically endured the same cut, followed by Lucian, who didn't flinch.

She didn't resist when Anca lifted her hand and Sorin's, pressing the palms together so that the blood mingled. She then joined Starr and Lucian the same way, before pressing Sorin and Lucian's palms together, sealing their union.

"Three lives made one. Bless the union of Starr, Lucian, and Sorin." As she spoke, Anca got to her feet and returned the knife to the altar.

As soon as the Protector stood, the reverent silence in the tower room dissipated. Starr accepted the cloth Helena handed her as she turned to greet the guests in attendance. She pressed it against the wound that was already coagulating and curtseyed to their guests.

Still between Sorin and Lucian, Starr walked with them to the silver bowl resting beside another knife on a crisp white tablecloth. The low table holding the items required each guest to bend slightly at the waist as they approached.

The end of the ceremony commenced as the newlyweds watched with solemn expressions. Each guest approached the bowl, lifted the knife, and nicked the vein on the side of their wrist. They stood with their hands over the bowl until a few drops of blood dripped inside. Then, with a formal bow from Sorin and Lucian, and a curtsey from Starr, each guest moved aside to allow the next in line to repeat the process.

Once everyone attending the small wedding had made an offering, Anca brought forth a silver chalice, which she dipped into the bowl of blood. She then held the chalice for Starr, who took the first drink. Lucian sipped next, and Sorin took the last drink before the chalice made its way to each of the guests, who sipped in turn.

When the chalice had been refilled twice, to allow everyone a drink, Anca poured the remaining blood back into the bowl and rested the chalice rim down on the previously pristine cloth. A pool of crimson formed under it in seconds. "By the blood of the people and the Protector, this union is sealed. Bound in blood, live by the life source."

With those final words, the air of formality seemed to melt away. Sorin and Lucian's arms came around her waist, and they turned toward her. She kissed first Sorin, and then Lucian, tasting the tang of blood on their lips.

For a moment, she had the sensation it was all a dream. She would awaken and find her lonely brain, drunk on longing, had conjured the ceremony and preceding events. Discreetly, she pinched herself and winced at the flash of pain. It was real, just as her union with Sorin and Lucian must be.

A heady sense of freedom filled her. She hadn't been the first spiritual leader to be led astray, and she definitely wouldn't be the last, but she wondered if any had been so well loved as she. Looking into the eyes of her mates, she knew she had received a treasure greater than even the life source of Corsova.

Their love was priceless, but even more precious was the ability to openly acknowledge their union, to show their love for each other to the world. No longer would they have to hide from their emotions or deny their desires. No one would ever ask them to deny their love for each other again.

Also by Kit Tunstall

Ablaze

A Christmas Phantasie

A Matter of Honor

Blood Lines 1: Blood Oath

Blood Lines 4: Blood Price

By Invitation Only

Eye of Destiny

Fortune's Fool

Heart of Midnight

Lions and Tigers and Bears

Only Love

Pawn

Phantasie

Playing His Game

Wrong Groom

About the Author

Kit Tunstall lives in Idaho with her husband, son and dog-children. She started reading at the age of three and hasn't stopped since. Love of the written word, and a smart marriage to a supportive man, led her to a full-time career in writing. Romances have always intrigued her, and erotic romance is a natural extension because it more completely explores the emotions between the hero and heroine. That, and it sure is fun to write.

Kit welcomes comments from readers. You can find her website and email address on her author bio page at www.ellorascave.com.

Tell Us What You Think

We appreciate hearing reader opinions about our books. You can email us at Comments@EllorasCave.com.

Why an electronic book?

We live in the Information Age—an exciting time in the history of human civilization, in which technology rules supreme and continues to progress in leaps and bounds every minute of every day. For a multitude of reasons, more and more avid literary fans are opting to purchase e-books instead of paper books. The question from those not yet initiated into the world of electronic reading is simply: *Why?*

1. ***Price.*** An electronic title at Ellora's Cave Publishing and Cerridwen Press runs anywhere from 40% to 75% less than the cover price of the exact same title in paperback format. Why? Basic mathematics and cost. It is less expensive to publish an e-book (no paper and printing, no warehousing and shipping) than it is to publish a paperback, so the savings are passed along to the consumer.
2. ***Space.*** Running out of room in your house for your books? That is one worry you will never have with electronic books. For a low one-time cost, you can purchase a handheld device specifically designed for e-reading. Many e-readers have large, convenient screens for viewing. Better yet, hundreds of titles can be stored within your new library—on a single microchip. There are a variety of e-readers from different manufacturers. You can also read e-books on your PC or laptop computer. (Please note that Ellora's Cave does not endorse any specific brands.

You can check our websites at www.ellorascave.com or www.cerridwenpress.com for information we make available to new consumers.)

3. ***Mobility.*** Because your new e-library consists of only a microchip within a small, easily transportable e-reader, your entire cache of books can be taken with you wherever you go.
4. ***Personal Viewing Preferences.*** Are the words you are currently reading too small? Too large? Too... ANNOYING? Paperback books cannot be modified according to personal preferences, but e-books can.
5. ***Instant Gratification.*** Is it the middle of the night and all the bookstores near you are closed? Are you tired of waiting days, sometimes weeks, for bookstores to ship the novels you bought? Ellora's Cave Publishing sells instantaneous downloads twenty-four hours a day, seven days a week, every day of the year. Our webstore is never closed. Our e-book delivery system is 100% automated, meaning your order is filled as soon as you pay for it.

Those are a few of the top reasons why electronic books are replacing paperbacks for many avid readers.

As always, Ellora's Cave and Cerridwen Press welcome your questions and comments. We invite you to email us at Comments@ellorascave.com or write to us directly at Ellora's Cave Publishing Inc., 1056 Home Avenue, Akron, OH 44310-3502.

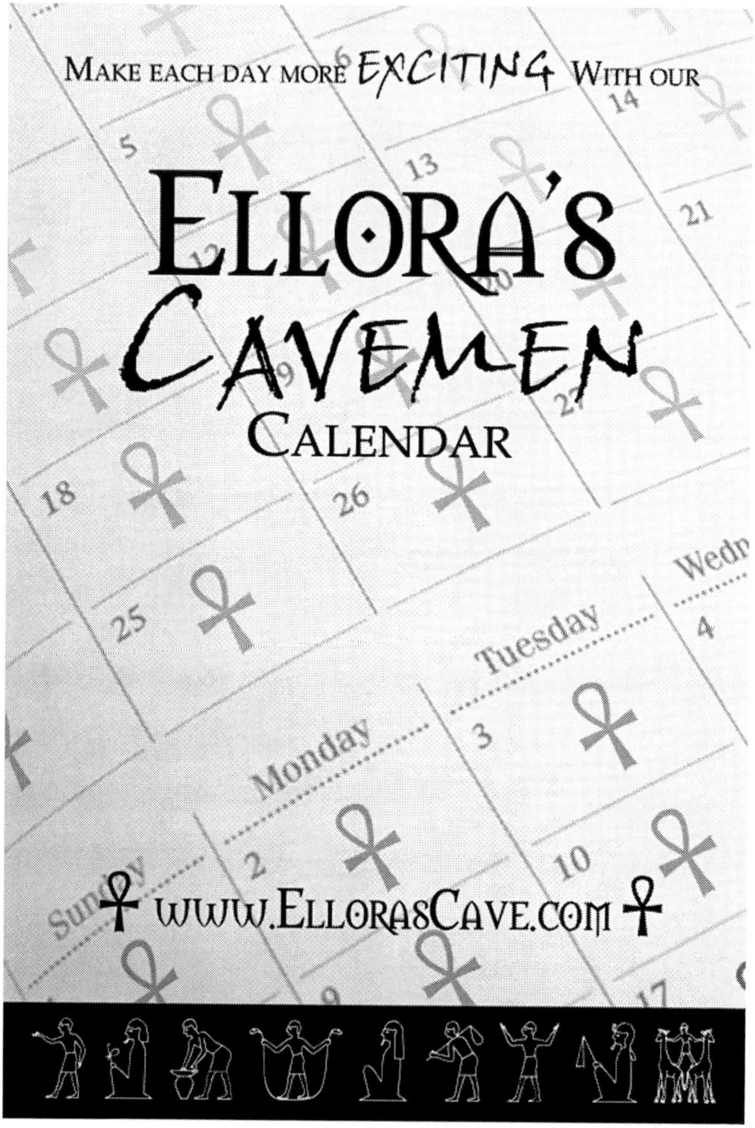
Make each day more EXCITING With our
Ellora's
Cavemen
Calendar
www.EllorasCave.com

2662514

Made in the USA